Past Praise for Mary Connealy

"A fun and engaging read from start to finish."

Midwest Book Review on *Whispers of Fortune*

"Nobody writes witty Frontier romances like Mary Connealy, and *Whispers of Fortune* made me smile with its sweet-and-swoony romance, layered characters, and exciting search for a mysterious treasure."

Reading Is My Superpower

"Mary Connealy's book draws you in from the first page and never lets you go! Her historical romances are well researched, and it does not feel like a history lesson. Instead, it feels like one is transported to her story, experiencing all the suspense, thrills, and romance."

Interviews and Reviews on *Into the Sunset*

"With a vivid setting, compelling characters, and a suspenseful, thought-provoking story, this will please fans of inspirational historical romance."

Booklist on *Chasing the Horizon*

"Connealy wraps up her A Western Light series with a breakneck ride through the late nineteenth-century American Frontier. . . . Brimming with high-stakes action, plot twists, and plenty of shady characters, Connealy's finale captivates while sensitively exploring the rights of women in the Old West. Series fans will be delighted."

Publishers Weekly on *Into the Sunset*

AMBUSH
OF THE
HEART

Books by Mary Connealy

ROCKY MOUNTAIN MARSHALS

AMBUSH
OF THE
HEART

MARY
CONNEALY

BETHANYHOUSE

a division of Baker Publishing Group
Minneapolis, Minnesota

© 2026 by Mary Connealy

Published by Bethany House Publishers
Minneapolis, Minnesota
BethanyHouse.com

Bethany House Publishers is a division of
Baker Publishing Group, Grand Rapids, Michigan

Printed in the United States of America

Library of Congress Cataloging-in-Publication Data
Names: Connealy, Mary, author.
Title: Ambush of the heart / Mary Connealy.
Description: Minneapolis, Minnesota : Bethany House Publishers, a division
 of Baker Publishing Group, 2026. | Series: Rocky Mountain marshals ; 1
Identifiers: LCCN 2025023198 | ISBN 9780764245992 paperback | ISBN
 9780764246067 casebound | ISBN 9781493452460 ebook
Subjects: LCGFT: Christian fiction | Romance fiction | Western fiction |
 Fiction | Novels
Classification: LCC PS3603.O544 A84 2026 | DDC 813/.6—dc23/eng/20250625
LC record available at https://lccn.loc.gov/2025023198

Scripture quotations are from the King James Version of the Bible.

Cover design by Design Source Creative Services, Dan Thornberg

Baker Publishing Group publications use paper produced from sustainable forestry
practices and postconsumer waste whenever possible.

26 27 28 29 30 31 32   7 6 5 4 3 2 1

This book is dedicated to *my* cowboy.
We're coming up on fifty years together. Yee-haw!

I will put my laws into their mind, and write them in their hearts: and I will be to them a God, and they shall be to me a people.

Hebrews 8:10

1

U.S. Marshal Owen Riley was riding beside Delaney Bridger and her brother, escorting them to Fort D. A. Russell in Wyoming, when a bullet whizzed past him, so close he felt the heat of it.

Owen threw himself at Delaney to get her off her horse. It was a reflex without thought. He held on to his reins and urged his well-trained buckskin mustang stallion to lie flat on its side. He saw fellow Marshal Morgan Sawyer hit the ground a mere second before he did. A third Marshal, Tex Mitchel, was already down, crouched low behind his horse, rifle drawn and aimed. Tex was bleeding.

Tex had Delaney's brother, Boone Bridger, lying on the ground as well. The team of Marshals had been paid to get the Bridgers safely to Wyoming, and fortunately Delaney looked all right. She lay next to Owen with her pistol in hand. Her horse, meanwhile, took off down the hill they'd just crested.

Assessing things fast, Owen noticed Boone sprawled on his back, bleeding from a head wound. Clive Duncan, the prisoner they'd been transporting, was facedown and not moving. Clive was right beside Marshal Marley Tweedt, who'd been leading Clive's horse as the man rode with his hands tied together. Just beyond those two, Deputy Marshal Stan Ross also lay flat on his back, arms flung wide, unmoving, and bleeding from a chest wound.

The horses that hadn't been forced down continued to stand. Owen knew they were well-trained horses, including their prisoner's horse, as he'd supplied that mount himself.

Gunfire continued to rain down.

Stan's spooked horse was trotting north, downhill, in the direction they'd been going. Other horses, trained or not, followed. Only Owen, Morgan, and Tex had managed to hold on to their mounts and had their critters down, acting as shields.

They had all just come out of a draw and then crested a hill. Of course, only someone from Colorado would call the rolling, rising mounds in these parts mere hills. Yet when you came upon a mountain close to hand, sure enough, they looked like hills.

They'd been skylined for just a few seconds on the trail to Cheyenne, riding north out of Denver along the Front Range of the Rocky Mountains, when they walked right into an ambush. Five of them shot, four seriously. Marley's leg bled, the wound bad enough that he'd let his horse get away. Marley had crawled toward Tex, the closest shelter, and got his gun out, not paying his injured leg much mind.

Another glance at Tex told Owen he was bleeding but still in action.

There was a pause in the gunfire, a rifle. It'd sounded to Owen like a Springfield rifle, which carried an impressive load of bullets.

One gun. The rifle fire let up, then came more bullets about the time it would take to reload. But was it one gun or just the same kind of gun and multiple riders close together? Owen had learned not to jump to conclusions. Then he heard something, a grunt maybe, and the gunfire stopped.

Owen was pinned down near the top of the hill. He had his rifle out of the scabbard, resting it over his horse's back, ready for the next round of gunfire.

But moments later, no one showed himself, and there were no more gunshots. Regardless, Owen stayed where he was, ready for someone to come charging over the hill. In the silence, a mountain breeze kicked up the acrid scent of gunfire, which to Owen smelled like brimstone. It was as if the whole world had gone dead still except for the buffeting breeze.

With a glance back at Boone, he saw Delaney leaving the safety of the horse, her only shield. He quick grabbed her arm. "Don't you dare go out there."

She turned to him, furious, and cried, "I've got to help Boone."

Owen's grip gentled. "He's down now. No one can get another shot in him. But if whoever opened fire on us comes over that hill, you need to be behind this shelter." He gave his poor horse a little pat. He hated to reduce the loyal critter to shelter.

No more guns sounded.

She nodded. "Yes, it would be foolish, I know that." She swallowed hard and swiped a wrist across her eyes. "I s-suppose he can't get worse in a few minutes' time."

"I'm sorry, but it's my job to keep you and Boone safe. I failed with him." It ripped at Owen's heart to see her cry, to see her brother bleeding from a head wound.

She calmed down and saw reason. It seemed she was a tough western woman. And pretty with her dark hair and blue eyes. He hated that he'd failed her brother, but he could still protect her. His hand on her arm felt a little too warm. He let go to face the hilltop and aim his gun again.

And then she was gone.

"Delaney! No!"

She'd dodged him neatly and was crawling, using her elbows to pull herself forward while staying flat.

He added *wily* to his other description of her.

He didn't go after her but instead focused on the hill, ready to stop anyone who posed a threat to her.

She was soon beside her brother, where she tore a strip off his shirt to bind his wound. But it was an ugly shot to the head, and Boone remained limp on the ground.

He, Morgan, and Tex had partnered up before. Two other Marshals had ridden with them today, both of them now laid out on the ground. Stan Ross's eyes were open, staring at heaven 'cause that was where he'd gone. Just a youngster. He hadn't been with the U.S. Marshals Service for a full year.

Marley Tweedt, a tough Civil War veteran, was the oldest of them and mean. Alive but hurt bad. Owen had seen gunshots like this before. Unless he got real lucky, Marley was going to lose his leg—if the wound didn't fester and kill him first.

Owen sensed his temper about to explode, but then his gaze landed on Delaney. The young woman had formed a bandage around her brother's head. She looked around desperately, her eyes locked on Owen's. "He's alive," she called.

Owen didn't believe it, and yet at the same time he had to. Then he did a blamed-fool thing. He left the shelter of his horse and crawled over to Delaney.

She drew out a wickedly sharp knife. For a second or two, Owen was afraid of the fury in her eyes and the weapon in her hand, but then she slashed at her brother's shirt, making another strip of cloth to bind his head before Owen reached them.

What Owen saw when he got closer to Boone gave him hope.

"The wound looks mean, but it's a graze," Delaney said as she tied the bandage around the pad she'd formed, just enough pressure to stanch the bleeding. "He's going to live!" She said it with such force and certainty, Owen figured God himself had assured her of the fact.

Delaney's pa was newly stationed at Fort Russell. Though she'd never made such a claim, it was said she was a distant cousin a few times removed to the rugged mountain man Jim Bridger. She sure seemed tough enough. Owen suspected she could've survived in the mountains with that old grizzly hunter. Same went for Boone, whose toughness just might save him.

They were on this trail because the train that ran from Denver to Cheyenne wasn't operating due to a wreck that tore up a stretch of track, which included a trestle bridge along the route. No one was making promises about when it would be running again.

A half day's ride by train had turned into a few days' ride on horseback. Clive Duncan needed to be escorted to

Cheyenne, where he'd been sentenced to hang. He'd broken out of jail a year ago. The Bridgers, Delaney and Boone, had been standing on the station's platform ready to board the train at the same time as Owen and his group. When they found out Owen was changing plans to ride horseback to Cheyenne, the Bridgers asked if they could come along. They wanted to get to Fort D. A. Russell, where their pa, Colonel Lionel Bridger, was the commander.

"Get back to watching for whoever shot my brother," Delaney instructed, crawling on toward Marley.

Morgan rounded his horse and scrambled on hands and knees for the crest. It seemed to be safe so long as they kept low. They headed for the top of a grassy knoll that rose from the rugged land. But the gunfire had come from over this same hill, and Morgan didn't like getting shot at more than any man Owen had ever seen.

And Owen feared that this time his friend was gonna die.

"Morg, no!" Owen hissed. "Let's fall back. Now. That's an order."

Owen expected to be obeyed.

Morgan looked over his shoulder. The pure fury in his eyes would have scared a lesser man, but not Owen. He respected it, but at the same time, Morg was going to do as he was told.

Owen lowered his voice so as not to give themselves away to whoever had been shooting at them. "We need to find a better spot to make a stand. Sure as shootin' they're after our prisoner."

Morgan gave the crest one more enraged glance, then turned back. Instead, he went to the prisoner. Tex, his blood-soaked arm now with a kerchief wrapped around it, got to work loading Stan's body onto his horse. They were far enough over the hill that the horses could stand, but no one was going to dare sit up high on their backs. Not until they'd put some space between them and whoever was shooting at them.

The prisoner was loaded next. Morg was a bit gentler with Marley, but he still hurriedly slung him, belly down, over his saddle.

Delaney guided her horse downhill, Tex leading the way with Boone limp across his saddle. Delaney kept her eyes fixed on her brother, and in her expression, Owen could see the anger that her injured brother was being handled like this. Yet along with her outrage was the grim acceptance that they had to get moving.

The men who'd shot them would be coming.

As they neared Boone's horse, Tex managed to grab its reins and swing up into the saddle while still leading three horses, one with Stan's body, another with the utterly still Boone, the third with a writhing but silent Marley. He had a tourniquet around his lower leg, almost ensuring they'd need to amputate it later.

Soon Tex was out of sight around an outcropping of stone.

When Morgan reached the rocks, he turned and rode uphill.

Then Owen mounted up, trotted around the stones, and caught up to Morgan. "Let's make a run for Fort Collins," he said.

Morgan glanced back at him. "That's too far, at least for Marley."

Usually when Owen gave orders, he expected them to be obeyed, but he knew how to listen, too. He looked at Morgan. "Where then?"

They were closest to Elk Point, Colorado. Going there meant Owen would be bringing danger to a small town ill-equipped to face it. While there was no longer a fort in town, Fort Collins was bigger and the nearest place to offer safety. But they'd have to make it there while fighting a running gun-battle the whole way, with Delaney right in the middle of it.

"I know this land. We're going right up that slope." Morgan pointed to the mountain right in front of them. A mountain with no way up, not on horseback.

"Move out, and fast." Morgan spurred his horse straight toward what looked very much like a dead end. If that was true, they'd be trapped and under the guns of the outlaws in minutes. Yet Owen didn't protest. Morgan was the toughest of a real tough bunch. If he said they could ride up the side of a mountain, Owen was going to spur his horse too and try to keep up with him.

So Morgan took the lead. Tex, without a word of complaint, fell in as well, leading his trio of horses that carried the wounded. Owen wondered if Tex was as worried as he was at the prospect of scaling the wickedly steep slope.

Delaney came next, her jaw clenched, her eyes flashing with grim determination.

Just minutes later, Morgan rode up a slope so steep it seemed impossible. Tex was next, trusting his horse, riding at a gallop. Delaney climbed right behind him as though she and her Thoroughbred bay gelding could fly. Owen glanced behind him before urging his own horse forward, half figuring he'd see gunmen coming after them any second.

Morgan was already out of sight, and Tex vanished as he rounded a jumble of rocks, Delaney not far behind him. After following, Owen got there in time to see Morgan climbing the jumble of rocks and setting himself up to shoot any attacker who dared to show his ugly face.

Tex moved Marley to the ground. Since Owen was the best of the three at doctoring, he went to Marley and got to work.

Delaney checked Boone's head wound, who had yet to so much as groan.

"It's not as bad as I feared." Owen removed Marley's tourniquet, and the gunshot wound immediately started bleeding again. Fortunately, the leg was still warm, as the blood flow hadn't been cut off for very long. And the leg didn't appear to be broken. A bone broken by a bullet was usually more than broken; it was shattered, with fragments of bone scattered around inside, making it near impossible for the limb to heal properly. Thankfully, it looked as though the bullet had penetrated deep into the muscle of Marley's leg but had missed the bone.

A gunshot sounded from below them. Their pursuer was coming fast, unloading his gun again. Bits of rock exploded right by Morgan.

Morgan opened fire. One shot.

There were none in return. Owen heard hooves pounding below, but they didn't come closer. If anything they were moving away from them. And no one did any more shooting.

"Morg can probably hold off an army from here." Tex looked away from Marley, who lay with his teeth gritted while Owen retied a new bandage, but not so tight that circulation was cut off to the stubbornly bleeding leg. "Reckon I oughta help him, though."

"Does the leg need to come off, boss?" Though his grizzled face flushed from pain, Marley didn't protest or howl or swear. A lot of men would have done all three.

"Nope, you're gonna keep your leg and heal up fine so long as the wound doesn't become infected. And we'll see it doesn't."

Marley, already flat on his back, seemed to collapse further as the tension leeched out of him. The man hadn't complained about Owen's rough doctoring skills, but that didn't mean he hadn't been fearing maybe losing his leg. "How's Ross?"

Owen looked at Marley, shook his head sadly, and didn't say a word.

"Good man, Ross. He was still a youngster and deserved better. It's the Duncan family's doing, I reckon."

This time Owen's eyes slid to their prisoner, Clive Duncan. "If the gang was coming to set Clive free, they didn't do him no favors. If he dies, I reckon those polecats will blame us even with their bullet in his gut."

"I got the first one up the slope, the one who shot at me," Morgan said from his perch on the boulder that overlooked the trail they'd come up on. "They can't get up here while we've got the high ground, and they know it. But they ain't goin' nowhere either."

"I had no hope they'd be easy on us," Tex said in his drawl that reminded everyone that he'd gotten his name from his days as a Texas Ranger. "They already broke Clive out of the jail at Fort Russell. It figures they'd keep at it. The fool had gotten away clean, but he had to wander into a Denver saloon and get himself rounded up again." Tex shook his head. "I'll see to him before I go shoot it out with his family."

"How far are we from where you're aiming, Morg? Or is this it?"

"This ain't it," Morgan replied, moving behind a stack

of boulders. But there was no more shooting from below, so Morgan just watched.

Owen noticed Delaney kneeling beside her brother, tending to the thick bandage around his head. He saw her lips moving and figured she was praying as she worked on him.

Owen had seen a graze to the head like that a time or two before. Usually there was a good amount of bleeding, but other than stanching it, there wasn't much to be done. Stitches maybe, once the bleeding stopped, but there wasn't time for that now. The stitches would probably bust open during the long ride anyway.

Tex gave Marley a pat on the arm and went to check on Clive, who was still unconscious.

"How's his belly wound?" Marley asked.

"Hard to say. I'll stanch it, then leave him tied up, even if he is unconscious. He's a mean one. I don't want him getting into a fight."

"I saw seven men, with six of them scattered among the trees at the base of the mountain. I thinned the herd by one—the one who was shooting at me." Morgan kept to his spot, still watching. "They can't get any closer, not with there being no decent cover. They'll be looking for another way up, but there ain't one."

"How do you know this land so well, Morg? You're from Colorado, right?"

"My pa has a ranch up here. But it's a rattlesnake of a trail to Pa's place. Long ways from here, but easier to defend. He ain't gonna be happy seeing me bring a group of strangers home for dinner with outlaws after us." More quietly he added, "He ain't gonna be all that happy seeing me either."

Owen didn't ask about that. He'd never learned much

about where Morgan Sawyer had come from. But Morgan was the finest tracker Owen had ever seen, and he'd seen some good ones. He was mighty good himself. But no one could top Morgan Sawyer.

Delaney rose from her brother's side and walked over to Owen. "What needs doing?" she asked.

"Nothing much, Miss Bridger. I think your brother will be all right, but he might be addled for a while. A bullet graze like that takes some time to heal fully." Owen looked up at her from where he was crouched next to Marley. He saw such fire in her eyes, he felt burned just looking.

"If there's no work to be done, show me where the men are who shot Boone so I can blow them all straight to the devil."

Owen flinched at the fury flashing from her eyes. He had a feeling the Duncan Gang oughta just run for their lives straight out of Colorado, maybe out of the country. She might not be able to find them in China.

But he knew better. The Duncans weren't gonna run. In fact, they were going to keep coming. And instead of Delaney being smart and hiding behind him like she should, she was going to give Owen all he could handle to keep her from unleashing her revenge.

And probably getting herself killed in the process.

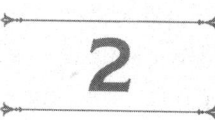

2

Stella Duncan looked with regret at her brother Leland.

Dead.

It'd all happened so fast.

Earlier, Leland had recognized their brother Clive and the lawmen transporting him back to prison and started emptying his gun.

Stella didn't know if they'd hit anyone, but she'd seen those riders go down hard and fast, and it had horrified her into action.

Leland had been in the lead, and he'd emptied his gun and reloaded and started shooting again even though everyone was out of sight, as if rage drove his trigger finger. Rage and stupidity. Never a good combination.

She'd leapt at Leland and pulled him off his horse. They hit the ground, and she'd landed a punch before Pa had pulled her off him long enough for him to give Leland a kick to the belly.

"Are you crazy? You could've shot your brother!"

"You could've shot a *lawman*." Stella wanted to start

hammering on Pa, too. "For all we know, he *did* shoot a lawman. If he did, he'd be in line right behind Clive for the hangman's noose."

Stella knew well how her family was. Her pa, Ralph "Sly" Duncan, wasn't the kind of man to let his son go to prison, even if he was a killer and a thief. Or in Clive's case, hang for murder. Clive had sworn it was self-defense, and Stella believed him just because he seemed like the sort of fool who'd boast about it if he'd really committed cold-blooded murder.

Pa's brother, Uncle Gordy, didn't have much mean in him, but he would fight for family. In fact, they had a motto from their Scottish Highland ancestry: The Duncan Clan Fights for Family. It wasn't much of a motto because all clans fought for family. It was practically the motto of every Highlander. And family unfortunately included her idiot brother Clive. The old ways of the Scottish Highlands were fading away, but a few idiots clung to them still, or maybe this ran in the blood of all Scotsmen because her family sure seemed to be displaying a fair amount of it.

The Duncans were an unruly lot, and they tended to strike out on their own and leave Pa behind to his wandering, family motto notwithstanding.

Stella sure hoped her turn to take off was coming soon.

Today, though, she'd ridden along with Pa because he wouldn't let her stay home alone anymore, no more than he'd let her just take off on her own. It made a certain sense since she was the lone woman now that Ma and her little sister and Uncle Gordon's wife were all dead, and they lived in a remote series of canyons with the reputation of a Robbers Roost. No place for a woman alone.

While it was reasonable, at the same time it annoyed her right down to the ground. And it meant she'd been on hand to see Leland rashly open fire not once, but twice—the second time after the lawmen had gotten away, dragging Clive along with them.

Tragically for Leland, the man who'd shot down at them from the rocks above had possessed a deadly aim. Even though Stella's next younger brother, Johnny, had moved fast to grab Leland and haul him under the cover of some nearby trees, it had been too late. Stella shuddered. She suspected that the lawman could have killed them all if he'd wanted to. She wondered if he was sharp-eyed enough that he'd seen who'd shot at them and deliberately killed the man responsible. Leland.

Johnny hadn't shot at anyone, and he wasn't apt to. But when he'd let Pa goad him into coming along to rescue Clive, he'd known what he was buying into.

Now they were hiding, and Pa was shaken and fuming. In fact, he was about one more burst of anger away from foaming at the mouth.

If only Leland hadn't gone after those lawmen again after they'd somehow managed to get up the narrow trail along that wickedly steep mountainside. What a waste.

Now there was only silence. No more gunfire from above, and no one down here quite reckless enough to open fire when the top of the cliff where the shooting had come from was out of range.

A warm mountain breeze washed over them. The trees, mainly aspen and pine, stood like sentries to block the sight of them from anyone overhead.

Stella noticed Pa had hunkered down over Leland. He was

so red in the face she wondered if he might have an apoplexy right here on the spot and fall over dead.

He wasn't roaring, though, and loud rampages were usually his way. Maybe he had the sense to know they might be within earshot of a man with a dangerously accurate long-distance rifle.

While she waited to see if Pa would survive his wrath, she looked down at Leland. Dead with a certainty. A rifle shot in the heart from probably more than two hundred years away.

A lawman for sure and probably a former soldier. She had no interest in riding into range of that man's gun ever again.

Leland had been of a kind with Pa, though Pa was no killer for all his dreadful temper. Leland hadn't been either before today. Now she had to wonder if he had indeed managed to kill someone because whoever had shot back at them from up there had shot to kill.

Stella moved with all the skill she'd learned living mostly on the trail with Pa and her family after Ma died. Pa had always wandered, and the boys had grown up and wandered with him. Stella stayed behind with Ma in the home she'd insisted on. Pa had come and stayed through the coldest weather. The rest of the year he'd been more of an infrequent visitor than a husband and father. When Ma died, along with Stella's little sister, in a house fire a little over a year ago, Pa had come home soon enough after the fire. Ma lingered long enough, he'd built another cabin and then helped bury his wife and daughter. Then he'd taken Stella along, and she'd been wandering too ever since.

She slipped along the line of trees like Ma had taught her when the two of them went hunting to feed themselves. Careful not to be seen, she dropped to her knees beside Leland.

She needed a moment to cry over her big brother, and Pa wasn't overly fond of tears.

He was still bent over Leland, holding him by the arms as if he could drag him back to this side of the Pearly Gates. For a second she thought of Leland meeting St. Peter at those gates and worried how Leland would fare. The thought made her want to cry some more.

She let the silence stretch until she thought Pa had relaxed a bit. The worst was over. Now it was time to use sense.

"Leland shot at them, Pa. They're lawmen—of course they were going to shoot back."

Pa's bowed head snapped up. He glared at her, pure rage flashing in his eyes. His teeth clenched.

She rested one hand on top of Pa's where it clutched Leland. "We can still save Clive, Pa. We don't have to turn this into a war."

Pa's chest heaved, but he was listening. Or at least she hoped he was.

"They're taking him to Fort Russell. Let's go there. We'll explain they've killed the man who shot at them, and then we'll explain the mistake they made with Clive. He didn't start the fight. We can end this without any more death, Pa."

Like a striking rattlesnake, Pa lashed out with the back of his hand. She dodged, used to his sudden bursts of temper, but also used to escaping them unscathed. Though he never landed a hit, she was royally tired of having to duck.

As was his way, he didn't swing again. Instead, he knelt there, almost gasping for breath, as he glared. He frightened her suddenly. She was a fool to never be frightened, but she never had been. Right now she was.

"No man shoots and kills my son and lives on."

She held his gaze. A lot of her strength came from him, she knew that. But she'd gotten a heart from Ma, which was the best part of her, along with the coloring of a Viking, blond and blue-eyed. And a faith in God that gave her a steel rod where some folks had a simple spine.

The silence stretched. The fear held her away, but she wished he'd let her hug him. Mourn with him. Head to the fort with him.

"I loved him too, Pa. We all did." She looked up at Johnny and Uncle Gordy. Johnny looked the saddest. He'd been close to Leland. He stood with his hands tucked in his back pockets, frowning down at his brother.

Uncle Gordy seemed close to tears. His sons, Macon and Beau, were sitting on the ground, knees drawn up, forearms resting on their knees, staring at the ground and looking defeated.

The menfolk in her family were of a type. Big men with dark, overlong hair that none of them bothered to comb beyond running their fingers through it. Faces that'd never known a razor until they looked more bear than man.

She knew every one of them wanted to follow her to the fort. She also knew every one of them would follow wherever Pa led.

"A woman's love is a soft and gentle thing," he said at last. "Fine enough for a woman, but this calls for a man's kind of love. The kind that doesn't let someone attack family. My Scots ancestors would be ashamed if I even thought of letting those men get away with killing Leland and taking Clive. I can't accept that. It ain't how a real man loves."

Stella knew that was wrongheaded. She thought of how her Heavenly Father loved. The greatest imaginable strength combined with gentleness. Like her ma, Sigrid, a woman proud of her Viking past, she prayed Pa would respect that and turn to Him for his salvation. She wasn't one to judge, but she feared her pa didn't believe.

Pa tore his gaze from Leland and looked around at his family. Grimly, Stella knew they wouldn't allow themselves to be thought of as weak, as less than *real* men.

"We'll bury Leland right here and stay down here for the night, then when those men up on the cliff move on, we find them and make them sorry for what they've done to my boys."

No one had such a thing as a shovel. But Uncle Gordy produced his knife and dropped to the ground and started cutting away the sod. Soon all the men were helping.

Pa paused in his digging. "Get a meal on, Stella. We'll eat right after the burial." Pa went back to work as Stella walked away to start cooking, still thinking of that deadly accurate bullet that had killed Leland and wondering if any of them would survive this madness.

3

Delaney knew she had the look of a gently raised woman.

Even though she wore sturdy clothing, it was a finely made riding skirt, with her brown shirtwaist fitting her well. She had her hair done up in a decent style. She wore a hat to keep the sun off her face like a citified woman might do. Of course, most country women did it, too. And men.

She also knew she could outshoot, outride, and out-track every man here. She knew how to defend herself, too. And she wasn't opposed to proving it.

Owen knew, at least a little. She'd assured him that she wouldn't be a burden to him when she arranged with him to be escorted to Fort Russell, where her pa, Colonel Bridger, was posted.

Delaney looked at her brother Boone and realized that she hadn't bargained on having to protect him as well.

Her brother! Her big brother! Owen said he'd probably be all right, but Boone looked terrible. The wound was so ugly. He was dead white, his breathing unsteady. She wished there was something more she could do for him.

Morgan Sawyer spoke up. "Tex, come up here and cover us. I'll lead us to Pa's cabin."

While Tex had ridden alongside Delaney and Boone, Morgan had talked with them a lot since leaving Denver. He'd heard her brother brag up Delaney's tracking skills and laughed at the bragging.

Later, after she'd tracked a mule deer across solid rock and brought it down from two hundred feet with her brand-new Winchester '73, a gun that wasn't even on the market yet outside of Pa's connections, Morgan had stopped laughing. Instead, he studied her and her gun with profound respect.

Now that she'd seen him on a trail, she knew he was good.

Delaney knew less about Owen and the others. Owen had helped keep watch over the prisoner on their journey. Clive Duncan had ridden on a horse led by Marley Tweedt, with the youngster, Deputy Marshal Stan Ross, and Owen riding on either side. Those fools she'd heard Morgan call the Duncan Gang had been trying to pick off the men watching over their brother and managed to shoot Clive.

Boone had been close enough to be hit by a wild shot.

A powerful mix of fear and anger swept through her. She forced herself to look at Boone. *Wake up, brother. God, please let him wake up and be his healthy, funny self again.*

Owen had Marley, the old-timer, bandaged well and up on horseback, while Morgan hoisted Boone over his saddle. Stan still rode along, draped over a saddle like Boone but beyond help.

Owen wore an aging Stetson over his thick dark-blond hair, and his eyes were a cold blue most of the time. Hard to say why since the man didn't talk much, and yet he made her feel safe.

She wasn't sure what Tex had done to assist Clive. Gut-shots like his were always serious. The outlaw was still unconscious, but they'd tied him hand and foot. Maybe lying across a saddle would put pressure on his belly wound and save his life.

Delaney didn't much care whether he lived or died. She'd heard of his crime. The man was on his way to be hanged. Being shot by his own family in a hotheaded attempt to break him free of the U.S. Marshals seemed like justice to her.

She looked at the still-unconscious Boone. There'd been no justice in his or Marley's being shot, nor in a Marshal being dead as a result.

Boone's dark hair, much like her own, was overlong from a neglect of barbering. It hung down, his Stetson gone. His dark eyes, also like hers, were closed. Pa had always said that their eyes were a matched set.

They'd been born two years apart, the stragglers in the family after three older brothers. With Pa stationed at Frontier forts, then gone to fight the Civil War, then gone back to the Frontier for a good portion of his marriage, the children were spread out in ages, and her older brothers had been gone a long time.

Now Ma lived with Pa at Fort D. A. Russell near Cheyenne. Ma had headed west, while Delaney, a schoolmarm and near spinster (oh, who was she kidding?, it was a lot more than *near* these days) had the school year to finish. Boone had offered to wait and ride to Wyoming with her to keep her safe. They were on their way to join their parents at the fort.

Delaney took one long, aching look at her brother. She was safe, but not him. She swung up onto her horse. She rode forward and took over leading Boone's horse. She'd see to him from now on if she could. That was something she could do.

"This trail is going to take everything we've got," Morgan warned. "Tex, don't stay back long or you might never find us again. Tracking on this rocky ground is almost more than I can do. Maybe Miss Delaney could manage it, but not me."

Owen gave her a sharp look and arched a brow before turning and heading after Morgan.

Delaney brought up the rear, leading her brother's horse. But before anyone thought to complain about a mere woman watching their back trail, Tex caught up and took over being rear guard.

It wasn't long before she began to see what Morgan meant about the trail. She didn't see one, and yet Morgan seemed to know exactly where they were going. There were canyons to climb down into, follow along, then scale again. Jumbles of stone, walls of granite, rushing streams, and stretches of solid rock. And all along, there were clumps of grass and scraggly scrub brush everywhere.

Delaney studied the ground for the tracks of the horses right in front of her and saw nothing. Their horses seemed content to move on. She said quietly to Owen, just in front of her, "I sure hope he knows where he's going."

Owen turned to glance at her. His eyes were lit with amusement, but all that had gone on had made a smile impossible. "Is Morg right? Are you that good a tracker?"

"I brought down that deer," she replied.

"Morg mentioned you found it when he'd've said it was impossible. But I figured him for being silver-tongued."

That jolted a small smile out of her. "Morgan? Silver-

31

tongued? I've heard the man speak very little, and mostly when he made a sound, it was growling."

Owen nodded. He smiled for a brief moment, but then his eyes went to Boone and Stan and the smile faded fast.

Morgan reappeared, way to the right and up about a hundred feet, almost straight up.

Delaney trusted to her horse, and the critter proved its skill because she was soon climbing, twisting, and rounding boulders that looked like they'd roll right off the mountain with little more than a breath of air.

And so the day passed. They stopped to let the horses rest a few times and to stretch their legs, to see how the injured were faring and eat some hard biscuits and jerky, and then they pressed on.

At some point, Clive woke up. They let him sit up, but he showed no fight. His hands were lashed to the saddle horn, his reins tied to the horse Marley rode.

Delaney thought if the gutshot hadn't killed him by now, he might just survive it. Boone, however, remained unmoving. And as the hours passed, her worry grew.

Their horses plodded onward, slow and steady, following the tail in front of them.

Delaney had seen no sign of pursuit. She couldn't make out if they were leaving any trail, though once when she glanced back, as she did often to study the way they'd come, she saw Tex off his horse, brushing out a hoofprint.

Toward evening, up among peaks she'd never seen before, they came over the saddleback on a mountain in air so thin it felt sharp when she breathed. Morgan pulled up and stared at whatever was over the mountain.

They all caught up to him and looked down at . . . nothing.

This was where Morgan had grown up?

Delaney didn't bother to ask. There was nothing below them but a valley full of scrub brush, soft grass, and quiet.

"Home sweet home." Morgan's voice was quiet, but everyone heard him. "We do have to climb down one more cliff."

Morgan gave his horse a gentle kick as if there was no sense hurrying on a trail this treacherous. The horse veered sharply to the right and descended on a trail Delaney couldn't see. But she followed along, her heart pounding with fear. She hadn't known that she had, it seemed, a fear of heights. Tamping down on her delicate nerves, she was determined not to be the slacker when in truth she wanted to loudly protest that she was *not* going down a trail that'd give a mountain goat the vapors.

She resisted closing her eyes, although being able to see wasn't going to help much. Either her horse would follow this ghost of a trail or it wouldn't.

Thankfully the horse did follow it.

Morgan had ridden all the way down into the inhospitable valley by the time Delaney caught up to him. Just beyond an outcropping of rock, she saw a ramshackle cabin and a log barn that was barely standing. A corral, more collapsed than standing, showed no evidence of livestock. Everything there was built of the wood and stone available around them and tucked back so that no one would see there was anyone here if they ever did find their way into the valley.

Morgan drew his horse up at the cabin. The roof looked solid, but the door sagged open. There was no sign of life, not so much as a trail worn from the house to the barn. No smoke was rising out of its stone chimney.

Morgan swung down and ground-hitched his horse, then righted a collapsed hitching post so that they could tie up to it. Hopefully it'd hold.

Delaney slid down from her own horse. Much as she loved horseback riding, she liked it now that the world wasn't moving under her.

Owen plucked Marley off his horse.

"I can get myself down, boss."

Not giving the man time to say more, Owen looped Marley's arm around his neck and took him inside.

Tex was doing the same for Clive Duncan while Morgan saw to Boone. Delaney was left to wonder if they'd bury Stan up here. Someplace where no one could ever visit his grave. But she didn't see that they had much choice.

Tex went inside. Morgan followed him and then emerged without Boone, saying he would take the horses to the barn.

Morgan stopped and studied her. Quietly he said, "I'm sorry about your brother, miss, but he'll be all right . . . I hope. I lost a big brother in the war. I didn't know about it for a year after it happened. I came home after the fighting was over and found a letter from Pa in Elk Point, the nearest town, telling me Gavin had died and I wasn't welcome to come home.

"My brother fought for the South, and that was my pa's idea of what was right. He grew up in Georgia before he came west and had his own notions about slavery, notions I didn't share. I went off to throw in with the Yankees."

"The war's been over for years. You can't have been old enough to fight."

He shrugged one shoulder. "A lot of youngsters fought."

It was more words than she'd ever heard Morgan speak since she'd met him three days ago in Denver to be escorted to Pa.

"Thank you. I'm sorry for the loss of your fellow Marshal."

Morgan nodded, then turned to lead the horses to the barn.

Delaney headed toward the cabin to see what needed doing. She watched Tex stride away in the direction they'd come from, rifle in hand. Posting a sentry.

But those outlaws had to be at least a full day behind them. And no matter how badly they wanted to free Clive, she couldn't imagine them finding their way to this place.

4

Delaney walked into the wrecked excuse for a cabin, took a hard look around, hands on her hips, and said, "Let's get this place cleaned up enough it's safe for a wounded man to lie on the floor."

Owen studied the remarkably pretty woman. It had been proper for her to come along on a ride with seven men since one of them was her brother. But an unconscious brother didn't count. Nothing much to be done about it, but it wasn't right.

He rose from where he'd checked Boone's head wound and nodded. "Your brother just needs time to wake up."

"It's been over a day. He shouldn't still be unconscious."

Owen understood worry. He didn't engage in the activity much but usually had better things to do. Still, he understood it. "No, he shouldn't, but he is and there isn't much we can do about it. Cleaning is probably a waste of time in this place, but I reckon it's better than idleness. Morg will bring water in."

"Right now he's tending the horses, then digging a grave." She paused to glare at Clive Duncan, as if she'd like to make

36

it two graves. But Clive was doing better than Owen had hoped. Well enough that they were keeping him bound, hand and foot.

Her eyes flashed, and he saw her thoughts. Her brother was unconscious still, while this murderer was awake and surviving a gut wound. She didn't like the injustice of that.

Owen didn't either. But hadn't he just seen that a hundred times over, good men wounded or dead while evil men rode free. Then he reminded himself he'd seen justice too, even helped it along during his years working as a U.S. Marshal, and he'd decided the rugged life he led was worthy.

Most days.

Delaney was back to looking around the room again. Not a stick of furniture. Gaping holes where there should have been doors and windows. She strode through the small front room to a doorless second room in the back. Morgan had told him while they rode that there was only the one bed-room. He'd lived in this main room with his older brother, while his pa had the bedroom. His ma had died before they'd moved to this remote, desolate area. They lived on what they could hunt or grow and traded furs for cash money.

Delaney came back out empty-handed. There was nothing in the cabin a pack rat hadn't dragged in. Shaking her head, she said, "Guess I'm going to need to build a broom." With that, she walked back outside.

He almost smiled. He'd wondered where she'd start fash-ioning something like that. But he figured the woman was as savvy as she seemed determined.

At least it was midsummer. Not much call for a fire unless someone brought down a deer. But they'd be wise to be quiet and to save their bullets.

Marley shifted up onto an elbow where he lay on a blanket on the dirt floor. How had Morgan stood living here?

"Got enough water to share, boss?"

Owen smiled at Marley and unscrewed the lid on his canteen. They'd worked together a few times. The crew was stationed out of Colorado. A lot of Marshals worked in federal courthouses, keeping order, providing protection. And a big part of their job was delivering warrants and a summons to appear in court. They also delivered reward money, which mostly came on the train these days.

So a Marshal would ride along to guard cash being delivered to a judge to hand out to someone who'd brought in a wanted outlaw. Marley had been well settled in Denver for a few years. He had a favorite judge, and the man reappointed him at the end of every four-year term. Owen was different. He'd gained a reputation, along with Morgan and Tex, of being a good man to send out on the trail. They got sent after outlaws who'd committed federal crimes, and stealing the mail was one of the most common ones. They'd chased down a lot of train and stagecoach robbers.

None of them had a regular judge they were assigned to guard. None of them had a home. They were wandering men, which suited all of them. Owen had just finished rounding up a band of vicious stagecoach robbers in Wyoming.

Marley took a slow sip, then another longer one.

He looked around the derelict cabin and chuckled, then winced as if the laughter had bothered his wounded leg. "I've stayed in worse places than this."

"Sleeping under the stars doesn't count." Owen managed a smile, but it didn't go very deep.

Then Marley gave him a smile so sly it sent a chill up

Owen's spine. "That's a mighty pretty young lady there." He said it like he was, what, matchmaking? Marley?

Owen didn't respond. It was a comment that didn't merit one.

The smile faded. "Ain't nuthin' proper about a young lady out here with us galoots," Marley added.

"You're right. With her brother laid up, he ain't much of a chaperone. Not much can be done about it at this point."

"Except hope her pa, Colonel Bridger, don't object when he learns about it. By all accounts he's a terror and a tyrant, as tough as old Jim Bridger himself."

Owen nodded, recalling how he'd looked for too long at Delaney Bridger a time or two . . . or three. He'd keep her pa in mind. "I've heard of him. Never served with him, though. Folks say he's a warrior to the bone who'd've single-handedly won the war for the Union if others hadn't thrown in to help."

Marley sat up and leaned back against the wall near the full-height fireplace. "Being proper is the least of our troubles. Her pa's gonna tear a strip off of us for his son getting hurt, and I won't blame him. I had a son who died fighting for the North. You never make peace with it; you only live with it because your heart keeps beating, and your breath keeps going in and out."

"I never knew you had a son, Marley."

"A wife and a boy. Lost her when she tried to bring a second child into the world. I went off to fight and left my son with neighbors. Minute I was gone, he ran off when he was too young to have a lick of sense. Became a drummer."

"I think Morg was a drummer, too. Another one who was just a youngster when he marched off to fight." Owen walked back over to take a longer look at Boone, reassuring himself that he was still breathing.

Marley went on. "Losing him sent me to the Western Frontier and into the Marshals Service. I still think of 'em both almost every day, and my mind wrangles around thinking of what I should have done to save 'em. And then the days I don't think of 'em, I remember the next day and feel guilty for forgetting them."

Marley was quiet a minute, and Owen wished he knew what to say. He carried pain of his own, but it didn't seem to make him any wiser when it came to moments like this.

After another sip of water, Marley added, "He'd've been a bit older than Stan if he'd lived. Reckon that's why I was so fond of Stan." Marley moved back to his blanket, then closed his eyes. "It's been a long day. I'm gonna see if I can sleep awhile."

Delaney came back in at that moment. She'd found a stick and a clutch of twigs and some vines. She lashed the twigs around the stick to make a likely looking broom. She sure was turning out to be a handy woman.

After a glance at Marley, Delaney went to the back room to work. Owen guessed from her closed-off expression that she'd waited outside to let Marley talk. She seemed to have a knack for knowing what people needed.

Owen wrenched his thoughts from the very pretty, very tough, very worried Delaney.

Morgan poked his head through the doorway. "Horses are taken care of. The corral didn't need much. I repaired it and dug a grave."

Owen saw Marley's eyes flicker open. The man was a Marshal, so he slept light.

"If you're ready, we can get Stan settled now." Morgan stepped back outside and brought in a haunch of deer. "It's safe to start a fire for cooking. I checked the chimney. Seems sturdy enough, and the flue's clear of any debris."

Just how long had Owen been in here tending Marley and Boone? But then Morgan got more done in an hour than any man alive.

"You got some game? I didn't hear a rifle shot."

"Didn't think it was wise when we don't know where those coyote Duncans are. I got it with my knife. Wandered right up close. I'll cut some steaks, and we can build a spit in the fireplace and roast the meat that way. I've got a big enough pan in my saddlebag to make up a stew for tomorrow. There should be some Indian potatoes and wild onions around here to flavor it some."

Morgan said, "Miss Delaney?" She appeared in the doorway of the sole bedroom. "You want to attend the funeral, miss?"

For a rough man from the wild, high-up hills, Morgan held more kindness in his voice than Owen could believe.

Of course, even knowing each other for years and working together now and then, he and Morgan hadn't done much getting to know each other. They were too busy chasing outlaws and making their way in the wilderness of the West. Not a lot of long nights spinning yarns and sharing life stories by the fire.

Out of the corner of his eye, Owen saw their prisoner roll onto his side, then flop over to his back again. Maybe he forgot he'd been shot.

At the sight of Clive's bloodshot eyes and pale face—so

young—Owen felt a pang of regret for a life wasted from the very beginning.

"Your saddle partner won't be the last to die in your posse. My pa won't quit coming for me," the young man warned them.

Marley, his voice menacing, said, "Then they won't quit dying, will they, Clive?"

"Right now I'm going to bury a friend. Miss Delaney, you should come along. Tex is standing watch, Marley ain't up to it, and Owen is guarding this polecat, who don't have the sense to stop threatening the men who hold his life in their hands. I'd appreciate some company."

Delaney set the broom aside. "It's right to have folks pay their respects. I can say some prayers while we bury him."

Owen would say his prayers for Stan, too. He'd've liked to go along, but Morgan was right—he had plenty to keep him busy.

Delaney paused to take a long look at her brother, then followed Morgan out the door.

Owen said to Marley, "Try and sleep. You haven't had much of a chance so far."

Truthfully, Delaney had been praying since they left Denver. She wasn't about to stop now as she stood beside Stan's grave.

Boone had to be all right. But he'd been still for so long now.

She felt like she was putting too much on Morgan. She'd've helped dig the grave as well as cover it, but there was only one shovel, and she knew men well enough to be sure Morgan wouldn't stop working to let her handle things.

"What next? Do we just hole up here forever?"

Morgan stopped throwing dirt over his saddle partner, turned, and gave her a grim smile. "As soon as we're sure Marley and your brother can handle the ride, I got a way out of here. We'll go through an abandoned ranch that used to neighbor us, and then we'll ride the winding back trails out of the mountains on our way to Fort Russell and your folks. And if we do run into any of those consarned Duncans again, we'll see if we can round up more of them."

Morgan emptied one last shovelful of dirt onto the grave. He dropped the shovel and removed his broad-brimmed hat and held it over his heart. Delaney appreciated that he offered a silent moment of reverence for the departed one.

She recited the 23rd Psalm, a favorite she'd memorized long ago, slowing to the part about "the valley of the shadow of death," then ended with another moment of silence.

"I should get back to tidying the cabin." Her throat had tightened as she'd talked, thinking of the young man, dead before his life had gotten a chance to really start. She didn't know him that well, but it could easily have been her brother, and he still might not make it. She felt a tear run down her cheek.

She and Morgan walked together back toward the ramshackle cabin.

"Do you have any idea where your pa got to?"

"Nope. I thought he might be here, but I reckon living here alone wasn't much fun. He probably went out into the wild. I wonder if he's still alive. I doubt I'll ever know."

Back inside, Owen had venison steaks sizzling while Marley slept and Clive glowered at the whole world.

God forgive her, but Delaney intended to be on hand for his hanging. Against her better judgment, she said, "We can't let the Duncan Gang kill a good man and be satisfied with avoiding them until we get to safety."

Marley's eyes popped open, and she regretted waking him.

"My family isn't a 'gang.' Why do you call them one?" Clive tried to shove himself to a sitting position but groaned and slumped back to the floor.

"Bank robbers, the lot of you," Owen snapped. "I've heard of your reputation. And you're far from innocent. You killed a soldier in Cheyenne. That's a federal crime, which is why the Marshals got the job of transporting you back. Add to that your family broke you out of a military brig, not just a town jail."

"We may live a rough life, but we live free. We're honest men. I shot that man in self-defense, and they were building a gallows right outside my window. My brother saved me."

"You can't claim honesty because I just buried a good man who died under your family's guns," Morgan growled. "I intend to hang every man jack of them. I counted seven men, killed one of 'em. Six to go, and you'll make another."

Clive gasped. "You killed one of my kin? Then you're a marked man." But furious as he was, Clive didn't try to sit up again.

Delaney's eyes slid to Marley, hurt mighty bad too but sitting up, not groaning.

"I killed that man in self-defense," Clive repeated.

Morgan shook his head. "A military court didn't see it that way."

"They weren't there when it happened. Of course they'd side with their own man. I saw a man grab a woman off the street in Cheyenne. Him and another man dragged her into an alley. I ran after them, Finlay MacNeil drew on me, and I defended myself."

"What did the judge say when you told him that?"

"He believed the only witness, a man called Calan Mac-Neil. Calan is a cousin to Finlay MacNeil, and he was after the woman, too. She got away and ran off, and then the gunfire started. She never came forward to support my story. No one believed me. If there was any way to keep fighting, I'd've stayed and faced up to it. But they said I'd hang soon. When my brother Leland came to rescue me, I did the only thing that made sense and rode away fast."

Delaney hadn't heard this part of the story.

"Maybe your family isn't a gang, Clive. Maybe they're a choir of angels. Maybe that killing was justified. But I doubt it." Owen shook his head. "Judge and jury is the system we have in this country, and I believe in it. 'Course, that was before one of your kin killed a U.S. Marshal. If the judge is feeling merciful, he might pluck one of your own out and accuse him alone of murder. But the rest of 'em will be locked up for being involved in a jailbreak. Until then, we'll hang on to you, watch our back trail for more Duncans, and head for Fort Russell."

Owen turned his steaks again. The smell of frying meat set Delaney's stomach to growling, though it felt almost wrong to think of enjoying food when Boone was so badly wounded.

"We should waylay the whole lot of them and take them back to Fort Russell with us." Delaney crossed her arms.

"I'd as soon stay and grab them too," said Owen, "but we have to get you and Boone to safety and Marley to a doctor. Then we'll come back."

"I'm coming back, too. I don't intend to sit idle somewhere while the men who shot my brother go on their way."

Owen narrowed his eyes and studied her for too long.

"Your pa would kill me if I deliberately let you hunt down outlaws. Not sure that's enough to stop me from allowing it, though. If it was my brother, I'd want the same. And the word is"—Owen glanced at Morgan, whose word was the only word he had—"you're mighty handy on a trail, and handy with a gun."

"It's decided then. We'll get Boone and Marley to a doctor, then turn Clive in and go looking."

Owen didn't nod, but neither did he tell her it was out of the question. Instead. he went back to his steaks. It didn't matter if he approved or not. Delaney seemed determined to hunt those men down, every one of them, and make them pay for what they'd done.

How Owen felt about it didn't interest her much.

"Something else you should know."

Owen turned back to her. "What's that, Delaney?"

"My pa expects us in a couple of days. I wired him when we left Denver and again in Elk Point. When we don't show up on time—and on time is tomorrow morning—he'll expect a wire from Fort Collins. And if he doesn't get it, he'll be coming. He'll probably bring my ma along."

"Will he bring the cavalry, too?"

"Probably not. The cavalry would just slow Ma and Pa down."

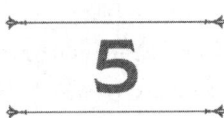

5

Owen sat up with Marley, and he was on hand to notice Clive was running a fever. It irked him, but he probably had oughta help.

He knelt beside Clive and pressed a cool cloth to his forehead. Clive was more asleep than awake, but wherever that bullet had hit him, it hadn't pierced anything vital or the man wouldn't still be alive. And the bullet had gone right through him, so it was a mercy that Owen and his hamhanded surgery wasn't required to dig a bullet out. Lucky for everyone. Owen had dug bullets out of people before, and it was a miserable business for both him and the patient.

Probably worse for the patient.

Clive's eyes flickered open, and though they had a glaze of fever about them, he focused on Owen. "You should just ride off and leave me. My kin will find me, and I'll tell them to let you ride on. Easier for you and me both."

Owen sat back on his heels and studied the kid. "Easy don't interest me much. You wouldn't last long on your own, and you're guilty of murder. I'm not going to let you go, Clive."

He got the rag wet again to cool it, wrung it out, and pressed it to Clive's forehead. "Don't you worry where you'll spend eternity, boy? You're getting ready to face it, so you should try and make peace with God." Owen figured he might be wasting his breath, but it was his to waste.

Clive made no response other than to shove weakly at Owen's hand, as if it bothered him to have his head bathed by another man, let alone Owen.

Owen would be in this room for the night with the other men. Tex had returned from standing watch, and Morgan took over to keep watch for the early hours of the night. That left Delaney the bedroom. No bed, no door, but at least she had a wall between her and the men.

He worried more every hour about Boone, still unconscious. It was coming up on two days now. A blow to the head like that from a grazing bullet could be tricky. It was way past time for the youngster to wake up.

"Rest of my family is in hell and playin' poker with Old Scratch," Clive said at last. "They'll deal me into the game."

Making a joke of it. Owen wasn't surprised. But it awakened compassion in him to see someone raised so poorly. The kid had little chance with that kind of learning. "That's not in the Bible anywhere, Clive." He tried to reach past the boy's arrogance. "There'll be no pleasure to be had. No family reunion to enjoy. I reckon hell is pure misery. Maybe you'll get a glimpse of paradise and then know you'll never see it again. Why would you want to abandon the hope of heaven when you have a choice?"

"Let me be, will you? Why try and cool me down if it's just to save me for eternal fire? Quit wasting both our time." Clive closed his eyes.

Owen eased back from him. The kid was so young, so misguided. Owen thought of the story he'd told about rescuing a woman. Shaking his head, he checked the ropes binding his prisoner, then leaned back against the wall to doze for a while.

◇—◇

Delaney had slept a couple of stretches and woke up to the early light of dawn. The house was in utter silence, and the realization that Boone was hurt slammed into her like a fist. Yet Owen was sitting up with the injured. He'd promised to wake her if Boone stirred.

She was mercifully alone in the back room and let herself quietly cry. No sense putting the menfolk through her weeping.

She tried to get it all out. Well, not all. Not when he was still so injured, but she needed to get out the useless waste of her tears so she could focus on what needed doing.

When the tears began to ebb, she stood to her feet and was mopping her burning eyes when Owen stepped into the doorway. He frowned at her tear-streaked face, then walked into the room and pulled her into his arms.

The shock of being held left her frozen for a minute, and then the floodgates opened again.

"I've heard it said that a woman needs a shoulder when she cries."

Delaney hadn't known that because she so rarely cried. But right now it was the pure truth. He tucked a crumpled-up kerchief into her hand, and that simple kindness made her cry all the more.

"I-I'm sorry. Such foolishness . . ."

"I don't do much crying myself."

That caused Delaney to laugh even as she wept.

"But if a woman can't cry over her brother being shot, then God shouldn't have invented tears."

Delaney burrowed closer, and Owen's arms tightened just a bit. His strength woke up some of her own.

"Morgan said you're a woman to ride the river with. A fine hand with a rifle and on a trail. Those are high compliments from Morgan. I'm afraid we'll be having a rougher journey than expected."

She buried her face into his chest. The simple kindness of Owen letting her lean on his strength knitted something together in her frightened, broken heart. Steadier now, she said, "We should be able to ride the trail from Denver to Cheyenne without having to fight for our lives. That's a settled land these days. But it looks now like we should've had the cavalry ride along with us. Who'd've ever considered that?"

"Right. We figured five Marshals would be more than enough."

There was a moment of silence as Delaney pondered how they'd started out with five, but now Stan Ross lay buried far from anyone he knew or loved. She felt the tension in Owen, and suddenly his arms around her felt selfish. She wasn't the only one who needed a shoulder; maybe Owen could use one, too. Her arms wrapped around him. She'd never held a man before. The unfamiliar feeling should have been awkward, but instead it was wonderful.

"We were told you and your brother were mighty tough. It felt more like extra warriors going along. But without need because there was no war."

Very gently, he said, "I didn't come in here to catch you

crying. Boone's stirring. I think he's waking up. Your brother has decided nap time is over."

Delaney pushed back far enough to see his eyes. The steadiness in them, together with the good news, helped her get ahold of herself.

Owen gave her a gentle smile. "He's not alert or talking, but his eyes flickered open for just a second."

With a gasp of excitement, she nearly knocked Owen over getting to Boone. She heard his soft chuckle and felt embarrassed for rushing away from him when he'd been so generous with his support. She dropped to her knees beside her brother. "Boone, can you hear me? It's Delaney."

His head tossed a bit. She saw his eyes open a bit, then close again.

"No, Brother, wake up now." She remembered Owen's words and smiled. "Nap time is over, Boone."

His eyes slowly opened, and this time they stayed open. He focused on her as she leaned over him. "Delaney . . ." he breathed.

She leaned down to kiss his forehead. The bandage was in the way, but she didn't mind. "Boone, you were shot, but you're going to be all right."

"Sh-shot?" Boone raised an unsteady hand to his bandage. "In the h-head?"

"You've been unconscious a long time. I've been so worried . . ." Her voice broke. "The bullet cut your scalp, but it didn't penetrate your skull. It would've done you no good rattlin' around in your brain." She tried to smile at that.

His eyes met hers. "T-tired. Need sleep."

"Have a drink of water first." She had a cup handy, and Owen came to kneel across from her and help Boone sit up.

She glanced at him. He'd stayed back to give her a moment with her brother, but he'd been close to lend a hand. She appreciated it so much, she had to shake off the urge to weep again. Enough of that.

Boone looked at Owen, and his brow furrowed.

Delaney didn't give him time to do any thinking. He needed to let his brain rest. She got the water to his lips and let him sip, then sip again.

Giving him a few seconds to see if the water would stay in his belly, she gave him another drink, and he emptied the cup. When it was gone, Owen lowered him back to the floor where the blanket from Boone's bedroll had been stretched out.

Boone was asleep in seconds.

Delaney raised her head from her brother and looked at Owen. She felt her lips tremble when she asked, "He is going to make it, isn't he?"

"Yep, your brother is probably good enough we can let him sit up on his horse. We'll tie him to his saddle horn. Better way to ride than draped over the saddle."

Studying Owen, she saw a rugged man. All of the Marshals were. In truth, her pa was such a man as this. And her brothers. Goodness, *rugged* pretty much described her ma, too. She reckoned she was rugged herself. She wondered if the U.S. Marshals allowed women into their ranks. She expected to see if Cheyenne needed any teachers, but she'd heard there were women Pinkerton agents, so why not women Marshals?

She thought she had the skills necessary for the job. Well, some of them anyway. She'd prefer not to get into a fistfight with a man twice her size. When it came down to it, it'd

probably be impossible to outfight a low-down polecat trying to dodge the law, but she'd bet she could outthink him.

She thought of the shiny new Winchester and how skilled
she was with it. Yes, she could be a Marshal for certain.

She realized then she was still looking Owen in the eye,
and he was looking right back—the man she'd let hold her,
let comfort her. That rugged face. His blue eyes. He hadn't
shaved in a week or two. He could sure use a haircut.

He tilted his head, staring at her with eyes surprisingly
kind for such a hard man. She was relieved to see that there
was nothing in those eyes that indicated he was thinking
improper thoughts, only concern.

"I suppose you don't deal with weeping women too often
in your line of work."

He laughed. "Nope, it's not the usual way things go for
me."

She smiled back at him. She could smile now without it
feeling like a betrayal of her wounded brother. "You have a
talent for it, I'd say. Though I can't recall ever having anyone
hold me when I cried before. Of course, I can't remember
the last time I cried."

"You shed a tear or two when Boone was shot."

Shaking her head, she said, "This will be a trip to remember."

More quietly, she said, "You have a talent for giving comfort, Owen. Thank you." Yet she regretted he'd come upon
her crying in the back room. Even so, he'd been nothing but
kind, and he showed no dismay at having a weepy woman
along. Instead, he showed decency.

"You're very welcome, Miss Bridger."

"Call me Delaney. We've been through a lot the last few days. It seems only right."

"It's Owen, then, Delaney. I'm sorry this trip has turned into such a struggle. But we'll get through it together."

"I'll not listen to you say you're sorry when your fast thinking saved us." She paused. "Except for Marshal Ross. Five men shot, but four of them will survive and heal. I thank you for that."

"We'll see how everyone is doing when we hit the trail."

She wondered if he was telling her they were moving out today. She thought it was too soon, but Owen was a man she could trust. If he thought it best that they get going now, she would follow his lead.

"We'll let Boone and Marley rest for another day or two, but your brother is definitely going to make it. The wound shows no sign of suppuration. He doesn't have a fever, and he's awake, if a little bit dazed."

"He said my name. Did you hear it?" She sniffed and swiped her hand across her eyes. She was *not* starting that again.

She wasn't sure just how she sounded, but Owen reached across a sleeping Boone and rested his strong hand on her wrist. "I did hear it. I also noticed he didn't seem to know who I was."

Delaney's breath hitched as she listened to what Owen might think about that.

"It's not uncommon to forget things that happened in the hours or even days before and after a blow to the head. Yet that's nothing to worry about, Delaney. He's going to be fine."

She nodded and took a deep breath, slowly letting it out

to steady herself. "Thank you." Then she swallowed hard and squared her shoulders. Time to get on with what all needed doing. "Would you like me to take over cooking? I saw what Morgan brought in, the wild vegetables as well as the venison. I can make a decent stew out of that."

Owen was still holding her wrist and only now seemed to notice. He tightened his grip on her arm for a moment, then released it and grinned. "That would be greatly appreciated. Thank you."

6

Owen managed a few hours of sleep a night for the next three nights. Clive was going to live. Marley was going to keep his leg. Boone was sitting up to eat, but was too dizzy to stand, so he spent most of those days flat on his back. Still, he was talking more and making sense. He still didn't remember anything from a few days before he was shot. Besides Delaney, Boone only knew Owen and the others because he'd been told who they were. But he knew they were headed for Wyoming and Fort Russell. He might never remember the time right around the attack.

Tex came into the cabin late in the day, along with Morgan. "I've just been watching the trail in, but Morg here, he's been hunting."

Owen looked at Morgan, dressed to fade into the landscape. He always wore buckskin and made his clothing himself. His broad-brimmed hat was the same tan color, the color of the earth. Morgan could sneak around in the wilderness without being seen, better than anyone Owen had ever known.

"Hunting men or wild game?" Owen asked.

Morgan gave Owen a narrow-eyed look, smiled but didn't answer. Owen figured that *was* his answer.

"We'll be ready to leave in the morning," Owen said. "You've got a back way down, Morg?"

"Yep," said Morgan, "but it won't be morning. We'll leave when we get back, whenever that is. Those varmints are a long distance away. They got to the top of that first hill, and they've been hunting tracks and not making much progress. I've got plans for them. Tex is standing watch with me." He and Tex had been taking shifts, but now they'd go together.

Owen didn't ask because he already knew. At least he knew what he'd've done.

"One more thing. I told you there were six of 'em. They're down to four now. Two rode off."

"Only four, Morg? Can you round them all up?"

He shook his head. "The way they lay out their camp, they've made it real hard to close in on them. There'd be shooting trouble, and there's no need for that."

Nodding, Owen said, "Careful on the hunt."

Delaney had more stew ready, and they all ate fast. Afterward, Marley offered to go along on the watch.

Morgan studied him for a while before saying, "You could handle it if you stayed on your horse, but two of us is enough, so you might as well rest up. Once we set out, we'll be riding hard."

Marley nodded. Owen was glad to see the man was ready to get back to work.

Morgan and Tex left the cabin and headed into the encroaching darkness.

Stella had awakened the day after Leland was shot to find Beau and Macon had ridden off in the night. That made Pa mad. Uncle Gordy complained along with Pa, but to Stella he seemed relieved. Still, she'd failed to stop her pa, Uncle Gordy, and her brother Johnny from going after the men who'd killed Leland.

She was glad her two cousins had gone. They might've just saved their own lives. Her only regret was that they hadn't told her of their plan or asked her to come along. As for Pa, she'd known he wouldn't quit, but she'd tried.

They'd waited a full day before Pa went up that steep slope, alone and in the pitch-dark of night. She gave him credit for doing what had to be done. He wasn't the sort of man who sent his children or his brother to risk their lives when he wasn't willing to do it himself.

Too bad he was risking his life on a fool's errand.

Once he'd crested the hilltop, he scouted around until he was sure the lawmen who had Clive had indeed moved on. By then the sun had risen and he'd come back to the cliff and waved them all up.

It had occurred to her to beg Uncle Gordy and Johnny to just ride off while Pa was gone, but she decided not to waste her breath.

Once they were together again, they began picking out a trail, proceeding a few feet at a time. They'd had to divide up and try different directions.

The men who had Clive were good at covering their trail. Her respect for them grew by the hour. She had no idea if they were getting close, but she thought they were going the right way. If the lawmen were setting a fast pace and knew a way down out of these peaks, they might be halfway to

Wyoming by now. She hoped they made it without another clash between their groups because she was grimly sure it'd end ugly for everyone.

⋄•————————•⋄

Morgan slid left and nodded at Tex, who slid right. They'd talked it through and felt sure they knew what to expect. These weren't the most original outlaws they'd ever seen.

The camp had settled for the night by the time the Marshals had arrived to watch over them. They'd posted two guards, one on each side of the camp, situated so that the guards couldn't see each other.

The Duncans were closing very slowly on Morgan's cabin. They'd been at it for days, and frankly, Morgan was impressed they'd come the right way. The guards took two-hour shifts, and it wasn't uncommon for at least one of them to set himself up for sentry duty, then fall asleep.

There were rumors about the Duncans, and yet Morgan, who'd spied on this band, couldn't identify the men from any wanted posters. The only crimes Morgan knew of for sure were the jailbreak and opening fire on a group of Marshals. Killing Stan was something the Duncans couldn't run away from.

There'd been some outlaw Duncans, and Morgan figured these were the men, but he couldn't be sure. Some men named Duncan had stirred up a good portion of Colorado and Wyoming in the last three years. Morgan suspected the older two brothers who'd brought their sons into the gang had been outlawing for most of their lives.

When they'd caught Clive Duncan, they hoped to reel in the rest of the gang by questioning him. There'd even been talk of letting Clive off with prison instead of a hanging if he helped bring in his family.

Before they got any information out of him, though, Clive had been busted out of jail in Cheyenne—although *busted* was the wrong word because busting was noisy. The Duncans had slipped in real quiet-like, gotten through locked doors and gates, past the guards, and slid out silent as ghosts. Clive had been missed only when one of the guards brought him breakfast and found the stockade door standing wide open. There weren't many tracks, but enough they were sure he'd had help. Naturally his family was suspected.

Clive and whoever helped him had vanished into the night. Then, over a year later, Clive had rode into town to have a drink at a Denver saloon like the blamed fool he was. Two town sheriffs had recognized him, arrested him, and then deputized ten men to stand guard over him, considering his earlier jailbreak.

They'd held Clive until Morgan and the other U.S. Marshals had arrived to transport him. Five Marshals should have been enough, especially when they were asked to transport two travelers to Cheyenne since they were going there anyway with the prisoner. The son and daughter of Colonel Lionel "Grizzly" Bridger were plenty wise to western ways and tough enough to make things easier, not harder. But they all knew now how that had turned out. Seven men in the gang had come chasing after Clive. Morgan had picked one off as they tried to charge up the cliff, hot on their trail.

Morgan should have brought the ten men along on the ride to Fort Russell. It might've headed off their troubles. He inched along, searching for the night watchman.

Finally, the guard came into view. In the dark, Morgan took a while to make out who he was dealing with and decided it was one of the older brothers. The outlaw stood there slouched against a tree.

The man rolled tobacco into a scrap of paper, making himself a smoke. In the flare of the match, which he should've known would give away his position, Morgan saw a big man but lean, as folks tended to be in the West, where they worked hard. He'd heard these two brothers ran the gang. He hoped both took this watch. If they captured the leaders, it might send the rest of the group into disarray.

Morgan watched and waited. The man wasn't on edge. He never moved from the tree, which made it hard to sneak up on him. After finishing his smoke, he slid down the tree and leaned his head back against it.

Five minutes later, Morgan heard snoring.

Asleep on watch.

With cold satisfaction, Morgan eased closer.

He wondered how Tex was doing but wasn't about to lose focus on this man. It was almost too easy, and that made him nervous. He kept a sharp eye out in case someone came to relieve the sleeping man, but the shifts were two hours long and they never varied.

When he was near enough, Morgan, silent as a striking snake—not a rattler—rammed the butt of his gun against the man's head with one wicked blow, then tied him up fast and tight like a calf at branding time. Once he'd gagged the man, Morgan lowered him to the ground and headed for where the Duncans staked out their horses.

When he'd untied all their horses, holding his breath that none of them made enough noise to wake anyone, he led the animals to where he'd left the old man, loaded the varmint up, then headed for his own horse.

He met Tex there with a bundle. Tex draped the other sentry over one of the horses Morgan had brought, and then they made a saddle string, with Tex bringing up the rear. They rode out quick and quiet.

They were well down the trail when Morgan heard thrashing and glanced back. One of the prisoners was awake. They were out of hearing distance, so Morgan said, "Tex, your varmint is conscious. You should have put him into a deeper sleep."

Tex was a hard man and had liked Stan, so Morgan had expected his friend to apply a sturdier blow to the man he'd caught.

"Keep on riding. The ropes will hold." Tex said nothing more, but Morgan heard a tone in his voice that set him on edge.

He did as Tex asked and kept moving. But he moved a little faster. The stretch they'd ridden in on from Pa's place was almost all solid stone. It was tough to follow a trail up here, especially in the night. Yet it was impossible to be as careful as they needed to be with all the horses, and surely they were leaving evidence of their passage behind.

The Duncans would find them now, but they were afoot, so they'd leave the gang far behind if they departed the cabin right away. As they approached, Morgan saw Marley sitting outside. His leg was extended in front of him, and he was holding a plate in his hand as he watched them approach. Morgan saw him turn toward the door from where he sat, and then Owen came out of the cabin, nodded at them, and smiled.

They'd started out with seven men hunting them. One was dead. Two had run off. They'd just cut that number to two and set those two afoot.

Owen ate his meal quickly, then headed for where they'd corralled their horses. As they drew near, Morgan smelled the cooking. Delaney had made something to eat, probably more stew. Morgan suspected the woman carried dried herbs or spices in her meager bags. Salt for sure, but he thought there must be something more because she made an unusually fine meal from few ingredients.

Owen had the rest of the horses saddled before Morgan rode up. He left their two prisoners on horseback. Tex came up beside him and said in a low voice, "No sense talking about it before now, but we got trouble."

Morgan frowned, looked in the direction behind them but saw nothing. He then turned his attention to the prisoner Tex had brought in.

The day was more than half gone when Tex said, "We need to keep moving."

"I agree it's best to push on. Good to see you outside, Marley."

Marley nodded but kept on eating, not saying anything.

Owen led their horses up. "Get some food in your belly and let's hit the trail. Good work—you took every horse they had."

Delaney came to the door, a gun in hand, which she kept pointed at Clive. Morgan thought her overcautious attention to the polecat showed good sense.

Morgan and Tex went inside to eat and saw Boone on his feet. Pale and unsteady but up and ready to go.

"You're looking better, Bridger."

"Head's still not right, but I can sit a horse."

"Good. Owen's got your horse saddled."

Boone left the cabin.

Whatever the trouble was, Tex didn't say anything more as they ate fast, packed up the bedrolls and saddlebags, then hoisted Clive to his feet while Delaney washed up and packed the pans away.

"We brought you some company, boy." Morgan moved him along even as Clive clutched his belly.

Clive saw their new captives and straightened, which made Owen wonder how much of his pain was an act.

Clive narrowed his eyes. "Pa?"

Pa? Morgan knew enough about the gang to know Clive's pa was Sly Duncan, supposedly the meanest of the group. His brother Gordon was bad, but Sly was the brains of the organization.

Clive's eyes slid to the other prisoner. "Stella?"

Morgan felt like he'd been slammed into a stone wall. He whipped his head around to glare at Tex, who was mounting up.

"You captured a girl?"

Tex tugged the front of his hat.

Morgan glared at Clive. "A girl is part of the Duncan Gang?"

"She's my sister."

The youngster managed to work the gag out of her mouth. "Your *big* sister, Clive, and don't you forget it!"

Morgan heard the female voice, and now in the sunlight, he noticed her long lashes and fine-boned face. He knew then she was absolutely a girl . . . well, a young woman more like.

"And you caught Pa?"

"If this trip takes long enough, we'll have your whole family hog-tied and draped over our horses. We almost grabbed them last night. Probably could have if we didn't mind a gunfight. There's only two of 'em left."

"Two? There should be more than that." Clive sounded peeved.

"Beau and Macon rode off. They knew we were riding into trouble," Stella said.

"They quit on the family when they were supposed to be saving me?"

"Yep." She said it like she enjoyed snipping at him. "I tried to talk the family into quitting this fool's errand and riding on to Cheyenne to try and talk you out of that hanging. Only Macon and Beau were smart enough to ride off."

"I told you we had trouble," Tex said.

"You bashed a woman over the head?" Delaney scowled at Tex, clearly disapproving. Morgan wondered if after she'd thought about it for a while, she'd decide that, man or woman, if you rode with a bunch of bloodthirsty outlaws, you might expect to get bashed over the head from time to time.

"I've never heard of a woman being part of a gang of outlaws." Morgan shook his head as he tossed Clive onto horseback and lashed his hands to the saddle horn.

Owen took the time to get Boone boosted into his saddle.

"I want to sit up, too," Stella Duncan demanded.

"It's time to stop jawing and get on our way." Owen mounted up. "I want these varmints locked up in a nice sturdy jail as soon as possible. One where they can watch as a gallows is being built outside the jail window."

Sly was still unconscious. Or maybe he was faking it. Only

a fool would trust anything about Sly Duncan. But more than his suspicion of Sly, Morgan trusted the knots in those ropes.

Tex dismounted, went to Stella Duncan's side, got her down off the unsaddled horse, and shifted her to sit up on Stan's saddled one. With her hands securely tied, he now bound them to the saddle horn.

Morgan considered their group. Boone was on horseback, pale but eager to get going. Marley had somehow gotten into his saddle without asking for help or uttering so much as a groan. Stella and Clive were sitting upright. Sly was still draped across a saddle. Morgan sighed, moved to his horse, and was soon astride.

They set out on the trail, along with the saddle string of extra horses. Three prisoners. Two men led, tied end to end, with one headed up by Morgan, the other by Tex. Five honest folks. A couple of them were pretty seriously injured. Though the outlaws were under control, the odds were not great that the Marshals wouldn't encounter more trouble.

Morgan saw Delaney staring at the mound of dirt that marked Stan's grave as they rode by. Her eyes were somber as she looked to Owen. He knew they were all in full agreement that whoever had killed Stan needed to be punished for what they'd done.

7

Delaney thought this was the slowest, hardest riding she'd ever done. And this was the way down! They were deep in the belly of the most rugged stretch of land where not a speck of the ground was level. Instead, it was all peaks and gorges, among which were narrow trails—if they could be called that. Even the streams they waded along dipped and rose with rough stones.

As they skirted mountainsides, they inched their way down into gullies that seemed to swallow them all in one gulp. Then they rode on in the shadowy depths of the gullies, sometimes along a stream, with the water curving one way while Morgan went another. They'd climb into the sunlight again and keep twisting along the snakelike trail. Delaney had ridden so long and hard that she was nearly asleep on her horse. And she needed to be in top form to survive the perils of such a rugged trail.

Thankfully, Boone was holding up all right. He rode in front of her, so she could see if he was pale or flushed, unsteady or steady or a little of both. But he hung on to his horse and never complained, and she did the same. When they reached one of the stretches that was part of a stream, Delaney pulled up her horse beside Boone's and reached her hand across to rest it on his arm.

"How are you?" she asked him. "I'm about to nod off."

Boone turned to smile at her. He was clearly exhausted, but his eyes were brighter, clearer. "This is the wildest place we've ever been."

She smiled back. "With the name Bridger, we probably shouldn't admit that."

He nodded but with tiny, slow movements, as if doing so made his head hurt. "The truth is, most of our hunting and tracking skills came from Ma. Pa was gone too much."

"It was always nice when he was home," Delaney replied. "Ma missed him something fierce. I wonder where our brother ever got to. It sounds like Bowie's been to the highest peaks and the deepest canyons."

"Well, he can't've been to higher peaks or deeper canyons than what we're riding through right now."

They grinned at each other.

"He might have us beat, but not by much. I wonder if he's still alive?" Delaney thought of their oldest brother. To her and Boone, he was more legend than family. "I wonder if we'll ever meet him?"

"Crockett and Jedediah wandered through Texas that time, remember?"

"Yep, but we knew them a little when growing up. Bowie, he took off before we were old enough to remember."

"Pa always said Bowie was born for wild country, and the house was getting crowded. Pa crossed paths with him a few times. And Crockett and Jedediah fought in the war. He met up with them pretty regular for a time, and they came through and visited us."

Boone seemed to look into the past as he thought of their wandering brothers. "Ma said they put out word that she and Pa are living in Fort Russell now. She'd heard all three of our brothers are in the northern Rockies, though maybe not together, and hopes they'll come for a visit. I can't imagine having a son who left over twenty years ago and has never come back."

"I'm glad we decided to join our parents in Fort Russell." Delaney had been teaching school in Texas, and Boone had lived there with her when their folks were stationed at a nearby fort. Then their parents had moved on, and for a time Boone and she were settled. Done with their wandering life. He'd done some sheriffing and worked as a justice of the peace, even spending a year doing the work of a cowhand. They'd done well there.

Ma wrote that she and Pa were planning to settle down in Cheyenne and stay put until Pa was done with his working years. Ma had invited them to come and live close to them. So they'd decided to pull up stakes and move to Wyoming. All of that had led them to this remote wilderness with four Marshals and three criminals tied up.

Seeing the trail was about to turn even rougher, Delaney said, "Looks like Morgan's turning off up ahead. It's getting real narrow now. I'd better drop back."

Their eyes met for a moment. "I'm so glad you're all right, Boone." She squeezed his arm. "Seeing you lying there, bleeding from your head . . . it was a sight that scared me right to the marrow of my bones."

"But I'm going to be fine now." He smiled and gave his head one slow nod.

She nodded and dropped into single file again. Delaney didn't say so, but she felt better riding behind Boone so that she could keep an eye on him. He was a savvy man. It was proof he was still somewhat addled or he'd've known why she rode behind and objected to being watched over so carefully. Or maybe he wasn't addled at all. Maybe he knew he should be watched.

Morgan started up another mountain. She knew better than to ever believe there wasn't a higher one somewhere, but honestly she'd thought they had to be near the top of the world.

She wondered how long this could go on. The question almost escaped her lips, but she clenched her jaw and kept quiet.

Once they'd reached the top, the group wound around a pile of boulders that looked to be clinging to the mountainside more out of pure habit than by anything holding them there. And then the trail opened up to paradise.

Delaney gasped. She heard Owen coming from behind her, leading Clive and Sly. Tex was now bringing up the rear with Stella and the saddle string. Sly had regained consciousness somewhere in the middle of the long day and was given water and a stick of jerked meat. He was allowed to straddle his horse now.

The man only grunted, and he had a look in his eyes so calculating that Delaney didn't like him riding behind her, not even bound tight to his saddle. She drew her horse to a stop alongside Boone and wanted to study him but couldn't take her eyes off what lay before her. Owen pulled up on her left and stopped.

Tex let out a whistle at the sight before them, while Clive seemed unable to find the words to describe it.

Sly spoke for him. "Who'd'a thunk there was a place like this on top of the world."

They continued on. There was a short descent into a bowl-like meadow that went on for hundreds of acres until it ended with a stand of oak and maple trees. The meadow was surrounded by canyon walls. A stream cut an arc at the far west edge of the meadow. Near the center of the meadow, a herd of longhorns grazed, along with a dozen or so horses, including four foals. Amidst it all was a tidy-looking log cabin. Smoke drifted up from its stone chimney.

A woman stepped out of the cabin, her rifle drawn. "You polecats ride on. This here's private—" Her words cut off, and then she said, "Morgan? Morgan Sawyer as I live and breathe. I never thought to see you again."

A young boy stepped out of the cabin behind her. His eyes were wide as he watched them ride up, awestruck. They were both white-blond and willow-thin. Both blue-eyed and seemingly dazed at the sight of company, especially company the woman clearly knew.

Morgan swung off his horse, spoke a few quiet words to Owen, then turned to stride toward her. "It is me for a fact, Roz."

She laid the rifle on the ground, spoke to the boy, then came a-runnin', throwing herself into Morgan's arms. He lifted her clean off her feet and spun her around, both of them laughing.

That's when a movement drew Delaney's eyes to the boy,

who'd picked up the rifle and looked more than capable of using it, even though he was only nine or ten years old. He looked for all the world like a youngster who didn't like seeing a man put his hands on his ma.

Owen swung down, then dragged Clive off his horse. Tex took charge of Sly, got Stella off her horse, and sat her on the ground nearby but out of reach of her brother and pa. No sense making it easy for them to untie each other.

While Tex watched over them, Owen released the extra horses, all bareback and wearing no bridles—only the halters they'd been wearing when they were staked out for the night by the Duncans. They walked, then trotted toward the lowland before them, wading into belly-deep grass. They went right to grazing.

Delaney shook her head. Probably stealing horses was one thing, but taking time to saddle them was something else. Of course, you couldn't steal horses that were already stolen, not if you were an officer of the law. Instead, they'd taken possession of stolen goods and would soon see them returned to their rightful owners. If they were in fact stolen.

She realized she was trying to work excuses around in her head for horse thieving and decided to stop. She decided she didn't care if they'd stolen horses from the varmints who'd shot Boone.

"When's the last time Morg was home?" Owen asked Tex.

Both men studied the woman, the child, the hug that'd gone on far too long.

"Longer than that kid is old, I'd say. Didn't Morgan fight in the war?"

The Civil War had ended in April of 1865, seven years ago. Morgan himself wasn't all that old either.

"He told me he and his brother fought on opposite sides," Delaney said, keeping her eye on the angry-looking lad. "His brother for the South, him for the North. He said his brother died in the fighting, but Morgan didn't know that until he came home and found a letter from his pa waiting for him in Elk Point, telling him to move on and that his brother was dead. Whether Morgan wasn't welcome because he was on any side other than his brother's or whether his pa had supported the South, Morgan didn't say. I assume that meant he left thinking he'd never go back."

"The war ended in sixty-five, but Morgan had been fighting a year or two. He's not that child's father," Owen said. "And he hadn't oughta be hugging that woman like that, seeing as how she's probably got a husband around here somewhere."

"Maybe," Delaney said doubtfully, "they're just old friends."

Morgan set the woman back down on her feet. She swiped at her eyes with the sleeve of her brown broadcloth shirt.

Delaney noticed she was wearing trousers and boots that looked about five sizes too big for her. Was this woman dressed in her husband's clothes?

Morgan turned and called, "Owen! Come here and meet my old friend."

Delaney had some old friends herself. They didn't greet each other that way.

Tex said, "Go ahead. I'll hold a gun on our prisoners while Morg has his reunion and does introductions with his . . . old friend."

Owen and Tex gave each other a look that said they agreed with Delaney. Neither of them greeted old friends that way either.

73

———◇•●————————●•◇———

"They're late, Hester." Grizzly Bridger tossed his napkin on the table. "I'm going after our young'uns."

Four days late, Hester Bridger thought while shaking her head. What should have been a two- or three-days' ride from Elk Point, where they'd sent the last telegram to Boone and Delaney, had stretched to nearly a week.

Hester shoved her chair back. "We're leaving this to you, Kimmy. The colonel and I are riding out."

Kimmy, the wife of one of the fort officers who'd hired on as housekeeper to the fort commander, nodded. "Ride careful, sir, ma'am."

They took five minutes to fetch a bedroll, to gather a few days' worth of beef jerky and hardtack, and to fill canteens, then headed out the door.

Hester already had on a riding skirt and a sturdy shirtwaist, so there was no need to change clothes. She grabbed her holster and black, flat-topped Stetson as she walked out ahead of her husband of forty years.

She glanced back to see Grizzly snag his Winchester off the rack over the back door and sling it over his shoulder, followed by his holster and Stetson. He never broke stride.

They'd been itching to go from the minute their children were an hour late. But several things could delay a trip, such as bad weather or a horse pulling up lame. Innocent things that made it foolish to go chasing out to save the day. Even so, it'd been too long.

"I'm irritated with myself, Hester. We should've told the young'uns to wait until the train started running again or ridden down to fetch them."

"No sense in it, Grizz. They should've been fine with five Marshals."

"Where you reckon they will've gotten to by now?"

"Don't matter where they've gotten to, Pa. Wherever they are, we'll find 'em."

Hester was proud of her son, Boone. Well, all of her sons. She and Grizz had three older boys. Then, after a span of years, while Grizz was posted out west and Hester couldn't follow, he came home, and they had their second family. Boone and the light of her life, a longed-for daughter, Delaney, who was their youngest. Hester had finally realized her dream of having a girl. After that, there were no more babies.

Grizzly barked out a few orders to his second-in-command as they rode out of Fort D. A. Russell.

"The last wire she sent was straight south, only two days' ride. That was a week ago. She'd been in Elk Point, the first town south of Fort Collins. I reckon we'll be riding south until we cut their trail, then pick up what became of them from there."

A simple plan, but Hester knew it was anything but simple. Something had stopped them or turned them aside. And it'd been too long for it to be something simple. Hester thought of the prisoner they'd been transporting, a man who'd already broken jail once. She had to fear he was the cause of the delay.

"Mighty rough country if they got driven into the mountains," Grizzly said. "I've been up in that wilderness, and some fearsome varmints roam those hills."

"More fearsome than our youngsters?"

Even in his concern, Hester saw a small smile bend his lips. Grizzly was thinking the same thing she was thinking. No one was more fearsome than their youngsters.

8

"We'll stay here for the night," Morgan announced, and Owen figured that was only sensible. Still, he itched to keep moving. The Duncans had been set afoot so they should be far behind at this point. He at least was glad to see that Morg had let go of that woman. And her boy had let go of the rifle.

Owen opened his mouth to ask a question, realized he had ten, and closed his mouth again. He had too many questions to even start.

"Roz, this is my boss and fellow U.S. Marshal, Owen Riley. And our partner, Tex Mitchel." He ran through the other introductions.

Roz, with her fine white-blond hair to match her son's, paid strict attention as if every word were fascinating. Owen had to wonder just how much time she spent alone out here.

He, Tex, and Morgan got the prisoners off their horses. He took Delaney along as lookout when their woman prisoner asked for a moment of necessary privacy.

Owen untied Stella and turned to Delaney. "Don't trust her for a second."

Delaney nodded, her eyes fixed on Stella. That was the extent to which she was mistrusting.

Owen stayed close enough to hear the low murmur of voices. But he kept a tree and some shrubs between himself and the women.

When they reemerged from cover, Stella extended her hands to be bound up, doing so willingly.

Seeing Boone talking with Morgan and Roz, Owen began gathering sticks for a fire. There was a blackened area with the grass cleared all around it. The woman must've built a fire there many times before.

Owen said to Delaney, "Is your brother up to this? I've known men who took a hard blow to the head like that, and they stayed dizzy for a couple of weeks. Sometimes their heads hurt for months. It can take a while to get over feeling light-headed and seeing double."

"He's holding up okay." Delaney glanced at her brother. Owen could see she didn't want him to know they were talking about him. "A *concussion*, that's the word for what happened to him. Good news is, the ground is softer here, not so much stone as we've been seeing."

"What difference does that make?" Owen took his eyes off the prisoner once her hands were tied again.

"If he falls while he's working around the camp, or if he passes out, he at least won't crack his head open. He should heal fine." Delaney sounded sure of herself, but gave her brother long, thoughtful looks often.

Owen figured she was right about him falling. It seemed he was building a fire outside rather than invading the rustic-looking cabin. The cabin was set against the canyon wall, so it looked as if the mountain formed the back of the house.

Morgan dug coffee out of his saddlebag, handed it to Roz, then set out on foot and vanished into the trees to the west of the cabin. In the fading light, Owen wondered where the man was off to, but he didn't waste his time asking.

The woman and the child went back inside the cabin with no invitation for them to join her, though Owen wouldn't have gone in anyway. He had three prisoners to watch.

Marley was limping around helping Boone build the fire, moving slow but steady. His leg still had a raw, ugly wound. Boone had a stack of kindling ready to go and a second stack to feed the fire later. Once he got the fire going, the woman came back out toting a pot, which sloshed with water.

Roz told Owen, "I'll help you get a soup going. I expect that's all you're eating on the trail. If I'd had more time, I could have fed you better." The boy was following close behind her, carrying a coffeepot nearly as big as he was.

"Can I help you with anything?" Delaney asked.

The woman looked at Delaney uncertainly with huge blue eyes. "I've got it handled. I haven't had coffee in a coon's age. I had water heating inside for washing up later, but instead I cleaned up my coffeepot and filled it with hot water. You'll have to add the coffee, of course, but I'll leave that to you." She jerked her chin at the steaming pot of water the boy carried as he headed toward the fire.

Owen wanted to wrest it from the hands of the child, who was too small to be carrying a heavy coffeepot. Yet the coffee might end up spilling and burning the youngster, so Owen stood back to let the boy set it on the fire.

"What's your name, boy?"

The boy gave Owen a suspicious look, then said, "Jesse. Jesse Beck. My pa died afore I could remember him. Ma and

I live here together, and we get by just fine." His tone was defiant, as if Owen was being disrespectful in some way. Or maybe others had disrespected him, and he was learning to fight back.

Owen nodded. "Good to meet you, Jesse."

Jesse's clothes looked like they'd come out of the same bag his ma's had. They'd been hemmed and taken in some, but it was clear both of them were wearing men's clothes. His pa's maybe? Did they go to town? Did Roz have what she needed to make clothes for the boy and herself?

Now wasn't the time to ask such things. But Owen had to wonder if he shouldn't offer to guide this woman and child out of this place along with the prisoners and the wounded. If the Duncans were coming, she didn't dare stay behind. At this rate, he'd be bringing a small town to Fort Russell.

Delaney approached Roz as the woman set a pot on the ground, then adjusted the layout of the fire a bit to make room for both her stewpot and the coffeepot.

When Roz had both on the fire, Roz glanced at Delaney and produced a tin coffee cup from her pocket. "Want coffee? Reckon it's plenty hot enough."

"I've got a cup in my saddlebag. I'll fetch it shortly. But what can I do in the meantime?"

Delaney saw Roz looking at her riding skirt, then her shirtwaist. It was a dark color, so she wouldn't stand out against the background while riding through the wilderness. No sense making a target out of herself. But it was well-made, definitely meant for a woman, and it fit properly. She suspected Roz was noticing all of that.

"I've got potatoes that need to be pared and chopped. I've got green beans from my garden. Jesse's picking them right now. You can help snap them. I've got a few other things to throw in too, and I'm counting on Morgan to show up here with a rabbit, a few grouse, or even a deer. I'd appreciate your help preparing everything."

She wasn't exactly friendly, but neither was she rude—more like she had no idea how to talk to another woman, or maybe how to talk to *anyone*. Delaney had the sudden urge to take Roz and Jesse with them when they left. Ma would know how to help them. Even though it looked like they managed on their own, and the meadow was breathtakingly beautiful, life here had to be hard as well as lonely.

Delaney got herself set up next to the stewpot with potatoes in her skirts and a paring knife while Roz got busy chopping onions. She shifted around in her head how to find out what she wanted to know. Jesse had already mentioned his pa had died. So that settled just how well Morgan had known this woman. But just what kind of "old friend" was she? "Um . . . have you known Morgan long?"

A sound that came close to a quiet huff of laughter, but didn't quite reach it, escaped Roz's lips. "You rode over here from his place. Long old ride in the wilderness. Funny, but he used to be my closest neighbor. My pa was out here same time as Morgan's pa and his two boys. Pa ran into them somewhere out scouting or hunting. In time we got real friendly."

Delaney had a hundred questions, most of them probably rude. One did seem fair to her, though. "You've got a beautiful place here, Roz, but do you want to ride out with us? Your cattle could manage well grazing even if you were gone for a time."

Roz gasped, and her eyes almost blazed with hope. "Can we come with you? I haven't left this place since my husband died . . . no, longer than that. Herman went to town some and brought things home, but he never took me with him." There was a long pause. "Pa hardly ever took me with him neither. The last time I went with him, there was trouble. Some men paid me attention in a way that scared me, and my pa was furious at the men. After that, we left town, and he never took me again and hardly ever went himself. When I married Herman, he went and found a parson, and Pa rode with me to meet Herman and hold the wedding. We didn't ride all the way to town. My boy has never been off the property."

"And he's how old?"

"Jesse is ten. I lost Herman when he was not yet two, but closing in on it, I reckon. He was born in the fall of the year, but then we've no calendar. I'd put his birth at the end of September. It seemed that the days and nights were about even when he came to be born."

"And how long did you live out here friendly with Morgan? How old were you when he left?"

Roz tilted her head as if she'd never had to figure such a thing before. "We never did such as birthdays. I'd say Morgan left when he was fifteen or sixteen. We'd been best friends most of our lives. Morgan's pa came to our place now and again, and then one day he came and told us his oldest son, Gavin, had died in the war. I knew Morgan and Gavin had gone off to the war, but I didn't know much about the fighting. Morgan's pa was on his way out of the country, next thing to a madman was my impression. I stayed well away from him. Pa told me later he was all torn up over

81

his son dying, and he'd told Morgan he wasn't welcome at home."

Roz gave Delaney a weak smile. "Only then did I realize I'd been living all that time, waiting for him to come back. I gave up then, and Herman came along. Before I knew it, we were married and there was a baby on the way. Then Pa and Herman died, and here I've stayed ever since."

Delaney focused on the potatoes as she considered how utterly alone Roz and Jesse had been. And how thrilled Roz had been to see Morgan. Not just thrilled, but desperate.

"Well, you're welcome to come with us. We're on our way to Fort Russell in Wyoming. That's near Cheyenne, the state capital, so you can look around there, too. Then decide if you want to come back here or sell off your cattle and make a new life with more people around you. My pa and ma live there, so I'm going to settle in. Maybe be a schoolmarm. That's the job I had in Texas." Unless she decided she needed to help bring those worthless Duncans to justice. "I'm planning to live with my folks. My folks would be glad to make your acquaintance." Delaney felt a pang of worry. "Knowing them, I'll bet they're on their way right now to find me and Boone. We're days late. No doubt they're awful concerned. But we're going to be powerfully hard to find up here. We need to get on the trail soon if we hope to cross paths with them."

Roz gave a big grin and said, "Suits me fine. We can leave at first light."

Delaney smiled in return. She realized then that under the men's clothing and rough ways, Roz Beck was a beautiful woman. Yep, they needed to get her out of here before some worthless man came along and she married him out of pure loneliness. A woman as capable and as pretty as Roz deserved to have the pick of the litter. Delaney decided she'd do her best to help make that happen.

She pictured Roz hurling herself into Morgan's arms, and Morgan grabbing hold and smiling and spinning her around. She wondered what it all meant.

Boone chose that moment to come up beside Delaney and sink onto a log that was positioned by the fire. The fire pit was well established. It looked as though Roz cooked out here a good part of the time.

Delaney realized she still hadn't gone into the house. Curiosity almost overcame her manners. "How are you, Boone?" She watched as her brother tossed another piece of firewood onto the flames.

He still had a bandage wrapped around his head. Delaney had been examining him daily, and he seemed to be on the mend now. It would soon be time to shed the cumbersome bandage.

"I'm seeing only one of things today—leastwise most of the time. My head still punishes me if I move suddenly or pick up anything heavy." He gestured toward the small stack of branches he'd gathered for the fire. "I'm a worthless saddle partner, Delaney. I'll make that up to you when I can see straight again."

Delaney knew her brother well. He always pulled his own weight and then some. "You're a lot better now than when you were unconscious after the shooting," she said. "Ma and Pa are tough, but I don't want them walking into the middle of a gang of killers who want to get their hands on horses. You know how Ma can be when she has to shoot somebody."

Boone shrugged. "I'll grant you she doesn't like it."

"The Duncans are still out there somewhere, although they'll have a hard time trying to follow after us. Those Marshals are skilled at covering their tracks."

He turned and looked at her, but very slowly. "You couldn't see the trail? Really?"

"Morgan said they'll never find it, but that was before we took their horses. Near impossible to hide the trail of so many critters." Delaney shook her head. "I forget you were knocked out. First, we climbed a mountain no horse should be able to scale." She went on to tell him about the trip they'd taken. Roz was listening as closely as Boone. "Roz and Jesse will be going with us. She hasn't been to town in years."

Boone nodded. "How do you manage up here with nary a trip to town? Don't you need supplies?"

"I remember the nice things Pa and Herman used to bring home from town," Roz said. "I had a liking for coffee and enjoyed what could be made with flour. But we don't *need* those things. We have a garden, and I'm a hand with my bow and arrow when we get really hungry. But I'm careful about saving our bullets. I usually take one of the cattle to get through the winter. A bit of beef is always welcome. Mostly I let the herd grow, although I'm not sure what I'm growing it for. I suppose maybe Jesse will want it someday. When I leave here, I doubt I'll ever come back."

"Those cows are valuable." Boone jabbed a finger at the small herd, which was better than fifty head, ranging from spring calves to fully grown cows and bulls with impressive spreads of horns. "Once we get ourselves out of this knothole, you should come back and get them to market. Cows go for twenty-five dollars a head these days, probably less for the young calves. That means you have more than a thousand dollars' worth of livestock here. That'd give you a good start somewhere closer to town."

"A thousand dollars! Why, I've never heard of anyone having so much money. Can we drive them out with us now?"

Not a lot of sentimental attachment to her animals. Delaney thought that was a trait most folks on the Frontier shared. Don't get too attached to an animal you might need to eat someday.

Delaney arched both brows. "Not now. Not when killers might be on our trail. We have to keep moving until we get shut of them."

"Fair enough," said Roz, nodding.

Morgan returned then with three dead grouse and a rabbit. They soon had them cut up and in the pot. Once everything was prepared for their meal, they had a stretch of quiet. Delaney rested with her back against a fallen log and sipped a steaming-hot cup of coffee, then caught herself waking up.

Then Jesse came running toward them, shouting something about a prairie fire. He had a stick in his hand, and he whirled around as if it were a sword and he were fighting a charging enemy. He turned and rushed off just as suddenly.

Roz laughed, ignoring him as she stirred her stew.

Delaney had four big brothers, and she was a schoolteacher. She was used to boys with their wild imaginations.

"Time to eat," Roz hollered.

Jesse skidded to a halt, spun back around toward them, and came running again. A starving boy, Delaney well remembered that.

Roz scooped the hot stew onto a plate as the boy chattered on.

Delaney noticed the men in their party walking toward

them from different directions. The sun was sliding behind the mountains that lined the western side of the beautiful canyon. Delaney saw Boone walking with Owen, the two of them talking with serious expressions as they kept their eyes on their prisoners.

Delaney and Roz filled plates as fast as they could and handed them out. Owen and Morgan saw to feeding the Duncans. Then, realizing how hungry and exhausted she was, Delaney collapsed back to where she'd been leaning on her log. Boone was already there beside her, finishing his meal as she began hers.

A few moments later, Owen sat down on her other side. "We leave at first light," Owen said after he scraped the last bit of his stew and ate it.

"Do you have things to pack, Roz?" Morgan asked. "I can help you gather what you need. I don't know if you'll want to come back here. It's a mighty long way to the next ranch, farther yet to a town."

"I'm done here, I believe. But I will want to herd my cattle to town and sell them. So I'll need to come back for them. I have little enough I want to take with me. For this trip, I've already packed what I need."

She jabbed her fork toward two bedrolls near the fire. "I've got saddles for two horses. The mustangs closest to the barn, the gray and the pinto, are the best trained, so we'll ride them. Jesse and I are ready to go."

"We'd best let your horses out of the corral so they can graze for a bit. Will they bother your cattle?"

"No, they're good friends."

"Friends? Your cows and horses are friends?" Morgan asked.

"Oh, yes. Friends with each other, and friends of mine and Jesse's."

Delaney considered Roz's longhorn cattle. She'd been taught to give longhorns, even seemingly gentle ones, a wide berth. They had a mean streak in them.

Yet Roz seemed to be done with the subject and took her stewpot off the fire to haul it into the cabin. Delaney got up and poured more coffee. Roz was back in time to have a cup and was eager to taste it.

Morgan gave Roz a smile of approval as he looked at her two bedrolls. He must like a woman who could pack light. "First thing in the morning then. We'll be out of the canyon before the sun rises. It's a tough trail getting out of the mountains, but we should be in Cheyenne in a few days' time."

A few days? Delaney remembered how they were two days away about . . . seven days ago. If the train were running, it was a one-day trip. She leaned closer to Boone. "I wonder where Ma and Pa would be if they did strike out looking for us. It'd be a shame if we didn't cross paths with them."

"We'll head for Cheyenne and round up our folks later. Hopefully, if we miss each other, they'll send a wire to the fort to see if we've turned up. So we should be able to bring them on home fast."

"I wonder if the Duncans have gotten themselves new horses yet." Delaney looked at the outlaws they'd rounded up. And the horses they'd confiscated. "And I wonder who they had to kill to get back in the saddle."

She saw Owen's face grow serious beside her. The flickering flames in the twilight set off his unruly blond hair and flashed in the blue of his eyes. He'd heard what she said and understood exactly what she meant.

It didn't mean they'd do things different. It just meant they were dealing with the lowest kind of folks, who all needed to be in prison.

Boone began snoring gently and drew Delaney's attention.

Owen said, "He held up well today. I reckon the food and the warmth of the fire and the long day caught up with him."

Delaney turned to see Owen leaning forward, looking across her to study Boone. Owen's shoulder pressed against hers. Then his eyes shifted, and their gazes held. She remembered how he'd held her when she'd cried, the alluring combination of his strength and kindness.

"It's been a long, hard day for all of us." She wished she could burst into tears, so he'd be forced to hold her again.

A small, private smile curved his lips, as if he knew just what she was thinking. And as if, maybe, he wouldn't mind holding her again, tears or not.

Morgan and Tex headed toward the prisoners. Marley had fallen asleep. Roz and Jesse got up and disappeared into their cabin. Suddenly, instead of there being a crowd, she and Owen sat side by side, alone together in front of the crackling fire—not counting the ones who were sleeping.

"What am I going to do about you, Delaney?"

She wished she had the courage to tell him what she'd like him to do. But she most certainly would not ask for a kiss.

"Roz seems to think she knows how to get to town from here." She managed to change the subject. "But if she hasn't gone to town since before Jesse was born, well, I hope her memory is good."

"Morgan has confidence in her, but he said he wandered this land as a youth and never noticed a trail. If there is one, it'll be more like what we've ridden through to get to Morgan's cabin than to get to Roz's."

"It's hard to imagine that there's a way through these mountains. But so far we've gotten through somehow. Nothing about it will be easy."

"You've done well, Delaney. As well as any of us."

"I might have made it harder if I'd gotten shot."

A gasp had Owen clasping her hand. "Don't say that. I couldn't stand it if you were hurt. I'm supposed to be leading this group, and I've failed as badly as anyone could. Adding you being hurt would be unbearable."

Delaney closed her own hand over his. "You saw your Marshal friend die. You saw Marley shot, Tex too. I saw Boone hit so hard I feared he was dead. However you felt about all of that, you kept going. You didn't turn killing mean and attack the Duncans." Delaney remembered that Owen had stopped Morgan when he'd been about to do that very thing. "You'd hold up. I-I guess so would I, although thinking of Boone, it would have broken something inside me if he'd died. I might've wanted to attack as much as Morgan did. I was furious at first, but Boone needed me. That's a good thing."

Owen managed to let go of the awful tension she'd felt when he'd gripped her hand. He sat back, breaking that spell, whatever it had been. Not just the spell when he'd reacted to her speaking of possibly being shot, but also the tension when they'd looked at each other and remembered when they'd been in each other's arms.

Delaney appreciated him leaning back and regretted it at the same time.

"I live a rootless life, Delaney. And I've lived it for years. It's gotten to be a habit."

"An interesting statement. Why do you bring it up now?"

He looked back at her and didn't speak for a moment. At last he said, "You know why."

It made her more than a little nervous to think she probably did. But it was more than she could speak of out loud. "Is it your plan to stay with this life forever, Mr. U.S. Marshal?"

The snippy tone got another smile out of him. "I haven't given it much thought. Never had a reason to."

"And now?"

"And now I'm giving it some thought." Owen ran a rough, callused finger down her cheek, then shoved himself to his feet and walked toward his fellow Marshals.

Beside her, Boone said quietly, "Mind yourself, Delaney."

Boone hadn't been so deeply asleep as they'd thought.

She turned to him. Her big brother, her best friend.

He said, "We've got trouble coming and need to be on our guard. Not much time for nonsense."

Nodding, she said, "Go get more comfortable. Your blanket's rolled out."

Apparently thinking he'd said his piece, Boone shoved himself to his feet much like Owen had, except Boone groaned while he did it.

Delaney didn't tell him, but she didn't think anything of what she'd just felt over Owen Riley was nonsense. And she'd be alert regardless of an attraction to a handsome Marshal who was giving his rootless life some thought.

She headed for her own blankets near Boone just as she heard Owen say to Morgan and Tex, "Let's post a guard over the prisoners and at our backs." Owen headed back toward the firelight, leaving Tex behind to keep watch on the Duncans.

Morgan said quietly, "I'll cover the back trail for the first watch. Boone, are you up to taking a turn?"

"Yep, I'll stand second watch on the trail."

"I'll do second with the prisoners," Marley said from where he slept, another light sleeper. Delaney wondered what Marley had heard of her earlier conversation with Owen.

The men worked it out between them. Delaney should have insisted she take a turn, but she knew without asking that they wouldn't let her, even though they admitted she'd handle the job well. But she trusted them, so she'd get some sleep and help get things moving early in the morning.

As she lay on her bedroll, she said a prayer for Boone and for the group's safety during the journey ahead, for lonely Roz and lively little Jesse. And for her parents, if they were searching for their missing children. And for Marley's healing, and Owen . . . plenty to pray about over him. Oh, she could pray for hours and not cover all their needs, but exhaustion caught up with her before she could finish it all.

9

"I don't know how in the world anyone found this meadow up here in the peaks." Owen hadn't had enough sleep in about a month, and it was wearing on him. He had three horses in tow, each with a prisoner on its back. Tex brought up the rear with the horses they'd retrieved from the Duncans while Morgan and Roz led the way. Jesse stayed near his ma. Delaney had started the morning riding alongside Boone, but he'd fallen into talking with the boy and the trail was narrow, so she'd dropped back. Owen found himself riding with her.

Shaking her head, Delaney said, "Followed a mountain goat, I reckon. No other way I can think of."

"Morgan said Roz's pa was an old mountain man. He knew the land better than Morgan's pa. A lot of what Morgan knows he learned from Roz's pa, Cap Sutcliff."

Owen took his eyes off the reckless stretch of rock they were descending. "Where'd you learn to be so handy in the wild?"

Delaney smiled at him. It made him realize no woman

had smiled at him for a long time, leastways not much. Years maybe. Never maybe. He was surprised how much he liked it.

"Pa was always going on about a child needing to handle himself in the woods. He'd taught all my big brothers to track and hunt, and when I came along, he never treated me any different from them. The older three were a lot older. Pa was serving in a fort for a few years, and Ma couldn't join him. The older boys took care of Ma. Ma put up with it, mainly because she thought it did the boys good, so they got real handy in the woods. It helped that my ma was also comfortable in the outdoors."

Boone looked back at her, still wearing his bandage. It was dirty by now, but Owen had to believe it had kept the dirt out of the wound, so it was a good thing.

"Then Pa came home, and Boone and I were born not long after."

"We were a good team, the four of us," Boone added.

"My big brothers sort of took off one at a time. But they were close in age and were mostly gone by the time I could have a hope of remembering them. It's said I met Bowie, the eldest, when I was a baby."

Tex said, "Bowie Bridger is your brother?"

"Yep. Heard he's in these mountains somewhere."

"I've heard of him. A fearsome man, more ghost than human."

"That sounds like Bowie." Delaney faced forward again. "So the four of us still at home went on adventures all the time. The next forts where Pa was stationed were mostly not in dangerous places: Ohio, Indiana, Missouri, and Texas, which was still mighty wild, but they had housing for a man's family. Boone and I were adults by then, so when Pa was moved again, we stayed in Texas. That's where we were living when Ma wrote and said she and Pa were done with their wandering ways for good."

Delaney smiled at Owen. "We'll see. We never settled for long. Wherever we were, we'd spend time in the outdoors, where Pa would test us, teach us every trick he knew, and challenge us to learn more than he could teach."

"We were living in Ohio when the war broke out—that was before Texas." Boone sounded somber about that.

Owen couldn't say if it was because the war was a mean business or because his pa had been in danger.

"All three of my big brothers had headed for the mountains by then. Two of them came back and fought in the war. They ended up serving with Pa in the Battle of Gettysburg with the Army of Northern Virginia, which later became the Army of the Potomac. They stayed with him and watched Pa climb the ranks until he was a colonel.

"He was sent to the Western Frontier after the war, and again he ended up in places no family could join him. This post in Fort Russell is, we hope, his final post. Boone has plans to enlist if the place suits him. He was too young for the Civil War. The knothead longs to serve in the cavalry."

"At least for a few years," Boone said.

Jesse broke in to ask what the cavalry was, and Boone turned his attention to the boy.

"You know, I think Morgan was in the Army of the Potomac," Owen said. "He was mighty young and served as a drummer, until they found out how good he was with a rifle. I wonder if he knew your pa?"

Morgan heard his name and glanced back. "What was that?"

Boone, closer to Morgan and following the conversation, said, "Did you know Colonel Bridger in the war?"

Morgan tilted his head. "I knew him because everyone knew him. Doubt he took much notice of me." He chuckled.

"Time to stop talking and pay attention," Roz cut in. "Single file now. This next stretch is a killer." She gave Morgan a look before taking the lead.

And she was right.

"You go first," Owen said to Delaney. "I don't want you anywhere near these low-down Duncans."

Delaney urged her horse ahead while Owen held back. He had to admit he liked a strong woman, especially one who'd listen to the occasional request. If it was smart anyhow. He suspected if he'd asked her to do something stupid, she would have something to say about it. He found he liked that, too. Of course, he was finding he liked most everything about Delaney Bridger.

Owen didn't know how anyone could call this a trail. It looked like they had stepped off the edge of the world. The gully in front of them was so steep, his horse would have to walk on tiptoes. But despite that, the horses picked their way down, down, down. The gully was in shadows even though it was near midday.

He wondered if wild horses roamed up here. Someone or something had to have gone down this trail before. No horse would've tried it if he wasn't following a scent or some other tracks that were invisible to humans.

Owen, who considered himself as steady as a man could be, felt his stomach swoop as they walked along the side of the slope. His foot scraped against the wall of the gully on the right, and his left foot dangled in thin air over a hundred-foot drop.

He let his horse find the way, doing his best to keep the reins loose to not interfere with the animal's concentration.

He heard a horse snort behind him. The jingle of a bridle. They were leading a parade with the saddle string of stolen Duncan horses bringing up the rear with Tex. He judged the jingle to be coming from the horse Stella was riding. She was third in line of their row of criminal Duncans.

He didn't look back for the sheer reason that it might throw off his horse's balance. He sure hoped that snort didn't have trouble behind it, but there wasn't much he could do about that right now anyway.

Directly in front of him, Delaney's horse stumbled. She was a fine rider, though, so she didn't panic. The strong horse regained its footing and plodded on.

Owen was proud of his ability to keep his head in an emergency, but he found his heart pounding. He thought of a few emergencies he'd faced in the war and with his family after the war when Quantrell's raiders came mighty close to his family in Iowa. The main reason he'd learned not to panic was because panic always made things worse. In fact, panic limited his ability to help. And yet here he sat, scared the woman riding ahead of him was going to suffer a deadly fall.

He studied the way down. The trail at this point was more like a scattered series of outcroppings that descended. He looked to his right toward a vast stretch of nothingness. He could hear water running and figured there was a river at the bottom of this slit in the earth. But he wasn't about to look for it. He'd see it when they got there.

Owen took a moment to wonder how he'd chosen such a

rugged, remote life. U.S. Marshals were supposed to deliver warrants and subpoenas. They traveled with reward money promised on wanted posters. They transported prisoners too, but most Marshals lived very routine lives. Not him, though. He'd sought out jobs that sent him far and wide. He liked investigating and doing undercover work, which meant traveling to places where no one knew him. He'd been settled in Colorado for a few years, but when a job cropped up that required travel, he'd volunteered. He'd just recently gotten back from chasing down stagecoach robbers in Wyoming. Morg and Tex had been part of that team.

It struck him right then that he was more a nomad than anything else. That life had suited him until right this second. Right now, clinging like a vine to the edge of the world, he had to ask himself what had given him such a blamed fool notion as to work at a job like this. His father had been an Iowa homesteader who'd worked as a carpenter besides the farming. Owen had learned the skill of building while at his side. But he'd never wanted to set down roots or build anything, not since he'd arrived home safe from the war.

He'd wandered for a time, hard-pressed to settle down after years of excitement and danger. Finally, he'd signed up for the U.S. Marshals Service and had never stopped moving since.

Brooding over the memories, Owen's heart almost came to a stop when Delaney's horse skidded for a few inches. It was then he had a bright idea.

Pray . . .

He'd been slow coming to it, but he was a believer. He needed to pray them all down this gorge, and high time he finally thought of it. Best to pray them all the way to Fort

Russell. He set himself to do just that as he and his horse picked their way down into the gullet of the mountain.

A man couldn't help but think of the valley of the shadow of death.

———◇———

Finally they reached the bottom, where one by one they waded into a fast-moving stream. Rather than cross it, Roz turned and rode alongside, and everyone followed. The water was knee-deep on their horses, and narrow enough that they remained riding single file, pushed along by a current that boiled at times.

The sides of the canyon they rode through rose up around them with no way to scale them. It might've been possible were they to abandon their horses, but then they'd be in the middle of nowhere on foot. And that was something Owen would never do unless it was down to a choice between life and death.

Delaney looked over her shoulder at him. She made her eyes go wide, comically so. "We made it down."

Owen turned to see everyone was in the stream now.

"Do you suppose a hard rain would fill this canyon up all the way to the top?" She looked around with some hesitancy.

Owen's stomach lurched again. "I might not have thought of that without you mentioning."

She smiled and turned back to ride on. They were all going faster now. No one wanted to linger down here.

A roaring sound brought Owen's eyes forward. Then he closed them. *White water.* Were they going to ride through that? It was a descent, too. A waterfall done the hard way through jagged rocks.

Then, just as they were going to have to wend through the rocks, Roz turned her horse aside, and though they'd been riding with walls on both sides of the stream that reached a hundred feet or more, there was a narrow strip of shore. Roz rode out of the water and along on that sandy shore. And then whatever she'd been looking for, she found, and they started to climb again. Another mind-numbing, bone-chilling, narrow trail. And Owen was being mighty generous to call it a trail.

He wondered where in tarnation they were.

Grizzly drew his horse to a halt and pointed to the ground. "That there's blood." He dismounted and knelt on one knee to study the spot. "Four wounded out of a group of eight, if each of these bloody spots is a sign of someone hit."

Hester wandered to the crest of a hill. "The bullets must've come from there," he said, looking downward. "This happened days ago. Let's go see what we're up against."

Grizzly mounted up, and they rode down to find the tracks of seven horses. "One man firing is all, I'd say. He was out in front and probably the only one able to see them as they skylined themselves on that crest."

Both of them took a long, hard look at the tracks. There was a good chance they'd be able to identify some of them if they saw them again, and Grizzly intended to see them again real soon.

"They rode down and to the west. Got off the trail." Hester stared at the tracks for a while longer, then rode downhill to where the group had rounded a boulder. The others, those who had done the shooting, picked up the trail and their prints mingled. And it was close enough, Hester had to believe the ones attacking were right on the group's heels.

"Grizzly, we can't go after 'em tonight. The sun is setting, so we won't be able to track them much longer. We should go on into town and ask around about these riders, then lay up more supplies if we're going to go haring off into the wilderness. We didn't pack enough for days, maybe weeks in the wild."

"You're right, Hester. It eats at me to turn aside, but we don't have a choice. The next town is only a few miles ahead. I'll send a wire to the fort and tell them to expect me to be gone for an unknown length of time." Because both of them knew they wouldn't be coming back without their children.

Hester stared at those bloodstains as they turned and headed back toward town.

10

When at last they crested the mountain slope, Delaney took her first deep breath in hours. They'd been all morning and part of the afternoon getting this far. A half-day's ride from Roz's cabin and she felt like they'd walked twenty miles when the truth was, as the crow flies, they might've gone five at the most.

She wondered where in the world "this far" was. They rode straight into a forest. They weren't on anything she'd call a trail, but Roz was still in the lead and seemed confident of her direction. Didn't the woman admit she hadn't been to town in years? Delaney questioned whether the woman was even on the right path.

The woods swallowed them up. The branches overhead were thick enough that only a few dapples of sunlight got through. Birds chirped as a soft summer breeze hushed through the branches of towering oak, quaking aspen, and juniper. The scent of pine and dirt, broken up regularly by rocky stretches, and the cool of the shade helped to ease the tension she'd been feeling while her horse climbed a slope that was the next thing to walking a tightrope, a thrilling act she'd seen performed once at a circus. She thought she knew how that felt now.

She was surprised to feel her hands trembling. She knew herself to be a woman with steady nerves. But letting the tension go had left her hands shaking. She'd kept her head, stayed calm, and hung on through the harrowing ride. But it was over now, and she could finally relax enough to fret.

They'd spread out some. Roz was making good time, as if her chance to get to town had finally come and she was determined to make it there before anyone stopped her.

Delaney wondered what it would take to drive Roz's cattle to market. They couldn't take the livestock this way, so it would have to be back past Morgan's place, and that was also treacherous. They'd gotten a handful of cows into that mountain valley years ago, and the herd had been expanding ever since. Longhorns, though, were tougher critters that maybe could scale these mountains. But *would* they? Delaney couldn't see herself convincing them to try it. Not a one of those cows living had ever taken on these high trails.

Morgan handed jerky to the boy, and it reminded Delaney that her throat was bone-dry, her stomach empty enough to echo after hours of living on nothing but nerves. She pulled food out of her saddlebags and chewed, drinking from her canteen in between bites.

She looked behind her to make sure the prisoners and the Marshals had food; they'd be ready for a meal on horseback. Boone smiled at her, then took a long drink of the cold spring water they'd brought with them from Roz's place.

Roz continued to lead them downward. It wasn't steep,

just a rugged, stony, winding slope through the woods. Delaney had hoped this would eventually lead her to where she could cut across on a trail to Cheyenne.

They finally arrived to where she could get a clear view of the canyon that loomed ahead. Its mouth was visible as well.

A blow knocked her off her horse. And a scream from behind her was sharp enough to cut flesh.

Delaney fell and smashed against a boulder. She drew her gun and turned to see all three of their prisoners running in different directions.

Clive vanished to the south side of the wooded trail, kicking his horse and moving at a breakneck pace, his hands untied. Judging by the way he'd ridden, he'd slammed a fist into her back as he passed her.

Sly charged at Tex, back the way they'd come. He slashed at Tex with something but had no visible weapon. His hands were supposed to be tied. Sly struck Tex hard across the face and then disappeared into the forest they'd just emerged from.

Stella went north. The trees were as thick on that side of the trail as on the south.

Why had they split up? They must've planned it, but they had no weapons and they'd been tightly bound.

Delaney then saw Owen tumble through the branches of a massive spruce. Hung up in the branches, he fought to get free, then landed hard on the ground. Looking all around, he tried to figure out what had happened. He gave her one assessing glance, then ran to his horse, swung up into the saddle, and took off after Clive.

She noticed a stripe along the side of his face, bleeding. He'd hit that tree trunk hard. He had to be at least somewhat impaired, and she didn't like him riding off alone.

Morgan shouted, "Boone! Marley! Mind the women and the boy. Go into the canyon." Then he took off after Sly. Another one going after the Duncans, who'd proven to be both dangerous and wily.

Tex was back in the saddle, storming after Stella to the north.

All three healthy Marshals had now abandoned them, though Marley wasn't too badly injured anymore. The Marshals split up in their pursuit of the prisoners. It could well be a trap, and Delaney wasn't going to stand idly by while more good men got killed by a bunch of ruthless outlaws.

This was all Clive's fault, including a man dead and her brother injured. As soon as Delaney could get on horseback, she galloped after Owen.

"Delaney, no!" Boone hollered.

She swept her arm backward and kept going.

Roz chased after Morgan. Another woman who wasn't going to let herself be tucked away while others were heading into peril. Delaney was starting to like Roz Beck.

She couldn't accompany all of the Marshals, so Tex was on his own in going after Stella. She hoped he could handle it.

As she rode on, Delaney spotted Marley, still hurting from his injuries, riding hard after Tex. He should've stayed back. That left Boone with the boy, wounded but still tough.

He wouldn't like being left behind.

Then she was gone, hard after Owen. The woods remained thick, probably why the Duncans had picked this spot to break free and run. How had they conspired to do it? Were they armed beyond whatever Sly had hit Tex with? Was it a tree branch he used?

Then she saw Owen ahead. She bent low over her horse, then slid as far to the side as she could to flatten herself as she pushed through the woods. The branches hung low, and if she wasn't careful, one of them could easily sweep her right off her horse's back. A wrong step and the horse might snap a leg bone.

It made her mad enough that she wanted to get her hands on Clive Duncan and wring his neck.

Instead, she was going to help catch him, then leave all the neck wringing to the authorities in Fort Russell and their handy noose.

———⬦•————————•⬦———

Tex went off the edge of the world.

His horse, a smart critter, skidded to a stop, while Tex flew headfirst off a cliff. He got one glimpse of the lady outlaw tumbling down ahead of him and set to keeping himself alive.

He rammed into a scrub juniper clinging to the edge of the cliff. It hit him so hard in the belly that it knocked the breath clean out of him.

Gasping, it stopped him for a second, but then the tree snapped and he went on falling, crashing through branches, knocking into jumbles of rocks too skimpy to stop him. While in midair, he twisted and got his feet under him and started running. Seeing the slope ahead hadn't one single spot for a man to set his foot, he skidded flat on his back, rocks rolling ahead of him. Dirt kicked up and choked him, yet somehow he managed to drag air into his lungs.

Stretching his arms wide, he tried to stop himself from sliding. He slowed down some but kept on going. An oncoming tree that was right in his path was going to break him in half. He quick rolled to the side and grabbed at the tree. He came to a hard stop, ripped a sleeve most of the way off his shirt, and then his grip gave way and on he went.

He hit a boulder feetfirst, and it stood him straight up for a split second before he somersaulted right over the top of it and was right back to sliding on his back again.

Then he was airborne. He sailed through the air and figured himself for dead as he slashed through the upper limbs of an aspen tree. He got whipped for a fact, but it also slowed him down. The slope he was on was wooded with aspens. They were growing straight up, but the land wouldn't cooperate and stood on end, which made the aspens appear to crawl up the mountainside.

Now Tex was grabbing at trees every few feet, nearly in control of his falling. He heard a bloodcurdling scream and focused beyond himself . . . just in time to see Stella fly over the edge of an even steeper cliff. Her scream died away as she fell and fell and fell. He regretted that he couldn't save her. He'd been pretty sure they'd never hang a woman and had hopes that the woman would still have a chance at a decent future.

Now that chance was over.

As he plunged onward, he shot a few prayers to the Almighty, figuring he'd be standing at the Pearly Gates in a few minutes. Best to have a word about any and all sins he'd committed since he last talked to God.

And he soared. He was in the wild blue yonder for a fact. No more tumbling and hitting anything, just wide-open air.

On he fell. He might've done some screaming himself.

Then he hit.

Water.

It was a blow as solid as a fist. He went under for a time before hitting a stony riverbed, or whatever water he was in, then by reflex he shoved off the bottom and was a long time finding the surface. As he came up, his head butted into Stella's back. The woman was flat out, stretched wide on the water. He caught hold on his way up, and she slowed him down something fierce.

Fighting upward, he got his head above water and dragged air into his lungs.

Towing Stella along with him, he got her flipped onto her back, wondering if the fall had killed her. Fumbling for her neck, he felt a pulse. Her face was pure white except where she was bleeding all along one side.

Blood welled up from skin that looked like it'd been raked by a ponderosa pine. Or maybe ten ponderosa pines.

He watched her draw a breath in without her eyes so much as flickering open.

Heartbeat, breath? That was about the end of his doctoring knowledge in this circumstance. He checked around some and didn't see any bones sticking out of her skin.

He hoped she'd be all right once she got over having her body pounded on like a Civil War snare drum.

And then he hit rocks and realized they were being swept along on a fast-moving river. He hit a boulder poking up out of the water, grabbed ahold of his outlaw friend, and fought a long, brutal fight with water as white as snow, foaming and roaring as it charged along to who knew where.

They were cast out into midair. A waterfall! A shout

escaped Tex's throat as they flew. He quit hollering and took a deep breath, knowing he was going to need it.

They hit water again, but deep enough it didn't smash them against the bottom, although it stung well enough. When he hit, he'd lost his grip on his prisoner, thrashed around and found she'd gotten ahead of him in the river.

Stella was facedown, and he came near to panic as he closed the space between them. He flipped her over and saw her chest rise and fall, and her eyes flickered open. He tried to get her to respond to him, but she was clearly dazed, and who could blame her?

As they continued on downstream, Tex hoped someone was taking care of his horse. At the same time, he knew his friends were all mighty busy.

———◇————————◇———

Morgan caught up to Sly Duncan in a few stretched-out strides of his horse. He got close and leapt off his horse to land on Sly and yank him off the saddle. The two of them fell, bounced along the stony ground for a bit before slamming into a tree.

Morgan got back on his feet, flipped Sly onto his belly, and tied his hands behind his back.

Sly fought his grip and howled like a wolf.

Roz came riding up and grabbed ahold of the riderless horses.

They were both well-trained critters, so Morgan could have rounded them up without much trouble. But he was glad for the helping hand, although he wondered why Roz had abandoned her son.

Roz was riding a mustang mare with brown-and-white

patches. Without dismounting, she snagged the dapple-gray mare that had once been Stan's, the one Sly had been riding. She had Morgan's black stallion, too. A good horse was often the only thing standing between a Marshal and death, so they made a point of having fast, well-behaved mounts.

Sly, his head bleeding from connecting with the tree, said some words so salty that Morgan wished he had a bar of soap handy to wash the man's mouth out. He remembered Roz's pa and knew she'd heard plenty of salty language. Still, it was offensive. And why wasn't Morgan surprised that such a low-down varmint was willing to offend others?

Morgan tossed a moaning and groaning Sly Duncan onto the gray's back.

"You're only alive because shooting you in the back isn't my idea of honor. Unless I was afraid you were getting away, then I'd've probably gunned you down."

"I'd expect nothing less from a cold-blooded murderer, who's hiding behind a Marshal's badge."

"You oughta know a murderer when you see one, unless you don't own a mirror."

Sly muttered such ugly threats, Morgan decided, even though his prisoner was wounded and bleeding, to take the man seriously.

"Why did you come along?" he asked Roz, thinking a ma oughta stay and take care of her son.

Roz narrowed her eyes at Morgan. "I remember you well enough, Morg. I'm not letting you out of my sight."

Startled, Morgan shouldn't have asked, but it slipped out. "For how long?"

Roz smiled, and it reminded him that they'd been a bit

more than old friends as kids before Morgan had ridden off to war. Too young to do anything about how they felt, but definitely more than friends.

She shrugged and said, "I suspect you need to get used to having me and my boy around."

11

Owen found a gap in the trees his horse could barely squeeze through. The terrain canted steeply uphill. He caught a glimpse of Clive Duncan ahead.

Owen ducked low to avoid the branches trying to snatch him off his horse and focused on gaining on his outlaw.

Where had Morgan and Tex gone? How were they doing? How had the Duncans gotten loose anyway?

Had they picked this moment for a reason? Did the Duncan Gang know this area? Was it possible they'd wandered onto land known to these outlaws?

They'd checked for hidden weapons, and he'd've said he and his men knew all the tricks. No, they hadn't come across a knife, and yet the Duncans had gotten one somehow.

But during the long, miserable climb down that gully, then back up, Owen hadn't been watching them because he was too busy clinging to his horse. He'd been fooled, and he didn't like it one bit.

Suddenly, dead ahead, Clive was off his horse and climbing. They'd come up on a steep rock wall. Owen got to the base of the cliff beneath Clive. There was nothing for it but for Owen to leap off his horse and go after him.

He was tempted to just draw his gun and start shooting. But shooting an unarmed man went against the moral code Owen had for himself, and he wouldn't do it.

Especially when he was gaining on the coyote.

Handholds were easily found, for it was almost like climbing a ladder. He pressed on, fighting for speed, closing the distance.

Dirt and rock rattled down from overhead. Clive didn't take the time to start an avalanche, but Owen figured he'd come up with that notion soon enough.

Owen kept pushing on. He looked up for a second every few paces to search for his next handhold, not wanting to end up getting a face full of dirt and grit.

He saw the top looming overhead and knew if Clive had a chance to think, he might gain the top, then turn and send boulders tumbling down on Owen, if he found any handy.

To prevent that, he had to catch Clive before he made it to the top.

Moments later, Clive was finally within grabbing distance. A ledge looked like it'd catch him if he fell, so he lunged upward and grabbed the leg of Clive's trousers.

A strangled cry escaped Clive's throat, and he lost his grip. Owen shoved sideways, and both of them fell onto solid, if narrow, rock.

Owen plowed a fist into Clive's face. He did it again, and yet again. He was at too much risk of falling all the way back to the bottom of the cliff. Mean and wiry as any sidewinder, Clive flailed at Owen. Owen gave no quarter but tossed Clive onto his belly and hog-tied him. Tighter than before. He'd need to let him go to get back down, but for now he tied up his legs, too.

And that was when he got company.

Delaney landed beside him. He hadn't noticed her climbing, but here she was, about fifty feet high in the air on a stone stairway that they'd now need to descend with a writhing prisoner.

"What are you doing here?" Owen hadn't meant to shout.

Delaney didn't seem all that fazed by his hollering. "How do we get him down?" she asked, not answering his question.

Studying the cliff, the prisoner, her own bloody fingertips, she turned to face Owen, one brow arched. Almost, he thought, like she needed some advice, which he sincerely doubted she did.

◇———————◇

With Sly back in his custody and lashed once more to a horse—this time with extra knots—Morgan rode his horse back the few yards to the canyon entrance. Roz brought up the rear to keep an eye on their prisoner.

Morgan studied Boone and the kid. Knowing Roz, she'd probably named her son after Jesse James. That was her style. Always a wild one. Had word of the notorious outlaw reached up into these hills? he wondered.

Boone had seemed much better the last day, though he still had the bandage on his head and probably had the granddaddy of all headaches. He sat on the ground in front of a small but growing fire.

The man was thinking ahead, but at the same time Morgan was a little bit annoyed to realize Boone didn't have a very optimistic nature, going ahead and building a fire like that. He clearly thought the Marshals would be a while rounding up the prisoners.

And where was Marley? He shouldn't have gone off with his leg as injured as it was.

No one else was back. Morgan began to think pessimism might be infectious.

Jesse was fetching sticks and tossing them on the fire. Morgan was impressed with the little one's willingness to work. Ten years old, his ma had said. Of course, Morgan had already started hunting with his pa by age five, so Jesse could handle gathering up some kindling.

Morgan remembered the long rifle his pa had given him. A lever-action rifle that was taller than Morgan. Then Morgan had gone off to war empty-handed because Pa was furious with him for fighting against his brother. Morgan had used his Army pay to buy a Winchester when the war had ended, and he still carried it with him today.

"We've got enough sticks for the fire, Jesse. Start a pile next to that boulder there." Boone pointed to a big rock that was a couple of yards away from the fire, all the better to keep it from catching fire by accident.

Boone studied them as they rode in, his expression grim. "Tex went that way chasing Stella, Marley after him." He jabbed his finger to the north side of the trail. Then he pointed the opposite way. "Owen went that direction, and my sister charged after him. No sign of any of them yet."

Morgan dragged a bleeding Sly off his horse to a shout of pain.

"He got a hard smack on the head. No sign of broken bones." Morgan pulled Sly's kerchief off his neck, formed it into a bandage, then tore a piece of Sly's shirt into a strip and bound the wound on the back of his head. No way would he use his own kerchief or cut up his own shirt.

Furious at the prisoner's escape and the extra trouble he'd caused, Morgan might've tied the bandage a little too tight. He admitted that, right now, he didn't much care if the man lived or died.

Morgan didn't like that part of him, but his fellow Marshals were gone and in danger. He blamed the man who'd brought it down on his own head by escaping. Add to that, battered though the man was, he looked like he would survive. So a few mean thoughts didn't do any harm, except maybe to Morgan's conscience.

"You'll live," he snapped at Sly. He sat the outlaw up and bound his feet, then tied the man to a tree.

"Ma, why'd you run off on me?" Jesse asked as he scooped up sticks from close around the camp.

"I knew you'd be safe here with Boone. I was afraid Morgan might need some help."

Jesse glared at Boone. "I should've gone, too. Or are you too wounded to be on your own?"

Boone gingerly touched his bandage, then jerked it off. "I reckon I'll be all right."

Roz went and checked Boone's head injury. She shook her head. "That's an ugly gash. You should've had stitches for certain."

"Yep, and probably a week in bed being tended by an army of nurses." Boone shrugged. "But here I am. How's the cut look?"

Jesse came close to his ma and studied the injury thoroughly. With that kind of close attention, Morgan had to wonder if the boy would be a doctor when he grew up.

"It's scabbed over, which is good. Safe to go without the bandage now. Too late for stitches to do any good—not that we have a needle and thread with us."

Roz tossed the bandage into the fire, then got busy at a spring collecting water in their coffeepot.

"The day's getting on. We'll bed down here tonight." Roz took coffee grounds out of Morgan's saddlebag. "This coffee you brought along is the first I've had in the years since Jesse's pa died."

Morgan gave his prisoner a hard look, still bothered that he didn't know how the man had escaped earlier. But the outlaw looked addled, so he'd stay put for now.

Morgan couldn't go after Owen or Tex without leaving the others here with the prisoner. After fretting for a few minutes, not liking how long his friends had been gone, he went back to his saddlebags and got out the fixings for a stew. Nothing much to do except wait.

He knew his friends well and trusted them. They'd be back soon, hopefully.

<hr />

Tex had no more strength to fight against the fast-moving river. It was taking all he had to keep his and Stella's heads above water. They went through another narrow stretch of white water and jagged rocks. The time narrowed down to seconds as he struggled to breathe. Then it narrowed to heartbeats. Just live through the next pulse in his chest, the next breath.

He prayed for God to add His strength to this battle.

The walls of the canyon rose up around him. He found

no way to get to the shore, such as it was. They were along for the ride the river was giving him.

Thankfully, Stella was conscious, but she seemed dazed still. Though she wasn't talking, her eyes were open, and she made some effort to swim to help keep them both afloat.

One more stretch of battering stones, a few that seemed to be angry they were going past, and then they were pushed out into a lake. Not a big one, and the current was still hard to fight, but Tex dug deep and fought his way to the shore. There was enough open space in one spot where he could pull himself and his prisoner onto the rough, stony soil.

He flopped over onto his back, panting, listening to Stella breathing hard beside him. He wondered if she had the strength for an escape attempt. He said a silent prayer that she'd just lie still for a while so he could rest a bit.

They'd gone into the water in the early afternoon. He'd lost track of how long they'd been bashed and battered. In this canyon, they were in deep shade. He couldn't figure, in his waterlogged brain, what direction they'd gone. Considering the twists and turns, they'd probably gone in all of them.

He had nothing. He'd left his rifle behind on his horse. Another check told him his Colt revolver was gone, too. He kept a knife inside his shirt, and he fumbled for it. With a sigh of relief, he found the knife was there.

He hurt everywhere on his body. He didn't think he had any broken bones thankfully, but he'd been through fistfights that didn't leave him feeling as badly assaulted.

Turning to look at Stella, he found her unconscious or maybe asleep. She was soaking wet. Her hair, long and blond, was swept back from her forehead and reached to her waist.

She was sunburned, the tip of her nose peeling. She had a bruise or two he could see and figured she probably had a dozen more he couldn't see. She was tall for a woman and slim, her neck slender, graceful. The attraction he felt toward her alarmed him. He tried to ignore it, to remind himself that she'd been living the life of an outlaw, robbing folks and running from the law.

He wondered if they'd settle the crimes her family had committed on her strong but slender shoulders when they took her before a judge. He wondered if that graceful neck was due an appointment with a noose.

There were hard things ahead for the pretty Miss Duncan, and he'd see that she faced up to them, but for just a few moments he let himself forget about that and instead think about how pretty she was. He sorted through the years of his past, going back as far as he could remember. Had he ever been alone with a woman?

That struck him as wrong. He lived a strange kind of life. Plenty of it riding with other men, but more of it alone. Riding with a group of Marshals wasn't the usual way.

He thought of Stella's reckless escape. She'd risked her life to be free. He had to wonder what all she had on her back trail to be willing to die trying to get free. Or was she just a wild spirit willing to take such chances?

Tex glanced at her wrists and saw she still had a rope tied around each of them, though the link between her arms had definitely been cut. How had she gotten a knife? He knew how to search for hidden knives, weapons of all kinds, and he knew he hadn't missed any stashed away on the prisoners. A wily bunch, these Duncans. He'd've sworn he'd been watching them real close. Bringing up the rear was his job.

118

But today that crazy rattlesnake of a trail had taken most of his attention. Was that what had given Sly and his family the distraction they'd needed to break free?

He couldn't really blame them for trying to escape. But he wasn't going to allow it anymore. He had a code he lived by, and being attracted to a beautiful woman didn't change that.

She'd be a handful when she woke up, unless the beating from the head-over-heels plunge down the cliff and the battering river ride had left her as stoved up as it had him.

For now, she slept. It was an idea with merit, and that was Tex's last thought for a while as his eyelids gained weight and exhaustion dragged him into sleep.

<hr />

Hester and Grizzly rode into Elk Point late in the day, starving, exhausted, and worried to a frazzle.

"I regret we didn't explain where we were going. You should wire Mortimer." Hester mentioned the man Grizzly had left in charge.

"He saw us heading south. He knew we were riding out to meet the youngsters." He called them that even though his youngsters were full-grown adults.

But Grizzly had missed a lot of their childhood, so maybe he wished they were still youngsters. He'd come home from the war to their older three sons gone. The two younger of them, Jedediah and Crockett, had fought with him in the bloody conflict, while Bowie had gone west before the trouble broke out. He'd never come back to throw into the fight, at least not as far as Hester knew. The raising of his two youngest had been left to her for a few years, but she knew what she was doing.

When her husband had returned from the fighting, his youngsters were nearing adulthood. He'd never really caught up with the details of the time he'd missed. Hester was delighted that Boone and Delaney had agreed to join them at Fort Russell. Hester hoped he'd get to know at least part of his family again.

"I'll let him know we're taking that trail that led into the mountains." Back to where they'd seen blood. "Then if Boone and Del do get to the fort, they'll know better where we are."

"What do you think happened?"

She must be upset or she never would've bothered asking such a question.

She watched him shake his head and look back the way they'd come. "Something bad, I reckon." He pulled her into his arms. "Hester, girl, marrying you was the best thing I ever did. How'd I get lucky enough to pick the perfect woman for myself?"

That got a smile out of her. "Have you been under the impression all these years that you picked me? Because I most certainly arranged this marriage all by myself."

"I was so determined to have you," Grizzly said, "I gave up these mountains. Best thing I ever did."

She'd been standing there in Jefferson Forge, Indiana. They'd both been about sixteen. They were married by their seventeenth birthdays, and Grizzly had joined the Army by the time he was eighteen. He'd built her a cabin and bought a cow and a few chickens before riding off. She'd known Bowie was on the way by then but kept it to herself because she knew how much he wanted to join the Army. He'd stopped by home a year later and met his son.

120

"Let's send a wire," she said quietly.

Grizzly nodded, then repeated himself. "Yep . . . something bad, I reckon. I want to ride back to where we saw blood on the trail and get busy finding our children."

"I wonder what happened to them." She could tell he was just as worried as she was.

"Can't say what happened, but it figures that something did, even if the place we came upon had nothing to do with them."

Hester gave a sigh and said, "Let's send that wire and get a good night's sleep. Tomorrow we'll pack a supply of food to last us in the wilderness, then go find our children."

"And we'll keep at it for as long as it takes, even if we have to tear down these blasted Rocky Mountains, stone by stone."

Grizzly walked to his buckskin stallion, where it stood patiently beside Hester's mousy-gray mustang mare. They'd gotten some beautiful foals out of this pair over the years. Now the horses were aging, just like she and Grizz were. But they were still strong, and still eager to do whatever needed doing.

She reached over and squeezed his hand hard, then spurred her horse onward. Grizzly would have his hands full keeping up with her.

12

Delaney was settled on the ledge, her feet dangling, breathing hard, her heart racing from the long, fast climb.

Owen swung his legs around so that he was sitting side by side with her. Clive lay facedown beside them, fighting the ropes Owen had tied tightly to constrain the man.

"If you wiggle much more, Duncan, you're gonna fall off this cliff. Lie still. I'm in no mood to grab you if you start tumbling."

Clive quit his wiggling and instead started yapping. "I told you, I don't deserve to hang. I shot that man in self-defense. You should just let me and my family go and—"

Owen yanked the kerchief off Clive's neck and gagged him. Delaney approved of Owen not using his own kerchief. And she approved of the silence.

"Have you got any idea how to get down from here?" he asked.

Actually, while Owen had been dealing with Clive, she'd given it some thought. "Sure, I've got a lasso on my horse. He's down there grazing." She pointed at her horse, standing near Owen's and Clive's horses. All of them were settling into a meal.

She went on. "I'll climb down, fetch the lasso back up here. We'll tie it tight around Clive's waist and lower him to the ground. Simple."

Owen leaned out enough to see how high up they were. "Got any better ideas?"

She turned to smile at him. "We can lower him enough that a fall won't kill him."

"You've got a little bit of a cruel streak, Miss Bridger. I like it."

She laughed.

"I'd like to catch my breath a little longer, but Morgan, Tex, and Marley might be worrying about us by now.

"The ledge right there." She pointed down about halfway. "That's within reach of my lasso. And behind you, that scrub pine growing out of the rock, it looks sturdy enough. We'll use that to lower him to that ledge. I'll wait down there for him and watch over him while you climb down. Then we'll lower him the rest of the way."

"It might work. But it's a narrow ledge. It'll be hard to keep him on it."

"It's close enough to the ground that if the coyote starts wiggling around again, I'll just have to let him fall. That's up to him."

"If he falls from there, it probably wouldn't kill him. And that plan will get him down to the ground while leaving him tied up. Yep, it'll work. I'd offer to climb down and fetch the rope and climb back up here, it'd be the gentlemanly thing to do." He turned to her and smiled.

She smiled back. "It's not gentlemanly to leave me up here with a killer."

"There's no real mannerly way to solve this. If you'd rather rest a few minutes before going after the lasso . . ." Owen paused and looked at her hands.

When he did, Delaney looked too and saw she'd ripped a fingernail below the quick, and it was bleeding. She hadn't paid it any mind before, but now she noticed how much it hurt.

Wincing, he reached for her hand and held it up for a better look. "Can you still make the climb, you think?"

She studied his hand holding hers. His hands were bleeding worse than hers. They were callused and battered and darkly tanned from his life lived outside. "Your hands are torn up, too. You climbed the same cliff I did."

Then she closed her hand over his and looked back at him. "Yes, I can do it. This sure has been a trip marked by pain, but the pain of fearing Boone was dead makes everything since then seem unimportant. I don't mind waiting a few more minutes to catch my breath, though." She touched his raw, bleeding index finger. "You're hurt too, Owen."

"I've gotten so I don't pay much mind to pain unless it's bad enough to stop me from moving forward." He lifted his right hand, revealing that the palm had been scraped practically raw.

"Lowering that worthless Clive Duncan is going to hurt as well and take plenty of strength."

Their eyes locked, and she smiled. She saw strength, kindness, and courage in his blue eyes. He was the kind of man who did what needed to be done and didn't shirk responsibility. He was a man who was used to being in charge and snapping out orders, usually to strong, highly skilled lawmen. Men who wouldn't take an order that didn't make sense to them, and yet they obeyed him.

"You're a strong, capable woman, Delaney, and a real pretty one to boot. Thank you for your help. I admit I wasn't happy to see that you'd followed me. That's mainly because I see it as my job to keep you safe."

"And now?" She arched one brow, amused.

"And now I'm glad you're here," Owen said. "I'm grateful to have your help. I'm also happy to have your company."

"I'd like to sit a little longer, until my heart stops pounding so hard I can feel it in my ears."

He nodded. "We'll take a bit of time then."

Delaney leaned forward and looked down. "You ever think about all the twists and turns your life has taken to get you to this spot, sitting on a ledge on a mountain with a woman and a killer?"

Owen smiled. "Nope. I usually think about what's ahead, not what brought me here."

"It does seem like an unlikely place to end up."

He squeezed her hand but gently, being careful not to hurt it further. But his hand, his gentle strength, made the hurt seem like nothing somehow.

"Are you from Colorado?" she asked. "Were you born here?"

"I grew up on a farm in Iowa. Pa went to fight the war, and then when it looked like my family could manage without me, I traipsed after him. Figured the war would last a few months at the most. Pa had said so before he left when Ma kicked up a fuss about his leaving us."

"Did she fuss over you, too?"

Owen was silent for so long, Delaney wondered if she'd asked him a question that opened up painful memories.

"She cried over me. Mad at Pa, terrified for me. But I was

too manly, too sure I had to fight for my country, to let her tears stop me."

"How old were you?"

"Nearly seventeen. A full-grown man—at least to my way of thinking."

"Ma said Bowie took off when he was about that age. Jedediah and Crockett weren't much older. I reckon you were a man by then, but a ma wouldn't see it that way."

"She sure enough didn't."

"So how did you end up all the way out here?"

He seemed to be staring into the far-distant past. Quietly, he said, "I went home after the war for a spell, then left. And I've never been back. I wonder if they moved on west or if they're even still alive."

"The train makes a trip real easy, Owen. When we get to Cheyenne, you can jump on the train and go see them. You could be out there and back in a week's time."

Owen turned to look at her. He wasn't looking into the past now, but right into her eyes. "I should go see them. I guess I've never considered the train."

"I've never met Bowie. I'm told he still lived at home when I was real young, but I have no memory of him. He headed out west with plans to settle there, try fur trapping or who knows what, and I've not seen him since."

Owen nodded. "Why do you think your brother left and never returned?"

Delaney heard the question he didn't ask. He was wondering why he'd done the same thing. She leaned her shoulder against his. Instead of answering his question, she said, "It's strange to miss a man I've never really met. I'll wager your ma misses you. Your pa too, but he's probably too tough to admit it. Even to himself."

She turned to him and realized how close she'd gotten. She was letting him bear her weight when he was more exhausted than she was. At least she slept at night, while Owen stood watch for part of it. She should probably move away, but she didn't.

Their gazes held for much too long a time. A mountain breeze blew a strand of hair across her eyes, and Owen lifted his hand and gently brushed it away, then drew one rough finger down the side of her cheek. He leaned forward, just an inch. She closed the space between them another inch.

His lips touched hers, and it was nothing she'd ever thought a kiss could be. The warmth and the emotion it awakened in her was a deep and wonderful surprise.

Then Clive squirmed and kicked Owen, and Owen moved fast to keep the varmint from falling off the ledge.

He was busy enough, so she found the grit to turn away before she was even close to done being kissed. "I'll get the lasso now." She started her downward journey before she got the reckless notion to stay and look some more, hold his hand some more, kiss some more.

They really did need to get back to the group. She sure hoped Tex and Morgan were having an easier time fetching their prisoners than she and Owen were with theirs.

"Everyone should be back by now." Morgan poked a smoldering stick into the fire as the sun sank beyond the horizon. He raised his eyes so that they met Boone's.

Boone rose to his feet. "We should've gone hunting for

them right when you got back. I'm going. I don't like the idea that Delaney is still out there."

Morgan shook his head impatiently. "You're right. But you're not going. I can track a rattlesnake over solid rock, sneak up behind him and slap him on the head, then get away before he so much as rattles."

A mighty bold claim, and one he hoped to never have to prove.

"I'll keep watch over the prisoner." Boone rolled his eyes, then looked over at Sly. He was sitting up, bound hand and foot, and besides that he was tied to a tree.

"I'm going too," Roz announced as she stood.

Morgan gritted his teeth. "No, you're not. You stay here with your son and Boone."

"Jesse will be fine with Boone. And I can out-track you any day."

"Shouldn't take much tracking." Boone jabbed a finger to the south side of the trail. "That way goes up. From here it looks like it's heading for solid rock. They'll be stopped soon enough. Go get my sister back."

Morgan knew it might take a whole lot of tracking. Boone did too. But the sun was setting, and if he didn't go after Delaney, he probably couldn't stop Boone from going. He looked at Roz, who was already on horseback. It appeared that the petite woman had set herself up as his bodyguard.

"All right then." Morgan looked at Jesse, afraid the youngster would ask to come along to hunt for an escaped killer.

Jesse arched a brow and shook his head as if he'd put up with his ma's nonsense all his life. He tossed another stick on the fire.

Morgan shared a long look with Boone, then when he

was sure the wounded man was paying attention, he slid his eyes toward Sly. The outlaw was a dangerous man. Even tied up and unconscious, Boone understood he needed to be on guard. The kid, well, he seemed to have inherited his mother's pluck, so he might be a handful for a wounded man.

Morgan had been studying tracks since they got back with Sly. He hadn't gone into the woods to look further, yet he knew right where to start.

There'd been no effort to cover any tracks. While the going was rough, passing through woods thick with underbrush, it was fairly simple to choose which way to go.

As they rode along, Morgan, knowing speed wasn't going to be a factor in this hunt, said, "What happened to your husband, Roz? You said he's been dead for most of the boy's life."

"Pa died right after Jesse was born," she said, "so I was thankful to have him. I found out soon after I'd married Herman that he was a no-account. But Pa pushed me into marrying the man when he showed up at our ranch and settled in to stay. Now I suspect Pa was feeling poorly and was worried about me being alone out there. He saw a chance to round me up a husband and did so. I didn't care overly. Herman seemed tough enough and reminded me of Pa with his mountain-loving ways. I soon realized he was different from Pa in some real important ways. Pa figured it out too when Herman took off on a long hunt about the time I started getting round with a child. Herman didn't come back for six months. And he died before Jesse was two years old. The boy doesn't have a memory of his pa, and I've certainly got no stories to tell about him."

129

Morgan nodded along as she spoke. He felt terrible that Herman hadn't done right by Roz.

"Oh, he was a charmer, good-looking—that much I can say. And I was lonely. Didn't take long after we were married to find out Herman liked his liquor. He rode off hunting it often enough. Fancied himself a mountain man, and I suppose he trapped furs. But if he did trap, he traded the furs for cash money without bringing any of it home to his wife and son. When I married him, he was the only man who'd come by for years, not including your pa and a few old-timers who stopped by on occasion."

"Sounds like Herman left not long after you got married. So it was just you, your pa, and Jesse?" Morgan shook his head.

"That's right," said Roz. "Then a few months later, Pa took sick and died. Jesse and I lived in the cabin alone most of his first winter. Eventually, Herman wandered by and stayed for a stretch. It didn't suit him that Pa had died, though. It took me a while to figure out that was because Pa saw to hunting food."

"Don't you have a herd of cattle? Why the need to hunt?"

"Pa always preferred wild game. Said he wanted to get the herd to growing so we'd have a steady income in his old age. He was 'building for the future,' he liked to say."

"If your pa looked to the herd for money, he must've had plans to drive the cattle to town. What trail was he planning to use? Not this sidewinder of a trail. Maybe a mountain-bred longhorn could tackle it, but it'd be hard to convince 'em it was a good idea."

Roz turned to look at him. "You know, you're right. We've got a few more hair-raising stretches to go, too. But the few times we rode to town, we went the way I'm going now. I've no idea if there's another trail to town. If there is, I've not seen it."

"What did Herman do next? You with a baby and with your pa gone, surely he figured it best that he stay for a while."

"Nope. With winter coming on and the pelts getting thick on the beaver, Herman took off again. He came riding in the next summer, but by then he was dying. He'd injured his foot somehow, and it was turning black. Red streaks most of the way to his hip." Her face twisted at the memory. "It was an awful sight. It needed to be amputated, but he wouldn't allow it. His condition grew worse and fast, until one day he lost consciousness. And there was no reason to torture him further by removing the foot when it was hopeless. I reckon it was hopeless from the start."

Morgan lifted his eyes from the trail. The sunlight was fading, and if they didn't find Owen soon, they'd be in trouble. "You had to dig holes for two men in a little over a year's time?"

"I did. Digging Pa's grave near to broke my heart." Roz fell silent for a minute.

Morgan didn't know if she'd go on, and he didn't know what to say next.

"Digging Herman's grave, well, he wasn't much help when he was home and was gone most of the time. A few dreams died when I realized he wasn't going to stay. I'd hoped he'd see our land as his now and decide to help out. My heart wasn't broken when I dug his. I was grateful, though, the ground wasn't frozen, and it was hard digging with a toddler wanting to climb down into the hole. Beyond that, I wasn't much affected."

Her tone, her expression, told him she'd been badly affected, but he didn't badger her to admit it.

"How about you, Morgan? You went to war. You were my only friend, and I thought we meant something to each other."

It was Morgan's turn to think a while before he spoke. "I don't know what gets into a boy, or even a man, but I was crazy to go to war. It was worse after Gavin left. Then I got to where the fighting was . . . and it was a living nightmare. I should've stayed home." He glanced over at her. "Should've stayed with you."

"A living nightmare? What do you mean?"

"Such a question, and not easily answered. I was a drummer."

"A drummer. They have boys playing the drum in war?"

"Yep, and other boys played the fife. The men would march along, keeping in step thanks to us. It seemed odd, but they recruited boys as young as ten to play the fife and drum."

"Makes war sound almost fun."

"It wasn't. I didn't pick up a rifle until one day a soldier ahead of me was killed. His gun landed at my feet. I picked it up because I was scared and the enemy was coming. It was a Springfield repeating rifle, which you can shoot for a time without reloading. When I added my skill to the battle, well, I won't say I saved the Union single-handedly, but I helped hold the line—helped a lot. My superiors found out my aim was solid, my hands were steady, and my thinking quick. After that I was one of the rifle brigade. I didn't have to do it for long, though. By that time, the war was mostly over, and we were cleaning things up. The renegade Confederates were brutal and killed without remorse, even when they

132

knew they'd lost the war. Fighting in the war led me to the Marshals Service."

He'd been badly affected, too, and hoped she wouldn't badger him about it. He'd been sixteen when he killed a man for the first time. He remembered that day like it was written in fire across his soul.

"Why didn't you come back?"

Morgan pondered her question. He'd wanted to come back. He'd planned to. But Pa made it impossible. He should have come anyway, except he'd been hurt by Pa's ugly letter and by the viciousness of war. Finally, he replied, "I don't really know. I can't say . . ."

They rode on in silence for a while, then, looking sideways at her, he asked, "You're not letting me out of your sight, are you?"

She gave him a quirky smile that reminded him of her as a youngster. "See if I don't, Morgan Sawyer. Just see if I don't."

"So you saw my pa for a while after I left?"

She nodded. "He left after he learned that Gavin died. Before that, he'd wander over to our place about once a month and stay to drink coffee and tell stories by the fire with Pa. Then one day he came and told us he'd received word that Gavin had died, and he was leaving the country."

"Did he accuse me of killing Gavin?"

Roz was suddenly busy straightening her reins when they were as straight as could be already.

Morgan took that to mean his pa had accused him of exactly that. He reached across to settle his hand on top of hers. "I didn't. I never fought near him. I got as close to home as Elk Point, where I found a letter waiting for me. It was from Pa. I tore it open and found the letter he'd gotten from

Gavin saying where he'd been fighting, and it was a long way from where I was. And there was a second letter, real short and real mean, accusing me of killing my own brother."

The two of them continued to wind their way through the woods, following the trail in front of them. Morgan could see that Clive, Owen, and Delaney had ridden through at a gallop, and they were lucky to have survived it and not killed themselves or their horses.

"I'll tell you true, Morg, when your pa came through saying he was heading west, he wasn't in his right mind, not in my opinion. He spoke against you, and I tried to stop him, tell him how sorry I was about Gavin. That he still had a son who was alive, and he owed it to you to be here waiting when you came home. He could grieve the dead without turning away from the living."

"He wasn't in his right mind? Pa was always a wild man and a loner. I never could figure out how my ma tamed him enough to get him to build a cabin and have two sons. But I'd've never said he was a madman."

"I think losing Gavin was just too much for him."

"He always preferred him over me. I think he blamed me for Ma's death. She died giving birth to me."

"I remember Gavin was his shining star." Roz shook her head. "But he loved you too, Morgan, and was proud of you . . . until you picked what he saw as the wrong side in the war."

"He didn't want anything to do with the war. He didn't think I picked the wrong side as far as what the war was about. I picked the wrong side because I'd made it to be brother against brother. That's what he couldn't forgive. Since Gavin went first and threw in with the Confederacy, he thought I owed it to my brother to side with him. I just couldn't do it."

"I remember the day you came by to tell me you were heading out. One of the saddest days of my life. Not as sad as losing Pa, I reckon, but far and away sadder than losing Herman. That man never did much but make more work for me, right up to the end when I had to dig him a grave."

"When you—" Morgan had a whole lot more to say just as the trees cleared a bit and he spotted a man being lowered on a rope down the side of a cliff. Owen was up top, Delaney halfway to the ground, standing on a narrow ledge. Clive Duncan hung halfway between. "Well, look at that. Owen and Delaney seem just fine. They got their man, too."

Morgan and Roz rode toward the steep slope. Since he was already here, he'd help out, although showing up now felt like he didn't trust Owen to handle his part of the job. He should have gone after Tex instead.

Owen looked up as Morgan reached the base of the slope and dismounted. His expression brightened, and being distracted, the rope slipped. Clive dropped a few feet and slammed onto the rock ledge. Delaney grabbed for him to stop him, but then she tipped over the edge, and both of them fell.

Owen yelped.

Morgan came a-running just in time to break Delaney's fall after they plunged off the ledge the last few feet alongside the cliff. He caught her neatly but didn't even try to catch Clive. Their prisoner hit a little bit hard, but the ground was soft there. He'd survive.

Maybe now the man would sleep through the next few days until they got him to Fort Russell.

Owen tossed the lasso down and climbed to where Morgan was setting Delaney back on her feet. She dusted herself off.

"Are you all right?" Owen studied her for scrapes and bumps, and just in case, for broken bones. She'd come through in good shape. Then he lifted both her hands, remembering how battered they'd looked up on the ledge. The fall hadn't made them any worse.

"That was my fault." He looked at Morgan, and then aware it was almost painful to look away from Delaney, he went back to studying her and knew it had nothing to do with checking for bruises. "I saw Morgan come riding into the clearing and was distracted for just a second, and I let Clive slip."

Delaney waved him back. "I'm fine." She turned to Morgan. "Thank you for catching me. Are you all right?"

Morgan picked his hat up off the ground, studied its squashed crown, punched it back into shape, and said, "Yes, I'm fine."

They all turned to Clive, who lay facedown again, breathing steady but unconscious.

Morgan said to Owen, "No sign yet of Tex. I took off after you first because Boone was itching to go after his sister himself, and I don't think he's quite as ready for that as he hopes. Roz and I caught Sly in a few paces, so we got to camp a while ago. We'd better get back before we lose the light."

Owen caught Morgan's arm when he started to turn, then narrowed his eyes when he saw the red welt that crossed his cheek. "What did you get hit with? You've got a slash across your face, but it doesn't look like a cut from a knife, but more like from a stick."

Morgan touched his face and seemed to look through Owen into the past. "I didn't think of it until you mentioned it, but he did hit me with something, and now that I know it's there, it stings. I don't know what he had or how they all got loose at once. I dove off my horse and had him hog-tied fast. I didn't search him again for weapons I might've missed. And if he had a stick, he must've dropped it when I took him down."

Owen's eyes were drawn to movement near where the trees opened up in front of the cliff. It was Roz. She had rounded up all the horses while still on horseback and was leading them over.

Owen gave Morgan a sly smile. "It was a good idea to bring help."

Morgan glanced over his shoulder, saw Roz, then looked away. Owen might be imagining it because it was faint, but he might've been a witness to Morgan Sawyer blushing.

So quiet Owen barely heard it, and for certain Roz couldn't, Morgan said, "Can't seem to get shut of her. But she's a handy woman."

Owen noticed the horses and that she'd led one of them over to stand near Clive. Owen reckoned that if they didn't get moving, she'd have the varmint loaded on his horse and hauled all the way back to camp.

Handy for a fact.

"We'll keep a closer eye on all of them." Owen headed toward Clive.

Morgan threw in to drag the man to his horse, untie his feet, and toss him over the saddle.

Delaney said, "We'll keep a closer eye unless we're scaling the sides of canyons."

Owen grunted, and they all mounted up. Not counting Roz Beck, who'd never dismounted.

They didn't talk much on the ride back to the campsite.

Owen had a firm belief in not worrying. He felt like it was a waste of time and energy, and it didn't sit right with his faith in God. Instead, if he had something to worry about, he set out to fix it. Because fixing it was something he couldn't do right now, he tried to keep his mouth shut and his thoughts on finding Tex, then eating supper and sleeping with one eye open, thanks to these lawbreaking Duncans. And do all of that before full dark. The lowering sun told him that wasn't going to be easy.

It'd solve all his problems if he got there and found Tex had returned with Stella—yet another troublesome Duncan.

When they finally arrived at the camp, Boone's eyes went straight to Delaney. He heaved a sigh of relief.

But there was no Marley, no Stella either. And precious little sunlight left. Owen had hoped to get out of the mountains today, though he had no idea where he was exactly.

"You'd think of the three of them, the woman would be the easiest to corral," Owen muttered. He didn't say it for anyone's ears but Morgan's because they had two feisty women with them, and he'd prefer it if they weren't mad at him. Especially the one he'd kissed less than an hour ago.

Morgan shook his head and looked at Roz, then Owen. "We can't track him until daybreak." Morgan was likely thinking the same thing they were. It'd been too long. Tex was in trouble.

Right then Marley came riding in, leading two horses. He

would have brought bodies back if others had died. Still, this was a bad sign.

"Tell us what happened," Owen said. "Can you take us to them?"

Marley shook his head. "They went over a cliff. Tex had caught up to her and was about to grab her horse's reins when their horses as good as sat down, they'd come so close to the edge. I saw them both go flying over their horses' heads. I was just far enough behind them I got my horse stopped."

"They're dead?" Owen's stomach wrenched. Tex had been one of his best friends in the world. He didn't have many.

"Not so's I could tell." The way Marley sank to the ground and poured himself coffee, like it was taking his last bit of strength, reminded Owen that Marley was still tender from getting shot in the leg.

"By the time I got to the ground and could look over the cliff, there was nothing left but a trail of dust. They took a header over the cliff and fell out of sight fast. Tex is tough, so I won't believe he's dead until I see his body. But one of the reasons I'm so slow getting back is that I scouted around for a long time trying to find a way down, and there ain't one. I got an angle on the bottom enough I could see a river. If they hit water, there's a real good chance they survived the fall."

"I've seen that river," Roz said, crossing her arms. "There's a curve of it closer to my place. It's a mean one. A fast current studded with rocks in the narrow stretches. More than one waterfall and plenty of sheer rock lining it. Hard to get out." She looked up at Morgan. "It's survivable, though, and you said your friend is tough. Stella strikes me as tough, too. But I don't know any way to get down there from up here.

The only trail I know out of these mountains veers away from that river. We'll never even see it."

"What direction does the current flow?"

Shaking her head, Roz said, "The wrong way. They'd be moved along west while we are headed east. We won't cross paths with them."

Still determined to find Tex, Owen turned to eating the food Boone had prepared. Somehow Boone had stood guard over Sly, who was unconscious, watched over Roz's kid, and rustled up a meal.

When they'd finished their supper, they set up a night watch between Owen and Morgan, though all four of the others—Delaney, Roz, Boone, and Marley—offered to take a shift.

Owen trusted them, except for maybe Boone with his head injury. But it was the Marshal's job, and they'd do it. He'd've trusted Marley to help, but his face was drawn, and his limp was back with a vengeance. Marley needed to rest that leg. They had a long ride out of here, and there was still a risk Marley's leg could fester and he might lose it.

Those in the camp settled in to sleep, except for Owen who'd volunteered to keep watch for the first shift. So he roamed around the campsite, leery and on edge, telling himself not to worry but failing miserably at it.

It was a beautiful night. The stars were glowing all around the sky like they'd been blasted up there with a shotgun loaded with diamonds.

Owen decided not to feel confident about anything, including the Duncan Gang's whereabouts.

13

Tex woke up with his hands and feet bound and with Stella Duncan sitting near him. She was a terrible mess of dirty clothes and wild hair. He saw her watching him carefully. Then she struck a spark on a flint that she'd probably fished out of his pocket, though she might've had her own.

The kindling was neatly piled, a little bird's nest ready to ignite. Because he was annoyed with himself for being caught, he kept silent as she started the fire while he watched.

Glancing up at him frequently as if he could escape as easily as she had, she said, "Before I untie you, I want to say something. I promise to cut your bindings after I've had my say. Although I doubt the word of a Duncan is worth much to you."

She had that right. He tugged against the ropes on his wrists and found them very securely bound.

He rocked himself up into a sitting position. Every move and breath hurt after yesterday's battering. She watched him through suspicious eyes, then got back to tending her fire.

"I have been trying to escape from my family ever since my ma died and Pa took me with him on his wandering."

She stopped talking and got a little curl of smoke to rise from the bird's nest, then gently blew on it, focusing on the fire. He got the impression she'd had it ready a while ago and had sat there waiting for his eyes to open.

"How old are you?" That was a dumb question to be the first out of his mouth, but they both had to live with it now.

"Twenty-five," she answered. "I have to tell you, I don't think my pa and Uncle Gordy are outlaws. I know you believe Clive is a murderer, but—"

"He *is* a murderer. He killed a cavalry private in front of witnesses."

"He escaped and stayed out of sight for months. I had plenty of time to talk to him. He's a reckless young man who makes plenty of foolish mistakes, I won't deny that. But I don't believe he's a killer. He admits he killed that man, but he didn't start the fight. He saw the man grab a woman and drag her into an alley. Clive fought him, and when the man drew a gun, Clive was faster. He was defending himself."

"Not according to witness testimony."

"The witness was Calan MacNeil, a good friend of the victim, Private Finlay MacNeil. And they weren't just friends since the time they met at the fort. They were Scots, cousins, who'd been together all the way back to Scotland. Finlay's cousin lied about the woman; he was in on that. He also wanted vengeance for Finlay and didn't care to be tied to what they were planning to do to that woman. So he accused Clive of cold-blooded murder."

Tex could see that Stella sincerely believed all of what she was telling him. He looked her in the eye and shook his head. "Your brother told you what he wanted you to believe. He cast himself in the best possible light."

"I'm telling you this story so you'll look into it when you take us to the fort. My brother Leland opened fire on you when he saw Clive. He always was a headlong fool. He died when you shot at us as we came riding up that first slope. The man who shot your Marshal is dead. No one else opened fire. And my pa is a stubborn, cantankerous old goat, but he isn't an outlaw."

"Him and your family are behind a rash of bank robberies all over Colorado."

"No, they're not," Stella insisted. "They're wandering men. They've always lived off the land. Pa and Gordy built cabins together in a hard-to-get-to spot west of Pikes Peak. I lived there with my ma and with my aunt Ethel for years while the men hunted and ran traplines and mined for gold. They'd pass through a few times a year, sometimes stay a few weeks or through the winter. Pa is a cranky man. We were always glad to see him go away, hunting or trapping. As the boys got old enough, they'd ride off with Pa when he left. I had a younger sister, Sissy, and she and I always stayed at home.

"Aunt Ethel died five years ago. Ma died two years ago, along with my sister, in a house fire. Pa rode in with his crew before Ma and little Sissy died. He rebuilt the cabin in hopes they'd survive, but neither of them did. That left me alone, so he decreed that I should go with him. He gave me no choice. It was a rugged life, but I was with them all the time for the past year since Ma died. There were no bank robberies. Fistfights aplenty and a few too many nights in the saloon. I was made to stay out of town. One of my brothers or cousins was always assigned to stay with me."

Tex was afraid that more went on in those towns than fistfights and whiskey drinking.

143

Stella wasn't done yet. "I liked being left behind. I could hunt, and it got to be my job since Pa and Clive and two older brothers were gone most of the time. While they were away, I'd go hunting with whatever poor, abandoned brother or cousin was with me. We'd feed the family. I learned plenty of what I know about living in the wilderness from my pa. But my ma was good with a gun and could fish and trap."

"But didn't you say you wanted to escape?" Tex asked.

"First of all, it wasn't the life I wanted to live. I didn't see how I'd ever have a home of my own because Pa never stayed in one place long enough for me to meet a man. And when a suitable man did wander close, Pa wouldn't let them near me. I believe my family is innocent, but they traveled through wild land, and some of the men we crossed paths with were criminals, maybe the bank robbers you mistook us for. I figured out we were running with outlaws. I'm not even sure that bothered me overly. I knew no other life. The only book in our house was the Bible, and Ma taught me to read with it. But there was no church, no preacher around. Anyhow, I didn't like riding with Pa, but I knew better than to say such a thing."

"If that was first, what's second?"

"Ma and my younger sister died. Our cabin burned down. We all got out alive, but Ma and Sissy were burned and breathed in too much smoke. They'd survived the fire, and we were so far out, I had no way to get to a doctor. I didn't even know where a town was. Then Pa returned home, and I begged him to help me get them to a doctor. He said none of the towns within a day's ride had a doctor, and with their injuries I knew they'd never survive a long ride. He said they'd live if they had the strength. I had to tend them for days. Ma had burns all along her back and legs. Sissy wasn't hurt as badly, mostly her arms got burns on them. I knew Ma was in terrible danger, but I thought Sissy would make it. It took Ma a week to die. Sissy lingered for a month before her wounds became infected and a fever caught hold. It was a dreadful thing to watch."

Tex had seen a few badly burned folks in his life. She was right. It was dreadful.

"While I tended them, Pa built a new cabin. But Ma died before he could finish it, and Sissy was moved to one of the two bedrooms. When she died, Pa told me to saddle up, that I'd be riding with them."

"And that's when you robbed your first bank?"

Stella's eyes narrowed. She threw a log on the fire. "I did *not* rob a bank. None of us did. But I didn't want that wild, wandering life. Pa as good as kept me under guard. I've been with them ever since. I'm telling you this because I don't want to be taken back to Pa. I want you to get me somewhere I can hide."

Tex studied her, probably for too long. He considered himself a good judge of liars. Of course, he dealt mainly with outlaws and Marshals. He assumed all the outlaws were liars and all the Marshals were honest, so maybe he was kidding himself.

Even so, what she'd said struck him as the truth. Or maybe it was just the truth as she knew it. Maybe her menfolk got up to things she didn't know about.

"We have no way back to where the rest of our group is." Tex looked at the wild river they'd come flooding down. He wondered if it was the Colorado River. If it was, they could have gone miles and miles to the south. Probably it was a smaller river or stream that emptied into the Colorado, and maybe they'd ridden it long enough that they were now in the Colorado. They'd been swept into a lake, but he still felt the current. He knew that lake had a way out that ran westward.

If they got back in the river, hoping to be taken to somewhere more hospitable, they could be swept all the way to Mexico, assuming they didn't drown first.

"Where would you go so your family couldn't find you?"

An expression of mulish stubbornness tightened her jaw. "I've been giving that some thought."

"Just now?"

"No, I've been thinking about it for years, long before Ma died. But while she was alive, I didn't feel quite so desperate. If you could get me to the train, give me enough money to climb on and head for California, my family would never find me there. I'm a decent cook, and I can clean rooms in a hotel or do their washing if I have to."

"Women are mostly either married or schoolmarms."

Looking chagrined, she said, "I can't be a schoolmarm. They'd probably want me to be able to read better."

"Most likely a requirement," Tex agreed. "Some women work in a store of some kind alongside their husbands."

"I've never met a man worth marrying, just wild-riding cronies of my pa's. And if I did meet and marry someone decent, he'd be in danger if Pa caught up to him."

"I wouldn't mind helping you, Stella. Near as I can remember, there's no wanted poster on you. I've never witnessed you commit a crime. But to just cast you out into the world like that is wrong. Come with me to find Owen and Morgan.

146

We'd have to check the latest wanted posters first, but if we don't find you there, we'll figure out a way to get you free of your family."

She frowned and replied, "No, that won't do. Pa would be angry if he got wind I was around and with all of you. What I'd prefer is to get myself on a train heading west, and you could . . . well, you could go on to find your friends and tell them I died. It's amazing I didn't. Then Pa would never hunt for me. I'd be safe."

"Except for being penniless and alone in the world."

"Yeah, except for that."

Stella turned her face toward the steep bank that rose high over their heads. "Maybe you could help me find a place to lie low. Or maybe I could sneak onto a train and ride in secret. I've heard of folks doing that."

Tex thought of the brutal men who guarded trains. "Conductors sometimes find hideaway passengers, and when they do, they toss them off the *moving* train. They tend to use their fists, too."

He considered at her pretty blond hair, a ragged mess but still a shining gold that might put the sun to shame if it wasn't so full of snarls and dried mud. Would they beat a woman like her if they came across her hiding on a train? Would they do worse than that? His stomach clenched.

"H-how much does a ticket cost? I'd pay you back, I promise." Stella's expression was earnest. "I'd prove I was honest by paying you back, if you'd just trust me this once."

Tex saw no reason not to admit the truth. "All the money I had in the world was in the saddlebags on my horse. I don't have the money for a train ticket."

Stella fell silent. He could see it had stung her to ask for him to pay. Now to be told no only deepened an already awkward situation.

Tex shifted around until he could rest his back against a boulder. He never took his eyes off her. Was she telling the truth?

Stella looked glum as she reached over, knife in hand— his knife, he noticed—and he tensed up, ready to fight even with his hands bound.

With quick, graceful moves, she cut the ropes binding his hands and feet.

A surge of relief coursed through Tex. This really did make her seem like an honest woman. When an outlaw comes at you with a knife, a man can't help but be wary.

He rubbed his wrists for a few moments.

"Can you tell me what to do?" she asked.

Tex thought of one job he had some control over. What's more, she was made for it. "This won't solve your problems with your pa." Although he was from Texas originally and a former Texas Ranger, he'd hired on to the U.S. Marshals Service to see more of the country. No reason he couldn't . . .

Their eyes met. He thought of a whole lot of reasons it was a mistake to say this. "I need to hire a deputy."

There was a long pause before she spoke. "A deputy?"

"Yep, and you have the skills for it, Stella."

"You mean I think like a criminal?"

Tex winced. "No, I don't mean that." Although, now that she mentioned it . . .

"Can women really be deputies?"

Tex couldn't exactly say he'd ever heard of one. But then he got to choose his own deputy, so why not? "Sure they can."

It wasn't against the law. Not one he'd ever heard of anyway.

"I've worked out of Colorado for a long time. By the time this is over, we'll have the whole Duncan Gang in jail."

"I told you—they're not outlaws. I just don't like the life they have forced on me. There are plenty of things wrong with my pa and cousins, but they're honest men for the most part."

"Including the jail-breaking killer?"

Stella swiped a hand at Tex. "Yes, including him. My family runs around with ruffians. I've got some no-good cousins who cast shame on the Duncan family name. But the men I ride with shouldn't have wanted posters on them."

Tex forged ahead. "You could work for me. Or if you don't feel safe here, we could find another place to serve. I could go back to Texas and work there as a Ranger. You know, not all Marshal work is this dangerous. There are documents to deliver and reward money to transport. Some Marshals stand guard during trials in federal court. I don't have to live in such dangerous territory. The posting is for four years. I have to submit papers to be reappointed, and it's nearing time to do that. I figured to ask for a second term, but it would be easy, I think, to change back to a Texas Ranger. By then we could find a place for you to live, and a job in some small town in Texas where it's safe."

After he finished planning her whole life, Tex smiled at her.

She was frowning. "I don't want to be a U.S. Marshal. I just watched your deputy get shot. And besides that, I don't want to go to Texas."

Tex thought she sounded mighty ungrateful considering

he'd just offered to upend his life for her. And he was mildly outraged that anyone would not want to go to Texas. He decided he'd concentrate on what he *could* do if she was too stubborn to let him manage things for her.

"The fact remains that we can't get back to Owen and Morgan and the others. I don't see enough shoreline that we can walk along, and I've no idea how to climb a cliff if we ever got back to where we fell. The current is too fast and deep to try wading back the way we came. Down here in the shadows, I can't even see the sun. I don't know what to do except climb out of here somehow, get a notion of where we are, and head for Fort Russell. I'm hoping Owen, Morgan, and Marley are already headed there. How about I find a place to hide you near the fort until I can figure out what to do with you?"

Her eyes narrowed.

He was making her mighty unhappy, and he had no idea why.

Since he couldn't seem to say the right thing, he decided to quit talking and get to work. They had no food, not a single bite. He slapped at his holster and remembered he had no gun.

She had his flint and had gotten the fire started with it. But he noticed now that there was no great stack of firewood. She must've picked up every branch and twig she could find down where they were.

So she had his knife and flint, and that was perilously close to all they had. Down in the belly of this canyon, there was no food to be seen. He glanced at the water. He might be able to spear a fish. He contemplated that for a few minutes but didn't feel up to going back in the water.

He wanted to stay here with Stella to protect her. But he got the feeling—considering he'd woken up to find she'd taken him prisoner—that she might be useful to have around to protect him. Yep, they needed to stick together, and right now the way to do that started with their staying put on land.

"I've made a bowl with a strip of bark. Here. Have a drink of water." She was a useful woman for a fact. "Then let's climb on out of here."

Tex decided to do his best not to start liking her. That would pinch if the law at Fort Russell came up with a wanted poster with her name on it.

"How about we get to the top of this wall." He turned to give her a look. "Can I have my knife back?"

She handed it over. Nope, not a criminal. Unless she knew she wasn't getting out of here on her own. She could still be a criminal, just a wily one. And the Duncan Gang had run roughshod over Colorado and Wyoming for years—unless Tex was wrong about that, too. And what had she said about cousins ruining the family name? Her pa was nicknamed Sly. So wiliness might come though the blood.

Tex just couldn't be sure.

Until he decided if he could trust her or not, he went and started scaling another cliff. He was on about his fourth today . . . or was it more than that? He'd lost count.

◇•••————————————••◇

"Delaney was here." Grizzly stormed out of the telegraph office, furious. "We should've turned off when we saw that trail. It could've been theirs."

Hester knew him well. Under that fury, Grizzly was scared for their children. She'd stayed on horseback, told him to go on in and that she'd hold his horse. She was tired and worried and saddlesore. She didn't admit it because sore and exhausted didn't matter. They'd keep going until their children were safe regardless of how hard it was. They were in complete agreement on that without saying a word to each other about it.

Grizzly had ridden hard to get here, and Hester had stuck with him every step. It was the end of the second day. Last night they'd slept in Fort Collins in Colorado, which was no longer a fort. Now they were in Elk Point, where the telegraph operator had already locked up for the night. But he lived above his office, so Grizzly had banged on the man's door until he came down to see what all the fuss was about.

"What did the telegraph operator say?" Hester asked.

"Delaney and Boone both came here. The operator remembered them well. They'd been riding with several other men. The telegrapher wasn't sure if it was five or six of 'em. He'd been busy sending the wire. The rest of the group had remained on horseback. They'd rushed through the request and payment, then were gone. The group galloped away to the north, headed along the Front Range. They used the road we came in on."

Hester clamped her mouth shut to cover her impatience, though she hadn't done a very good job of it.

"In the morning we'll head back north," Grizzly went on, "where we saw the tracks. We'll follow those tracks and hopefully catch up with them. If I remember correctly, you're the one who made the point that we couldn't follow their tracks in the dark."

"I know that." She swatted at him, but he was out of reach

152

and was just frustrated anyway. "Let's find a meal and get some sleep. We can be moving again before sunrise."

Grizzly and Hester spent a few minutes studying the ground at the front of the telegraph station.

"The Marshals I've known ride top-quality animals, always well shod." Grizzly crouched beside a clear set of tracks. "I'd say there are eight folks riding together. But the light is about gone now. It's the plain truth we couldn't have followed any tracks into the mountains."

"Elk Point is a quiet little town. Not a lot of hoofprints, especially off on this side street by the telegraph office." Hester nodded as she came and stood by his side. It was almost full dark, the sky moonless. "We can only see them because there's a light on in the telegraph office."

Right then the lantern went black, and their tracking was done. "We'll study them for a few minutes tomorrow at first light." Then, being a practical woman, she added, "Let's get some rest. Someone opened fire on our children. They bolted into the mountains, and whoever shot at them went after them and fast. We might find ourselves fighting our way to get to the youngsters."

"If we have to fight, then we'll fight." Grizzly swung back into the saddle and rode toward the darkened livery stable.

They hoped to find the hostler sleeping behind the stable, but if not, they'd put up the horses themselves and pay him in the morning.

"Then it's for the best we get some rest and a good meal under our belts before heading out. And we'd better stock up on ammunition as well, just in case we need to fight a war."

"Remember me asking who was riding with her? Which Marshals?"

"Yes," said Hester, "you said you knew one of them, and he was a good man. Morgan Sawyer."

Grizzly nodded. "I knew him in the war, and I only remember him because his pa and I ran the hills together as youngsters."

"Ran the *hills*? You mean the Rocky Mountains?"

Grizzly turned to her. "Yep. Ma died when I was a youngster, and Pa had no heart for the wilderness. We went back east. And then I met and married you as fast I could talk you into it."

Hester smiled. "I didn't put up one speck of a fuss."

"Morgan's pa stayed here because he'd found a place he wanted to settle in. He always craved a hidey-hole, and he'd found one a bit north of here. If Morgan was in trouble, I'll bet I know right where he'd run to. Hard place to find, but I think I remember how to get there."

"We were riding along some mighty steep hills right where they turned off. You're saying there's a way up into those mountains?"

"That's right," he replied. "We'll ride out in the direction of Morgan's pa's cabin and see if it doesn't lead us straight to our kids. There's a decent chance they might have gone there if attacked and injured." Grizzly was quiet for a moment before adding, "I wish we had time to explore these mountains a bit. The Rockies are beautiful. Dangerous but beautiful."

The two of them found the livery empty just as Hester had expected. They made short work of stabling their horses— stripping off their leather, brushing them down, and giving them hay and a bit of grain.

Hester stepped out of her horse's stall at the same time

154

Grizzly did his. She reached for his hand. "We'll do that sometime. Maybe we can take a real trail ride and try to ferret our sons out of the mountains. You were always good on a trail, Colonel."

"It's a wonder I didn't die of loneliness being away from you so much, Hester. I'm glad we're finally done wandering in opposite directions."

"I followed along when I could, but five children slowed me down some for certain." Her eyes turned bright with love and admiration. "But this time I can keep up. Just see if I let you get away from me again."

"It ain't gonna happen." He gave her hand a squeeze, then pointed and said, "Look, there's a light glowing in that building there. The sign over the door says it's a boardinghouse. Let's see if they have a room available and can rustle us up some dinner."

They walked hand in hand in the dark to the only place in town with its lights still on, and those were turned down low. The man who ran the boardinghouse was sitting behind the front desk, head rested on his folded arms. He woke up when they came in.

"We'd like a room if you've got one." Hester did the talking. Men had always responded better to her than to him, unless he needed to scare cooperation out of them, like he'd done with the man in the telegraph office. In that case she let Grizzly do the talking. But when it came to sweet-talking men, that job was turned over to Hester. "Some hot food would be welcome, too," she said.

The man handed over a key. "Your room's right at the top of the stairs. And I've got plenty of fried chicken in the icebox. I can warm it up if you want."

155

"Cold chicken is fine. We're eager to eat and eager to sleep."

He nodded and said, "Follow me into the dining room."

They were soon well fed and ready for some rest because the trail ahead was sure to be a hard one.

14

Tex had to claw his way up the canyon wall that surrounded the river. He was near done in by the time he reached the top of the gorge.

He dragged himself over the ledge, looked back and saw Stella close behind him. She looked like she was on her last legs, except it was so steep, they were both more on their bellies than on their legs. He slid sideways so she'd have room on the ledge, then looked at what they had to do next and was stunned into silence.

He sat unmoving while Stella reached the top and scooted far enough away from the cliff they'd just scaled to make sure a wrong move didn't send her sliding back down to the bottom. She peered out at what lay ahead, and her mouth gaped open.

They stared blankly at mountains upon mountains—some rolling, some rocky peaks, along with trees and grass and endless wind. It all stretched as far as the eye could see.

How far into the mountains had they been swept? He opened his mouth to talk but could not think of a single thing to say. At least he could tell which way was which from up here and knew they needed to head north. Only trouble was, north was a mighty long stretch to go. West was worse. East looked nigh to impossible, but maybe it'd get them out of these hills sooner than any other direction. Maybe they'd even cross paths with Owen. South was back across that wild river. He dismissed it completely. They'd burned off most of the day climbing, and now here they stood, stunned by the majestic beauty of what looked to be eternal peaks cast in a gold-and-red sunset.

Still, the beautiful view wouldn't get them any closer to Fort Russell.

It took some effort, but finally Tex turned to look at her. "The sunset makes your pretty blond hair a glory, Stella. Like you're wearing a halo." He gave her a rueful smile.

Her gaze was drawn away from the sunset, which he knew for a fact wasn't easy. The sky was bathed in red. Clouds streaked the red and gold with white, with violet cascading from the sliver of sun that still lingered on the horizon.

She smiled back in wonder, and he had to ask himself if she might never have heard a kind word from the lunkheads that made up the Duncan Gang. "It makes me inclined to trust you, and that's probably a foolish thing to say."

Her smile shrank away. "Are you saying you'd be a fool to trust me?"

He tried to be casual about it, but he moved a few paces away from the edge of the cliff they'd just climbed. No sense making it easy for her to kick him over the edge. "I didn't say that." Except he did, sort of. "I just meant I'm inclined to trust you. The foolish part is me trusting my instincts. I tend to insist on proof and not take someone's word for much."

He didn't think she looked impressed with his fumbling explanation.

"I do trust you, Stella. Hang on a second." He gathered some stones and fashioned an arrow pointing north. Using more stones, he shaped a T, then an S.

"You're leaving a sign?"

"Yep. Let's see if we can hike down this slope while heading north." He pointed, then set off. Maybe about the time they were clinging to the side of a cliff and starving to death, she'd forget what he said. He glanced back and saw she'd fallen in behind him.

"Have you ever heard the saying 'a journey of a thousand miles begins with a single step'?" Her voice, when he wasn't looking at her, struck him as musical.

"Nope, never heard of that one. But we don't have to walk a thousand miles." Unless they had to climb up and down so many mountains, it amounted to that many miles.

"Well, a journey of one hundred miles begins with a single step, too. However long our journey will be, we've taken the first step at least."

Tex had to admit that was indeed true.

The sun disappeared, the sunset blazing now. A cool mountain breeze in the thin air of the high altitude made walking a pleasure.

Tex's stomach began to growl. "We won't be able to hike for very long. Keep an eye out for scrub brush or a thicket of some kind where I can build a snare." He found a fork in the trail that headed eastward on the mountainside and decided to take it. "We can make a slingshot using the knife and get a bird or a rabbit with that for our supper."

They soon were walking into spindly woods that grew into more mature trees as they descended, where they came upon a spring with its cool water burbling up from the earth.

"Let's stop here to get ourselves a drink. Then we can keep going for a while longer and hope our passing flushes out a rabbit or bird. And let's pray we don't disturb a grizzly or anything more than we can handle."

Tex handed her the knife while he got a drink. When he was done, she'd found a small branch and had begun whittling away what was to be their slingshot.

"Let me work on it for a bit. Get yourself a drink."

She handed over the knife and went to the crack in the rocks with water bubbling out of it. With her thirst quenched, she took back over working on their weapon. He was close to wrestling with her, as he wanted to keep working on the slingshot. A man was supposed to do the hunting after all. Instead, he bit down on his foolish protest and gave her back the knife and stick.

"How long do you think we rode that river?" Tex asked as he looked around from where he sat. He honestly couldn't remember a time when he'd been this tired and this battered.

Stella paused as she considered the question. "We made our break about midday maybe. We rode along on the river all afternoon, and I fell asleep as soon as you hauled me out of the water." She stopped working on the slingshot and looked him in the eye. "Thank you. I'm not sure I'd've gotten out of there without you. I know I was knocked out or at least dazed more than once, and you kept my head out of the water." Looking serious, she reached across and took his hand. "Sincerely, Tex, thank you. You saved my life, and I thanked you for it by waking up before you did and tying you up." She shrugged and gave a sheepish smile. "I needed you to let me talk."

"You did need to do that. But then you untied me and

returned my knife. That went a long way toward me trusting you."

Testing the forked stick and the strip she'd cut from her skirt, she gathered a few stones and stood. "We slept the night through, it seems. Down in that gorge, I woke up once in the pitch-dark. Then I slept again until morning. We were a time having our little talk and climbing up the cliff, and now it's nightfall."

Shaking his head, Tex said, "Owen won't believe I'm dead until he's seen my body, but by this time—assuming they rounded up Clive and your pa—they'll have given up on finding me. I doubt there's any way over the cliff where our horses tossed us. I reckon they'll head for Fort Russell and come back for us—*if* they can get out of the mountains." He paused and let out a sigh. "It amounts to us being on our own with nothing but a knife and a sling. The living won't be easy. You've already proved you can light a fire. I suppose if we take too long getting out of here, Owen and Morgan will find us and lend us a hand."

"How could your friends ever begin to find you out here?" she asked.

"I don't know how, but I hope to make it as easy for them as possible. But they're smart men and loyal saddle partners. They'll come sure enough."

Tex finally had some starch back in his legs. If they didn't get to hunting soon, they'd be going without food for the night. And his belly was so empty, it thought his throat had been cut.

"Let's go," Stella said, straightening her back. He thought he heard a little groan come from her, but she stifled it instantly.

161

"If we don't flush anything out, I can take threads from my shirt and set up a snare to catch rabbit or grouse. That way we'll have something to eat for breakfast. Or maybe I could use the knife to make a spear to catch a fish with if we happen upon a stream or a lake."

"Let's also keep our eyes open for nuts and berries," she said before setting off.

Every muscle and bone in his body ached, as hers must be aching as well. Even so, Tex had his hands full keeping up with her.

He had many worries and things pressing on him to do, but despite all that, he enjoyed walking with the beautiful Stella Duncan. He hoped it turned out she wasn't an outlaw after all.

⬦———————⬦

Delaney kept busy with supper—eating it, that is, because Boone had cooked it. She kept busy collecting more firewood, although they probably had enough. Jesse too had kept busy while everyone else was running after escaped prisoners. She also tended Boone's head, which was healing nicely with little tending required really.

All that busy didn't make her forget she'd kissed Owen Riley.

He and Morgan and Marley had ridden off. Roz went along, of course. They'd gone off to find Tex, even though Marley had told them it would be all but impossible to find him in the mountains.

Yet having Owen out of sight did not put him out of Delaney's mind.

She'd never been kissed before.

She'd almost never had a man pay her any attention. And now the very first time a man had interested her, and he'd seemed interested in return, she couldn't stop thinking about it. She couldn't stop wanting him to kiss her again. She wondered what he was thinking. Besides, of course, thinking about his missing Marshal friend.

He'd gone right back to taking care of business when Morgan had shown up. She admired that about him at the same time she wished he had acted . . . different.

As she lay down, Owen and Morgan returned. She watched them move about the camp, splitting up night-watch duty. Sighing silently, Delaney wondered what love was exactly. She felt so much. She wanted to take care of him. Talk to him about his lost friend, kiss him again . . .

For a few seconds, Owen, ready to leave the camp and take up the watch for the Duncans who were coming after them, probably looked at her for too long. She was bathed in shadows in the night. Could he see her watching him? Did he want to come over where she lay near Boone and ask how she was feeling?

It was hard to know since he didn't do it. Instead, he waved at her, a little salute to what was between them. She lifted her hand in response, surprised that his vision was sharp enough to see her eyes were open, that she was staring at him.

A firm jerk of his chin said he was thinking of what had passed between them. He was remembering that he'd told her he finally had a reason to stop wandering. He'd said a lot and yet not much. He was a confusing man.

Her ma had managed for years with a wandering man. The love they'd shared had survived all of those years. But

Delaney had witnessed Ma's loneliness. Did she want to start up a life that followed the same path as her ma's?

A week ago she'd've said no. Absolutely no! Now, if that life was with Owen and she felt the abandonment her ma must've felt, but it was for a special man she loved and respected and was willing to wait for . . . her no was far from absolute.

Closing her eyes to break the connection with him, she thought maybe yes. And with that turmoil and attraction and doubt, she fell into a sleep haunted by dreams of being alone in a wild land.

———⋄———

Grizzly and Hester got an early start. They'd eaten breakfast, bought supplies from the general store, had their horses saddled and packed, and were riding out of town just before sunrise.

They found the turnoff to the west and took a good look at the tracks and bloodstains once more before setting off into the mountains.

Grizzly headed straight for a mountain that looked too steep to climb. She admitted to a few qualms.

Before they began climbing, Hester saw something that about scared her to death. "Grizzly, look at this." She pointed at the spot.

Her husband drew his horse to a stop and stared down at a freshly dug grave.

Someone had been killed. Had it been one of her kids? Was it Boone or Delaney lying cold and dead here beneath the ground? Then she studied the tracks again and knew.

"It's the same men who attacked Pa. Mind the tracks.

They're coming straight from over the crest where they lay in wait like the low-down cowards they are."

Grizzly headed up the steep slope, his horse walking as if he were climbing a set of invisible stairs. The critter must be following a scent because there was no visible trail, and yet the mountainside was passable enough as her horse followed Grizzly's without any hesitation.

Before long they reached the top of the cliff they'd just walked up, and Grizzly said, "It's just the beginning."

"Do you see all these tracks?"

Grizzly pulled his horse to a stop. "I do." Together they stared at the ground. "It looks like Morgan is headed for home, and he led a parade up that cliff." He swung down next to a patch of blood on the ground. "If they were being pursued, and they made it to the top—which it looks like they did—then they'd've found cover. It appears someone here, watching their back trail, killed one of their attackers."

Hester rode beside him as they picked up a trail with the hoofprints of different horses. Likely the riders were her children, their Marshal escorts, and the men pursuing them.

It didn't take long for the trail of the lead party to vanish, while the folks who were following them were easily tracked. Whoever the varmints were, they'd worked hard to follow the trail they were on but hadn't bothered to cover their own tracks.

"Let's keep going, Grizzly. Get to those outlaws before they catch up to our youngsters."

Grizzly fell in beside her, and on the stony, steep path, the two of them pushed as hard as they dared. And maybe a little harder.

—◇———◇—

"They went over the cliff right here." Owen couldn't read the signs as well as Morgan, although no one could, so he didn't let it bother him overly.

But he could read it well enough. Especially since Tex's hat was lying on the ground here, and his rifle was on the ground far below. On the shore of a river.

At least Tex's body wasn't down there. He must've hit water. Stella too. If they survived the fall, they had a chance.

"We can't get down there." Morgan lifted his eyes, and the frustration in them was vivid, almost frightening.

Owen might've been frightened if he didn't know his friend so well.

"Let's get back to camp. Get the two prisoners we've got down out of these mountains and get on the trail to Fort Russell. We've got no choice but to ride up there and deliver the Bridgers and the prisoners, then come back and search for Tex."

Morgan said, "I think we should start our search on the far side, because if Tex can, he'll get to the other side, climb out, and head for Fort Russell. Maybe he'll beat us there."

Their gazes met. Neither of them believed it'd be that easy. Assuming Tex had survived the fall, he had no supplies, no horse, and likely no weapons either.

And somewhere out here, the rest of the Duncan Gang still roamed. Maybe still on foot, but stealing horses was an easy enough trick if they could find some. The trail they'd followed to come to Roz's place was rugged and stony. Very hard to follow, especially on foot. Tex had brought up the rear, and he'd done his best to hide their tracks. But they had a herd of horses with them and three wounded riders—four counting Tex, which Owen tended to forget about. He'd as good as shaken off the bullet graze to his arm.

Following that trail would slow the Duncans down but not stop them.

"Do you know how to get out of these mountains?"

Morgan looked a little sheepish. "Roz does."

Owen sighed, reached down, and picked up Tex's hat. He'd loved that hat. That's when he caught himself thinking of Tex as if he were dead. Well, he wasn't.

If he'd gotten himself into a tight spot, they'd find him and drag him out of it, then find that no-good Stella Duncan. She was to blame for this since she'd been in on the escape and was the one Tex had gone after.

Owen looked forward to seeing Stella locked up along with her no-account family, a bunch of outlaws. "Let's get back," he said.

"Grizzly, there's a campsite." Hester pointed to a thick grove of trees.

They swung down and hitched their horses so they could munch on the grass. It was time for a break anyway. This was the second camp they'd come upon. The crew who'd shot at her children had been working out a trail mighty slow, not caring that they were leaving their tracks behind them.

Grizzly and Hester walked into a small clearing with the remnants of a fire left behind for all to see.

"The embers are stone-cold. I'd say this isn't from last night." Hester noticed where four men had bedded down.

They were good at setting up camp, like men who'd done it a lot.

Grizzly laughed as he wandered around the edges of the campsite.

Hester found the laughter jarring considering how serious their business was. But she knew Grizzly. Whatever had tickled him would be worth checking out.

She went over to where the group of riders had picketed their horses. Once there, she saw the tracks of horses as they were being led away on what she figured to be a saddle string. Riderless horses judging from the tracks, which showed a lighter weight than what the horses had carried before. And it looked like two men had walked away on foot from the camp.

"Look," Grizzly said, pointing. "Saddles left lying there on the ground, as well as bridles and a fair amount of supplies. Someone must've stole their horses." Which was something Delaney might do.

"Started with four of 'em in the camp, but then two walked away for some reason. And then there's these tracks." Grizzly crouched down and brushed his hand over one of the hoofprints. "This horse here led the way up the first cliff and has been in the front of the pack ever since. I'd say this is Morgan Sawyer slipping into the camp. The hoofprints right alongside tell me someone came in with Sawyer and rode out bringing up the rear. This second rider was with Morgan for certain."

Hester nodded. "Probably another Marshal. I doubt they'd let a civilian, even one as talented as Boone, ride out to capture prisoners. Sawyer is leading them all to his home. I'd say he and his fellow Marshal came back to see how close

168

their pursuers were. They stole the men's horses and took two of them captive."

"It's all easier to read now," Hester said. "Morgan and the Marshals were doing excellent work covering their trail from the first, but now with a saddle string, it's much harder to hide. And the men chasing on foot are leaving an even more noticeable trail. We can catch up to walking men a whole lot faster." She was ready to move on.

"If there are two of them," Grizzly said, "maybe we can just sweep them up and bring them along as prisoners for when we catch up to Boone and Delaney."

The trail was narrow, so Hester fell in behind Grizzly.

"You said Morgan's good in the wilderness? You met him during the war, is that right?"

"I did, but I didn't know him much then. I'd heard his name, and I figured he was the youngster I'd known when I roamed these hills long ago. Morgan started out as a drummer, just a kid, maybe fifteen years old. I told him I knew his pa. He said they'd parted on bad terms because his brother was fighting for the South, while Morgan had signed up for the North. He ended up as a sharpshooter, and I doubt he was even sixteen yet. I don't know how good he is on a trail, but I doubt his pa would let his boys grow up without teaching them such skills."

"U.S. Marshals are strong, savvy men." Hester had known a few. "Looks like they're thinning the herd. Least we can do is try and help 'em."

15

Owen had the prisoners, only two now, on horseback and moving before first light. They didn't string their horses one after the other this time, just in case they'd escaped before by working together somehow.

Sly seemed dazed still, but he'd been acting mostly dazed since the day they'd dragged him away from the Duncan Gang. So Owen was mighty skeptical.

Roz was back in the lead. She'd told Morgan she knew the way to town even though it'd been years since she'd ridden there. The woman was knowing in the ways of wild country, but was it possible she was following a route she didn't remember right?

At one point they'd found a game trail left by a herd of elk, probably years old. But Roz ignored it, and Owen decided to keep his mouth shut. That trail would've been easier to follow than the trackless land they were walking along, but then why would an elk go into town? An elk would follow a natural path that led to water and maybe more easily traversed land, but these elk weren't going anywhere Owen

170

wanted to go. So he kept quiet and continued to follow Roz toward the town, assuming there *was* a town.

The land was as wild as it could be. Picking their way up and down mountains, crossing streams, rounding boulders as big as a house. And doing it all a dozen times an hour, it seemed.

The day stretched long. As the hours dragged on, Owen was starting to lose track of time. He caught himself daydreaming, following the tail of the horse ahead of him, and snapped to attention. Not paying attention was a good way for a man to get himself killed out here.

And the Duncans had already broken free once.

And what about Tex? Was it possible he was dead and swept down the river? Maybe he was nearing Mexico by now.

Owen wouldn't believe it unless he was standing over his friend's dead body. Tex would take a lot of killing. Owen believed Tex was alive, and he wouldn't let himself think anything else. And he wouldn't let himself worry. He'd had the wishful notion that they might find him out here. If Tex could make his way back to them, he would.

But *if* was a mighty hollow word in this wilderness.

His attention shifted to Sly. The man was up to something, fidgeting in a way that didn't strike Owen as normal. "Hold up," he said to the group and raised his fist in the air. His Marshal friends stopped immediately.

Owen trotted up to Sly's side and grabbed his arm, still tied to the saddle horn . . . and cut himself.

Sly glowered at him but didn't say anything.

He twisted the man's wrist around and found his shirtsleeve, which looked normal enough. Then, upon closer inspection, he saw a glint of iron along the seam in Sly's sleeve.

171

And the rope around his wrists was frayed, sliced most of the way through.

Owen pulled his own knife and cut the sleeve off Sly's shirt. He checked his other wrist and found the same thing. A hidden razor. Owen wondered if he had more of them in his clothes. He wondered if Clive was also hiding weapons.

Morgan rode up, and their eyes met. Owen dismounted, walked over, and dragged Sly off his horse. Morgan moved past him toward Clive to see if he had any blades hidden in his clothes.

Marley was limping mighty bad, but he came up to stand watch over the scene unfolding before them with Sly and Clive.

"You Duncans have an uncanny knack for slipping out of trouble," said Owen. "Seems this is how you do it."

"We ain't never been in any real trouble." Sly jerked his arm away from Owen, but Owen hung on. "We're just ready to handle it in a pinch. We've told you, Riley, we're honest men. You may have heard gossip, but we've never been charged with a crime until that man attacked Clive there."

"Until Clive killed a soldier, you mean? What other tricks have you got up your sleeve?"

Sly didn't reply.

"Never mind," Owen said. "Morgan, Marley, search these men's clothes for razors and whatnot." Owen couldn't help but wonder what other tricks these two polecats were up to. And he wondered how much luck Tex was having with catching up to Stella Duncan.

<hr />

"This is the most delicious meal of my life, Stella, and I owe it all to you," Tex said. The grouse meat was tasty, perfectly roasted over the fire. "If we wander around out here much longer, maybe you can teach me how to use that slingshot."

He'd watched over Stella as she made the slingshot out of a forked stick, her belt, and a small stone. He was wondering if he was about to play the part of Goliath to Stella's David when he saw her lightning-quick reflexes spring into action as a grouse burst out of the bushes, and she brought the bird down with one skillful whip of the slingshot. They'd built their fire close enough to a large oak so that the smoke rose up through its broad branches and dispersed. It was good enough for daytime, but at night—Tex gave a mental shake of his head—the fire had to be put out.

"One slingshot is enough." Stella licked her fingers, then tossed the drumstick bone into the flames. The scent of roasting meat was heavenly after such a long, hard day with no food.

Tex wasn't really full, but splitting the grouse had at least taken the edge off his hunger. Stella had given him more than her share, and he'd put a stop to it. Neither one of them could risk losing their strength.

"And I hope we aren't out here long enough for me to teach you how to work it." She washed her fingers with water from the nearby spring. "Tomorrow maybe I can get a couple of grouse or a rabbit."

Tex had been watching her lick her fingers and was glad she'd turned to washing instead. Since they had no canteen for carrying water, they had to drink their fill from the spring and travel along with their eyes always open for water and food, as well as for the trail east. So far they'd just been meandering in that general direction.

"I was afraid we were going to have a hungry night," he said. "We were pushing hard to get out of these mountains, but it feels as though we've hardly made any progress."

"We'll be days getting out of the Front Range," Stella said, looking toward the east.

Tex's eyes followed the direction she studied. The peaks seemed endless. "I'd hoped we could make it out in a single day. Tomorrow we can stop earlier. Take time to hunt or fish, maybe dig up some Indian potatoes or find ripe berries."

"It gets cold at this elevation at night." Stella looked at the fire, which crackled as it sent up smoke.

"The light from a campfire shows for miles up here." Tex knew the flames would shine like a beacon, no doubt summoning trouble. "We'll have to put it out soon." He shook his head. No fire. No shelter. No blankets. "But I could rig some pine boughs and such so you don't have to sleep on the hard ground."

Stella jerked one shoulder in a shrug. "No need. I've slept rough before. Most of the last year, in fact. Our cabin, the one that burned, was at Robbers Roost. Pa rebuilt it, hoping Ma and my little sister would survive. When they died, Pa wouldn't even consider letting me stay behind when he wandered. He made me go with him, and we've never gone back. The men in my family are like a band of nomads. We're used to sleeping on the ground. We usually have blankets, but we're fine without 'em."

Tex could see she meant it. The woman wasn't afraid of sleeping on the ground in the cold. He had to admire anyone who didn't whine about harsh conditions.

"Robbers Roost, did you say?" He'd heard tell of such a place in the Rockies. He knew there was an outlaw trail that was traveled by no one honest. Finding Robbers Roost and arresting the men who lived there would clean out a good portion of the crime in this part of Colorado. He was sure there were more remote canyons than just that one, and they might all have the name Robbers Roost. But finding even one would make the West a better place. He couldn't exactly go arrest a whole hideout full of outlaws if he didn't know where he was. "Have you traveled in this part of the country before?"

Stella shook her head. "Mostly my family did our hunting to the south of Colorado City. That's close to where Ma and I lived, though we were deep into the mountains to the west. I've never been this far north." She finished the last piece of her grouse and tossed the bones into the fire. "Do you think I'll be able to hide from Pa in Cheyenne?"

Nodding, Tex said, "Yep. And it's unlikely you'll go to prison or even be arrested. You'd be tagged as part of the gang but not arrested for that alone."

"My family aren't outlaws. We're not a gang. We're a family of wanderers. I've told you that time and time again."

Tex raised his hands in surrender. "I remember, but your family's got a reputation. You can't blame me for your family's strange ways. But you don't get arrested for being nomadic." He gave her a narrow-eyed look but didn't say what he was thinking. Only a foolish woman would expect him to trust her on her word alone. She knew this, so there was no need for him to repeat it. Even so, he was starting to trust her. He didn't mention that'd make him a fool. He'd run into that saw blade before.

He met Stella's eyes. As they'd worked to get a meal prepared, he hadn't paid much mind to where they ended up sitting. They'd found a sheltered spot, where the gentle evening breeze wouldn't blow the fire around and would reflect off the stone wall, with the oak branches overhead taking in a lot of the smoke. They'd settled in between the fire and the stone and leaned back to watch the bird cook, then stayed there to eat it.

He noticed now that they were sitting shoulder to shoulder. Not touching, but almost. Far too close to almost. The fire was dying down. The sun had set. An owl sang its question *whoo* into the night.

Tex wondered if she'd still be here in the morning. She hadn't run off when they'd crawled out of the river. He'd woken up with his hands and feet bound, but she said she just wanted to force him to listen. And he had listened, so he felt confident she'd stay with him. If not, he didn't think he'd chase after her.

Stella wasn't a wanted woman after all. She'd been riding with outlaws. Or maybe just Clive was an outlaw and not the rest of her family. Of course, her family had helped Clive bust out of jail. Which, to go round into a circle of his thoughts, made them all outlaws. That was reason enough to take her prisoner. There was no real crime to accuse her of, unless she'd helped with the jailbreak or helped with the shooting that killed Stan. Tex wouldn't underestimate her.

But for now, he was exhausted and battered from his long fall, followed by the wild ride downriver. He'd like to hope she was the same. Sleep would come easy for them both, and he'd be hard-pressed not to sleep the night through. He could only hope she'd stay close. He wanted to protect her, and he admitted to himself, considering the bird she'd caught and the only food they'd eaten today, he liked having her along.

He looked around. "This has got to be the wildest, most remote place I've ever been in my life." He wanted to add *loneliest* but decided it best not to.

He rose and moved to the far side of the campfire. She'd be a little warmer between the fire and the stone. "I don't think we need to extinguish the fire. It's down to embers now. With the rocks to the west side and being tucked under the tree branches, there's no chance it'll be spotted. Another hour and it'll die completely."

Stella nodded and said, "The warmth is mighty welcome. Honestly, it wouldn't break my heart if someone did notice the fire—unless it was my family, of course."

"I wonder if Owen and Morgan caught up to your family and brought them back in. I wouldn't bet against them."

Stella stared across the fire for a long moment. In the dim light he saw something in her gaze. He couldn't say what exactly. If he had to guess, he'd say she wanted to tell him something but didn't think she should. That'd be the way with a woman in an outlaw family. Always needing to keep secrets.

She then looked down and stretched out on her side, curling one arm under her head to use as a pillow.

Tex did the same and looked at her across the glowing red coals. Then she closed her eyes, and he followed suit. He could still feel her presence nearby, though, and thought about how much more comfortable the night would be if . . .

He jerked his thoughts away from that notion and said his prayers, mindful to spend time praying for Owen and Morgan and the whole band he'd left to fend for themselves.

A lawman lived a hard, dangerous life. He'd become a

praying man years ago. When he prayed, it always steadied him and gave him a strong heart to face whatever lay ahead.

He remembered a Bible verse a parson had quoted one day when he'd wandered into a town in time to hear the church bells peal. He couldn't remember the chapter or verse, but it was something like "God writes His laws on every man's heart." He'd always remembered those words and intended to borrow a Bible from somewhere to see if he could find the exact words. The passage reminded him that even without Bible reading or preaching, a man knew what was right. Deep inside, with no excuses, he knew what the right thing was to do.

Tex lay there, alone with a woman who probably wasn't an outlaw after all, and he didn't know if it was right to trust her completely.

Did his trust stem from some deep place within him where God had written the truth? Or was his head turned because Stella was so pretty, and because she'd had a chance to hurt him and hadn't taken it? Was it because she was good company, or that she'd taken down a grouse with her slingshot and had left him impressed?

A woman alone in the wilderness might risk letting a man live if she didn't know where she was and had limited means to take care of herself. She'd fetched that grouse, however, and she'd proven herself able to start a fire. She most likely could have survived on her own.

Probably.

And if she persuaded the law in Fort Russell that she was honest, then she might be allowed to go on her way. Not all outlaws make themselves known enough to get their own poster. He was reminded then that *all* outlaws tended to practice lying to get by. She might well have a talent for it, but for good or ill, he found himself trusting her all the same.

Tex wasn't sure if God had written that very law on his heart or not. But he was sure that having certain thoughts about a woman he was alone with in the wilderness was wrong.

The owl hooted again, and a different night bird called back. Warmer inside than out, he thought of the peaks and valleys they had yet to cross, prayed a little more, and fell fast asleep.

Grizzly pushed as hard as he could, and Hester had her hands full keeping up. She sure as certain didn't tell him to slow down.

It was a miserable trail, but easy to follow. With four men walking after a herd of horses, it couldn't have been more obvious if they'd left men out here pointing in the right direction.

They were three days on the trail and reached the Sawyer cabin midday on the third.

"I'll make sure those men following Boone and Delaney aren't lingering." Grizzly set off while Hester poked around the cabin. Grizzly was back five minutes later.

He'd found trouble. Hester cocked her rifle from behind the tumbledown cabin.

"I found another fresh grave, Hester." Grizzly's voice was as solemn as the news he brought.

She followed him until soon they were standing shoulder to shoulder beside the lonely grave. It hurt Hester's heart to think of anyone buried out here in such a wild place. And yet plenty of men had been. Plenty of folks on the wagon train had been. It was the way of the Western Frontier. But what if it were one of her children?

"I think these are a woman's boot prints." Hester crouched beside one of the prints. It was one of many, but too small to be a man's.

Clive Duncan was being transported. It stood to reason that the attack on the Marshals had been an attempt to break Clive free. Others had helped him escape the stockade at Fort Russell over a year ago. That was before Hester had moved there with Grizzly. He'd been recaptured only recently.

Grizzly knelt and brushed some dirt aside to reveal a small piece of something. Rising, Hester recognized it. "A Marshal's star. This was one of their men." She let out of whoosh of air.

"Delaney told me names of several of the Marshals along," said Grizzly, "but Morgan Sawyer's was the only one I recognized."

"It looks like that spot where they attacked was the only place the Marshals' group shed any blood." Hester peered down the trail to the west.

"Let's go on before night falls." Grizzly was reading her mind. "We can't make out their tracks in the dark, but we'll push on for as long as we can. We've got jerky and our canteens—let's eat while we ride. If we don't catch up to the sidewinders tonight, we can hope to find 'em tomorrow. They've tried to kill 'em once already and only got one of five Marshals. That leaves four tough Marshals and Boone to protect our girl."

Hester whacked him gently in the belly. "Delaney will be protecting those Marshals, if I know our girl."

Grizzly smiled, but she didn't see much happiness in it. "Well, if I were those Marshals, I'd be burning mad about losing one of my men." He heaved a sigh and added, "I don't know much about this land, but it seems to me what lies to the west is as wild as land can get."

They chewed jerky as they rode toward the lowering sun. Hester found Grizzly's dire warning about the way west to be true. Were they closing the gap? The horses had no chance of picking up speed to a pace that was faster than a man could walk.

◇—————◇

"There's no end to these mountains." Tex was whining, he supposed, but it was the bitter truth nonetheless.

He was footsore, and his belly ached from hunger, even though they'd found enough food to stave off starvation. But they were burning energy like they were stoking a steam engine. They couldn't live on half a grouse a day for long.

Stella was following along not far behind him when she stopped. He noticed the lack of footsteps rather than any noise she made.

Turning back, he saw a stone go flying from her sling, then another and a third before he could turn his head to see what she was shooting at.

She'd bagged three rabbits. He kept his eyes on the critters to make sure they were dead, then turned to her and smiled. "You're a mighty skilled hunter, Miss Duncan."

She gave her head a little tilt that almost seemed like modesty. Then she gave him a look of regret. "We can carry them along until suppertime, or we can stop here and—"

A sharp shriek cut off her words as a stone rolled under

her foot, and she plunged over the steep slope and slid out of sight.

The ride was no fun for her, but Tex didn't see any cliffs. He followed her down at a more reasonable speed.

Throwing her arms back so she was lying flat, she finally stopped. By the time she gathered herself, he was there. He extended his hand, and she reached up for him and stood, looking dirty and disgruntled.

"Are you all right?"

She shrugged. "It was an improvement over the ride I took down that river."

"You sit a spell and rest. Sit on something level."

She nodded and managed to stay upright as she walked a few paces to a waist-high boulder.

He looked closer and saw a rivulet of blood trickling down the side of her head. Pulling his shirt out of his waistband, he used his knife to cut the bottom two inches of it into a long strip. He folded it into a ragged excuse for a bandage. "Stella, you're hurt. Behind your ear."

She took the bandage and pressed it to the back of her head. "Thank you. Sorry about your shirt."

He waved her off. "I'll get a new one."

"I wonder if we'll be hiking these mountains for the rest of our lives," she said glumly.

Tex chuckled as he put away the knife. It was a wonder he hadn't lost it in the river. "I reckon we'll find the eastern edge of the Rockies someday. And until we do, if you can keep bringing down the game, I'll keep on cooking it."

Stella lifted her eyes to take in the vast wilderness, and Tex couldn't help but look around, too. The desolation was staggering.

"I suppose my pa can't find me if I can't find myself."

"Too bad that amounts to a bright side." Tex turned back to her, as looking around only seemed to make things worse.

"Call me Stella from now on. I don't ever again want to hitch the name Duncan to myself."

"I'm sorry you're hurt. Get some rest while I skin the rabbits. Rabbit fur is soft—maybe I can make you a pillow with it."

Nodding, she went back to tending her cuts and scrapes.

Tex turned his attention to preparing their first meal of the day. Before he was done working, Stella had finished up her resting, found a stream down the slope a bit, and washed her head wound, drank some water, then came back to get a fire started.

"Let me take over with getting supper on, Tex. You go get yourself a drink of water."

He handed his knife to her and turned to walk toward the water as if he trusted her completely, which he probably did, wise or not.

16

"That held us up for half a day," Morgan growled as he set up camp.

"Those two are gonna get cold tonight." Owen tried not to smile, and thinking about Stan helped with that.

Clive and Sly Duncan looked mighty foolish with the cuffs cut off their shirtsleeves, the buttons cut off their shirts, the pockets from their trousers, and a few inches cut off the bottom of each pant leg. Morgan and the others had found razor-sharp edges hidden in all of those places, tucked between the folds of cloth and almost impossible to find if a person didn't know they were there.

Owen had never seen anything quite like it. They'd searched the two men's clothes thoroughly, and that included checking some extremely personal articles of clothing. Every button on their shirts and pants was made of metal, and their edges had been sharpened with a whetstone. They all had to be cut off. They were wearing longhandles, and except for the sharpened buttons on the shirtfronts, their underwear was left intact.

And now they'd used up the day and had to settle in for the night.

Getting out of these mountains had become annoying. Owen couldn't stop himself from occasionally wondering if Roz—who was supposedly leading them to the nearest town—knew where she was going. Still, she probably knew as well as anyone. The land was so rugged, peppered with cliffs and canyons, that he'd be able to find his way out of here only by trial and error. Morgan admitted he'd never gone so far into the mountains in this direction. And between the slow trail, the escape attempt, and frisking their prisoners very thoroughly, they hadn't made much progress today.

Of course, none of that could be blamed on Roz and her supposed knowledge of the mountains and the location of the town. Owen made the decision to leave Roz to her guiding for a couple more days, and if they were still wandering deep in the wilderness after that, then he'd speak up. Time to try something else.

They ate in the full dark and settled in for the night. Again, Owen had to stand watch. Tonight Boone offered to help and declared himself well enough to stay awake.

Roz and Delaney offered too, but didn't argue much when Owen turned down their offer. They were as exhausted as everyone else.

Owen sat up until Morg took over. As the two men passed in the night, in a voice lower than a whisper, Morg said, "I wonder where Tex got to."

It was all there. Unspoken, but there. The fear that their friend had met with a deadly fate. Nothing of that was said out loud, for what good would that do?

Owen rolled himself up in his blanket and was asleep before any more dark thoughts invaded his mind.

◇━•━━━━━━━•◇

Stella awoke to a vivid red sunrise. *"Red sky at night, shepherd's delight."* Her ma often quoted that old saying as she woke to another day of living without a husband's help. She said she'd gotten used to such a life, that it didn't bother her much anymore.

Reading her own meaning into it, Stella wondered if life wasn't easier with her pa and her brothers. When they came home, rough and growly after living in the wilderness, it was like having a family of ornery bears stop by.

Thinking about her family confused her. She loved her pa and her brothers, but being dragged into the wilderness life they loved didn't suit her. Despite the red sky, with the beginning of another long day that might lead to a reunion with her family, Stella was far from delighted. She dreaded what lay ahead.

But this wasn't night. This was a sunrise, the morning. The rest of the saying was "Red sky in the morning, shepherd take warning." She took that warning seriously. Still, it was a spectacular sunrise.

With a full belly for the first time in days, and whether a good omen or not, the sun rising in the east gave them the right direction to head.

She studied Tex—asleep near the now-cold ashes of the fire—and wondered how she'd ever get control of her life. Not wanting to wake him just yet, she tried to move silently as she rose. Only then did she remember her fall yesterday.

Every muscle hurt. Stifling a groan, she walked to the stream and washed the sleep out of her eyes.

They'd eaten every bite of the rabbit meat last night. Now she had no real job to do, and there was no rush to get on with the day. Gazing at the glorious sunrise, then turning to the downhill slope before them to the east, she realized that time didn't matter much. And the sooner they accepted that, the better off they'd be.

Tex's eyes flickered open.

"Good morning," she said with a smile. Her voice was a little scratchy, her eyes heavy from sleep.

He smiled back. "Are you hurting from your fall yesterday?"

She gave a little shrug. "Some new aches added to the ones the river dealt us. Nothing to slow me down."

He nodded. "Might as well get going then."

"I wonder how long it'll be before we find our way out of here."

"However long it takes, I reckon."

"That's the answer of a man who's just too stubborn to moan and whine and complain. How am I supposed to do it if you won't?"

Tex chuckled, then got to his feet to ready himself to hit the trail again. Within minutes, she was falling in behind him, not one bit interested in being left alone in the mountains in the middle of nowhere.

❖——————❖

The next morning, Owen and the others were moving before the sun was up, and for once Roz seemed to be going somewhere, acting as though she had a destination in mind. She took the lead, with Jesse right behind her. Morgan was leading Sly, who still looked the fool with his clothes trimmed short and the buttons all missing. Owen came next with Clive behind him, then Boone, then Delaney. Marley brought up the rear, leading a saddle string of Duncan horses.

A wider spot in the poor excuse for a trail brought Delaney up to Owen's side. He preferred it this way. He told himself it was because he wanted Marley and Boone right behind Clive and himself behind Sly, but he also liked her company. He remembered that kiss. He'd done his best not to let that happen again, yet he hadn't been able to stop thinking about it.

She leaned close to him, and it was almost shockingly pleasant. She spoke low enough that only he could hear her, and he was forced to lean even closer to her.

"We shouldn't have left those horses at Roz's place," Delaney said.

Owen furrowed his brow. "We brought them along."

"I don't mean the Duncan horses. I meant Roz's extra horses. She had a few horses there beyond the ones she and Jesse rode. I didn't think of it at the time, but if the Duncans came after us on foot, and they kept following, they could find Roz's place and get back on horseback. I've been fretting over it."

Owen wasn't the worrying kind usually, but this fact grabbed his attention. "You're right," he whispered.

He tried to remember just how many horses Roz had. They'd been wandering in and out of the woods on the edges of Roz's mountain meadow.

"I remember a big old gray stallion, and there were two

188

spring foals. So there at least had to be a couple of mares. Mustangs, one white and one chestnut, but there could have been more than that. Maybe there were two brown mares and they never stepped out into the clearing at the same time. I never thought to count them."

Delaney said, "Roz didn't have any more saddles. There were two in her barn, and we took both of them. Two bridles that I saw, too. We took them too. But they could rig a bridle with rope and ride bareback. I've wondered how tame her horses are."

"Only two Duncans left. We have to figure now that they're on horseback."

Delaney nodded. "Stella and I talked some. She said there were seven, but we've captured two, Morgan shot Leland, and two of her cousins abandoned them after Leland was shot. Yep, there should be a pair of Duncans still after us— assuming she's telling the truth."

Owen doubted very much that she was. Why hadn't Tex and Morgan captured the other two? After they'd grabbed the ones standing watch, they could have done it. Yet Morgan didn't think he could get to them without shooting trouble, and he wanted to avoid that.

Owen gave her an admiring look. "You have really thought this all the way through, Delaney. We'd be wise to consult you every time we make a decision from now on."

She gave him a perky grin. "Yes, you would."

Owen couldn't help but return her smile. Then he started thinking again. "Boone and Marley need to keep a closer eye on our back trail." He slapped himself on the forehead. "It's been all of five seconds and I am already underestimating you. "You can watch our back too when you're not up here with me. 'Course, it's hard to watch when we're winding through the woods."

"It's been more woodland than open space since we started moving this morning. We should be well ahead of the Duncans. Still, we'll keep watch."

He turned to look at her fully. "Don't hesitate to tell me what occurs to you, Delaney. I appreciate it."

Her worry seemed to ease some. He wondered if he should mention how pretty she was.

But before he could pay her the compliment, she said, "I'll drop back and have a word with Boone and Marley. Then I'd like to ride up here for a time. Neither Boone nor Marley are talkers, and they don't like me talking either."

Owen laughed. "I like talking with you just fine."

"Even with all this madness, I'm glad I decided to come west."

A smile bloomed on Owen's lips. "I'm glad you decided that, too."

"All my life my family's been busy moving around, following after Pa or making our lives without him. I wonder if Pa will finally stop moving. He says he plans to. It'd be nice to have a real home, put down some roots."

Owen thought of his life. He lost any urge to smile. "That's the way of the West. Too busy building a cabin, building a business to support yourself, building a life and a family. And if you're not building, you're forever moving on."

"Have you always been a rootless man, Owen?"

"I guess I've always liked moving. Never thought of myself as 'rootless,' but it's probably true of me."

"You say you're from Iowa? And you haven't seen your ma

and pa since right after the war? That's years ago, and the train's been running for most of that time."

"I grew up in eastern Iowa on a farm along the Des Moines River about twenty miles from the Mississippi, where the Des Moines flows into it." Owen shook his head. "I wonder how my ma and pa are doing. I haven't written them or received a letter, not even telegraph. No reason for it really."

Delaney leaned forward and rested her forearm on the saddle horn as if settling in for a long talk. "And you have nowhere you call home?"

Owen sighed. "You have a talent for making me see my life and wonder about it."

"I guess it suits you. I've been so lonely for my parents. I miss my brothers, too. Are you planning to live your whole life this way?"

"I've settled down for a spell at times. Lately I've been in Denver, mostly when I'm not on the trail working. But I went to war straight from my ma's house. Pa had gone ahead."

"That sounds like my pa. Only he didn't just go off to fight in the war. He was always in the Army, always traveling hither and yon."

"Not my pa. He was gone for four years. I spent three years fighting. He was back to stay, but by then I'd started wandering. I had a younger brother and sister. I stayed behind when Pa left for a while, but I was on fire to go to war. Save the Union and teach those upstart rebels a lesson they'd never forget." He shook his head in disgust. "I was a fool kid. I thought we'd whip 'em in a couple of months, which turned out to be dead wrong. Pa had already been gone for a year, but I expected to be home in time for spring planting. I thought the war would be some kind of lark."

"It's a wonder you didn't stay at the farm when you got home from the war," Delaney said.

Owen nodded. "Our farm was prosperous enough. The hunting was good, the soil rich, and the rain came faithfully. Ma had chickens and a few milk cows, and she grew a big garden."

"What happened after the war ended?"

"Pa got home before me. My little brother had headed west on a wagon train the minute he saw Pa walking up the road. I had an older sister who'd gotten married while I was fighting. She and her husband had fallen in with a wagon train to Oregon. I stayed a few weeks, but I couldn't settle down. The war had stirred me up, and I couldn't shake off the feeling of restlessness. So I moved on. Besides, it didn't seem like home anymore with the youngsters all gone."

Smiling, Delaney said, "They couldn't've been too young if one went west and the other got married."

"I reckon not." How had Owen got to talking about himself? It was his least favorite thing in the world. He lapsed into silence before he started yammering again. It was awkward because he'd been doing all the talking.

As if she realized he had no more to say, Delaney said, "Marshal, you are past due to settle down and find yourself a home."

Owen laughed quietly, glad for an excuse not to talk any more about his family. He'd left his old life behind when he headed west. He wondered if his brother and sister were out west somewhere too by now. He should find out. Go visit his ma and pa maybe. With the train he could do it. Strange that he never thought much about them. It seemed like a betrayal somehow, especially of his ma, who'd tried to talk him into staying near her.

"Tell me about your folks, Delaney," he said. "We've got nothing but time."

"I reckon I can dig some stories out of my head. But first I'll go warn Marley and Boone to keep watch, and then I'll be right back."

<hr />

Hester had gasped when the tracks they were following opened into a majestic mountain valley, acres of grass waving in the breeze. The stunning mountains rose up all around them. The rustic cabin had been built into a mountainside, and the valley was dotted with longhorns and horses.

"The two men on foot got themselves mounts now," Grizzly almost growled, which he was fully capable of doing. In fact, it had earned him his nickname. "We should've tried harder to close the distance between us and picked them off when they were on foot."

Hester knew her husband. He'd fought in the war and on the Frontier. But he wasn't a man to just go to shooting when trouble started. He was smarter than that and kinder, wiser. He wouldn't have picked them off. And if they'd ever caught those two, they'd've taken them prisoner if at all possible. But they'd had to slow down some.

"We weren't that far behind 'em." He shook his fist at their hoofprints, overtop of earlier prints he'd decided long ago belonged to Boone, Delaney, and their crew. "We should've settled things before they found mounts. But who'd'a thunk there'd be a cabin and horses and cattle out here? We've ridden so far out into the wilderness, maybe we're back to civilization now."

A few minutes later, Hester headed into the cabin and then came out with a report. "Two people, one of them a child, I'm thinking the other a woman. They must've joined up with our group and ridden out with them."

Grizzly looked around the beautiful meadow. "Who'd live clear out here? A woman and child alone? Makes no sense."

Hester said, "There's nothing inside that isn't made from the land right under our feet. Not a can of peaches, no salt, no sugar, and no flour. The clothing is all men's sizes but cut down to be smaller. That's why I think it's a woman and child. There's some buckskin being used, so maybe that's what they're both wearing. Judging by what I saw inside the cabin, they've been living alone out here for a long while, and there's no town nearby."

Hester had searched the cabin, Grizzly the barn.

"There's a root cellar," Hester said. "Honey in there and jars that look like she knows how to preserve the bounty of her garden."

Grizzly said solemnly, "I found three graves."

That got Hester's attention. "Old ones?"

He nodded, and her shoulders relaxed. "There were rough crosses marking them. Two with the last name Sutcliff. The woman, June, died fifteen years ago, and the man, Cap, six years ago. Her parents, I'd say. And another man with a different last name, a Herman Beck, who died four years ago."

"If she had a child," said Hester, "the third grave might be her husband. I'm only guessing, but it strikes me as such. You knew Morgan's pa, Grizzly. Does Cap Sutcliff sound like someone you knew once?"

Grizzly shook his head. "The American Frontier's a vast place, and there aren't that many people really. And a man who had a daughter who'd been living out here, possibly for years, she'd've been a child back when folks were settling the land around here. I'd've remembered a child. A man who chose this place was someone who knew how to survive in the wild. How else could his daughter learn to do so, too?"

"That sounds about right," Hester said.

"We need to push on." Grizzly swung up on his horse. "Now that the outlaws are on horseback, they'll be moving faster. That puts our children in even more danger."

When would it ever end? she wondered.

They rode over to where it looked as though a landslide had cleared the side of the mountain some years ago, and it scraped every tree clean off the slope.

There was still no trail except the tracks left behind by others.

Tex came up to a cliff and sat down, dangling his legs over the edge. He was exhausted, and he was stranded. Again. Honestly, Stella was holding up better than he was.

Stella dropped down beside him and sighed so deeply it about created a breeze.

Looked like she wasn't holding up that much better after all.

"We'll have to go back and find another way forward." She swung her legs like she was out for a hike and taking a break by sitting on a fence rail.

Tex turned to face her. She noticed and looked at him with a wry smile. "I never thought I'd be walking my way out of the Rockies. We should have been able to walk east and reach the edge of the mountains and just move right on down the trail."

"It's not a busy trail from Denver to Fort Collins to Cheyenne, but it gets some use. I had hopes that we'd be able to hop onto a farm wagon and just roll on north."

She chuckled. "You strike me as a realist, Tex. Now you're just talking like a dreamer."

He smiled as he shook his head. This wasn't the first dead end they'd reached. They'd climbed down a few slopes that were just barely manageable. And they'd gone around a few. Right now he didn't see any way forward. How far would they have to go to get around this massive canyon?

"Do you like being a Marshal?"

"I've liked it well enough. This mess we're in now sure takes some of the shine off it."

"With a name like Tex, why aren't you a Marshal in Texas?"

"I had a chance with the U.S. Marshals Service at Fort Smith, Arkansas, but that's the last town before Indian Territory."

Her brow furrowed. "So you'd be sent in there to arrest Indians?"

"You'd think it was like that, but it wasn't Indians I'd've been after. All manner of outlaws run for Indian Territory to hide out. No local lawmen could go into the territory; they had no jurisdiction there. As more and more outlaws ran across the border into Indian Territory, they decided to make the Marshals into a kind of federal police force. Part of the job was to go in there and arrest them, bring them back for trial. I'd been told that was a harsh business, and it held no appeal to me. Not that things are simple here in Colorado, but I was interested in seeing the Rockies."

"Do you miss Texas?"

"Like an ache in my chest. Yep, best state in the union."

Stella smirked at that and didn't reply.

"I need to decide if I'm going to stay a Marshal. I've been yearning for Texas here lately. My folks are still alive, and I've been down to see them twice since I left home."

"You haven't seen your parents but twice in nearly eight years?"

"Nope, but it's the way of things when a man grows up. A woman too, I reckon."

"If you can escape them."

Tex reached over and patted her on the shoulder. Then his eyes met hers for a moment too long, and he pulled his hand back and jerked his head around so he was looking at the scenery again.

He hadn't thought an encouraging little pat to be much of anything, until he'd touched her and noticed . . . well, he'd noticed he hadn't oughta do it.

"We've been walking around in these mountains for five days, Tex. Are we ever going to get out of here?"

"I believe we're generally heading east." He was a man who knew the land, and when the sun or the shadows were visible, he could be sure of where he was going. And he would swear they'd been moving east for five days now, and yet they never seemed to reach the end of these blasted mountains.

"How come we haven't found a trail yet?" Stella asked. "It's not just passing through the mountains; it's passing through them without so much as a trail."

"A few times we came upon a game trail, but none that

led in the right direction. I reckon this is about the wildest land any man ever saw. You'd think by now we'd've stumbled on some indication that someone had been in this country before."

Finding food was an ongoing worry. They'd found some berry bushes and a few nuts that were ripe enough to eat. They were high up in rugged country. Not above the tree line, but it wasn't exactly grassy pasture either, certainly nothing welcoming to a deer herd.

"I doubt I could bring down a deer with this." Stella tapped the slingshot she'd made. She was full of ideas and self-sufficient. He'd done all right ending up stranded in the wilderness with her.

"Nope, and I doubt I could sneak up on one and take it down with my knife." Tex heaved himself to his feet. "But there's water down there." He pointed at the depths of the canyon, where a stream flowed through. Could it be the same stream that'd swept them away? He couldn't say. "Let's try and wind our way down there to the water. Maybe I could get us a fish or two while we're at it. That'd make a good meal."

"Or we could keep moving east for a time before we try scaling another cliff." Stella looked doubtful as to what they should do next.

"I suppose we don't have to have meat, right?"

She nodded but didn't answer.

"I'll go looking for more berries." Tex surveyed the stark, stony land. "And I can bake Indian potatoes in our fire if we find any. Looks like it'll be a while longer before we get to Fort Russell."

"Until then we'll have to keep on spearing fish and bringing down birds and rabbits." Stella gripped her slingshot. "I don't know how we got so turned around out here, Tex, but the truth is we're lost."

He was not about to admit that. "We may not know where we are exactly, but that's been mostly true since we turned off the trail when your low-down family shot at us. I don't count it as 'lost.' We know where we're going generally. We're walking on land that's maybe never had a man's foot upon it, not since creation, but we know where we're going."

"North and east." Stella snorted, and it almost got a smile out of Tex. Things were a bit too grim for a real big toothy grin, but her snort did lift his spirits a little.

"Yep, north and east, so let's get moving. And since north is straight off a cliff, and east is up, we'll have to go south and west for now."

That got another snort out of her, and he did smile this time. He figured being grouchy didn't make the trip go any faster.

He reached his hand down and helped her to her feet.

"We have to start hunting more intentionally. We need more food, and we need it soon. For now, we're going to have to go west and a little south, then up a steep slope before we turn east and north. If we do decide we need to get down to that water, this isn't the route to take. I'll leave another marker for Owen, Morgan, and Marley, then we'll go."

Tex remembered the slope Morgan had ridden up, which was nothing resembling a trail. And yet the horses had just gone on up, easy as you please. He wondered if he had his horse, if the critter could find a trail where he couldn't and get them out of here. Might as well wish for the moon.

"We have to walk up and around whatever way is easiest to walk and do it now. We need food."

Tex pictured his friends, who were all the way to Fort Russell by now. They were probably enjoying a meal of fried chicken and gravy, mashed potatoes, and apple pie.

17

Owen ate stew for the tenth meal in a row, if he was counting right, and he might not be.

He'd triple-checked the Duncans' tied wrists and legs, then checked them again.

Delaney and Boone had gone to sleep on the far side of the fire. Roz and Jesse were over there too, with Delaney near her brother, who needed to be beside her for the sake of propriety. Being proper in the wilds of the Rocky Mountains struck Owen as a strange business.

They'd separated the Duncans and let Marley sleep for as long as possible. He was going to be all right, but even after all these days, his leg was still causing him pain, and pain wore on a man. Marley needed sleep.

Owen had second watch. He passed Morgan, they exchanged a few quiet words, then he'd gone on out while Morgan had rolled up in his blanket to spend another night on the hard, cold ground.

Owen didn't sit down. He didn't trust himself to stay awake. Instead, he wandered, checked in all directions from the camp, also checking the horses, remembering how they'd taken the horses from the Duncans. He didn't want anyone to return the favor.

Everything seemed to be peaceful for the night when he heard a twig snap in a way that only meant one thing. Someone was out there. And they'd gotten too close.

He fired once, straight up in the air, then vanished into the forest. Morgan would be awake and moving. Marley too, though he was considerably slowed down these days.

He hoped Delaney took to cover and stayed there. Boone would help. What about Roz and little Jesse? They were all a tough bunch. And what about Clive and Sly? To them, that shot would mean rescue was at hand. They'd be doing whatever they could to help themselves, which made them even more dangerous.

Before the gunshot was fully fired, he'd gone to ground, crawling on his belly as silent as a slithering snake, or he sure tried to be. His gunshot would warn the scum as surely as it had his fellow travelers. They knew they were being hunted even as they were doing the hunting.

He slipped along toward where he'd heard the twig snap, knowing they'd be moving. He assumed there'd be two of them, but assumptions could get a man killed.

Owen finally reached the spot where he'd heard someone but found no one there. Not a surprise. Then he set out to hunt down the two vermin in the darkest hour of the night, with no idea where either of them was.

◇───────────◇

Delaney rushed for the Duncans, Clive and Sly, and had them gagged as quick as a striking rattler. It sped her up that

Boone had Clive done before she could take care of him. Boone got to him in time to cut off a holler for help.

They knew what that single gunshot meant as well as anyone.

Boone stashed Sly behind a massive oak tree that had sheltered them as they slept. Delaney threw her back into it and dragged Clive behind another tree. No sense letting the two of them near each other. Gagged and tied up or not, they couldn't be trusted for a second.

Soon Roz was next to her and helping out. Clive, wide awake, struggled against their grip. Delaney lashed him tight to a smaller tree behind the big oak.

Jesse went to his mother's side and handed Roz's rifle to her.

Boone came rushing back. "Split up and lie low." Boone had to know he was wasting his breath. If the need for silence wasn't so acute, Delaney would've told him so. Instead, with a quick scan that told her Owen, Morgan, and Marley were all gone, she strode behind a copse of aspen and set out to find and capture two men, single-handedly if she had to.

And while she was at it, she had to remember that there were a whole lot of her friends slipping around in the woods too, including her brother. In the pitch-dark, she wasn't going to be able to start shooting unless she was absolutely sure who she was aiming at.

<hr />

Grizzly hadn't let up, and they'd ridden long into the night.

In the dark of the night, Hester saw Grizzly slow up, then stop. It'd felt as if they were keeping up with the trail as well as everyone else. The Duncans, most likely, and her children's traveling party were following what was close to being a trail. Whoever was leading this parade had to know where they were going because all day they'd wound around, avoiding canyons and rivers, cliffs that plunged deep, and rock walls that went straight up.

Hester guessed it was someone from the high mountain meadow who'd joined up with them. This was more her territory than anyone's. She felt sure it was a woman, regardless of the manly clothes. Just because she never went to town didn't mean she didn't know where one was.

Neither Grizzly nor Hester knew which way to go.

Then a rifle fired into the night.

Way too close.

Grizzly took off on foot, Hester right behind him. It was too close to the gunfire to ride.

Grizzly didn't bother giving her orders. He knew better. She glanced at him, and a split second later, he vanished. She ran for the noise, thinking there were few things more stupid than running toward gunfire.

But her children were out there. No power on earth could stop her.

———◇—————————◇———

Owen couldn't think of much that was stupider than crawling straight for a rustling noise in thick brush in the pitch-black night.

Oh, wait, he could think of something. Knowing there were sneaking, wily outlaws in the dark around your camp and *not* moving out, tracking them down.

So he eased forward, trying his best to use every trick he'd ever learned about staying quiet. He tried his best to open his senses wide—listening, smelling, touching, and even though it seemed futile, seeing.

He didn't know what was up there. He was certain it was human, but he couldn't shake off the fear that he was rushing straight into the arms of a grizzly. The image of him crawling straight into the arms of a hungry bear kept slapping at him.

And yet he didn't slow down.

Then he heard it again. It was human, no doubt about it. But one of them? Two? Six? And were they the type to just start shooting? He thought of how Clive had ended up shot when the gang tried to break him free. They hadn't proved to be the careful type.

He froze when another noise coming from a different direction caught his attention. Would he have to fight two men at once? And where out here in this black pit of night was Morgan?

Waiting so as not to earn anyone's attention, and afraid he already had, he listened hard in two directions. He thought he heard yet another sound, this one coming from behind him.

Owen inched forward just as a hand clamped over his mouth.

◇━━━━━━━━◇

Morgan dove into the woods, moving without thinking. He did just exactly as he needed to do without considering where to go and how quiet he had to be. All that came with instinct as natural as drawing his next breath.

They were being followed, they knew that. And no doubt the Duncans had gained on them, mainly thanks to Sly, Clive, and Stella's escape attempts, although it wasn't really an *attempt* in Stella's case. The woman had indeed escaped. He hoped Tex had her corralled somewhere.

Even as these thoughts rushed through his head, he never stopped moving. Staying low, hoping these sidewinders didn't just open fire, he listened and eased ahead as silent as the grave. This was his gift, his best skill, moving silently in the wild.

He'd once snuck up on a nervous, well-armed woman with two guard dogs. No one he wanted to arrest, but someone he didn't mind impressing. Then, when her alert gaze turned away from him, he'd just stood up. He had his Marshal's badge raised where she could see it before she could open fire.

She was a tough, savvy woman, and she'd been impressed.

He snuck in a moment of pride, then went back to paying strict attention to the hunt.

He heard someone ahead. He was almost certain it was one of the Duncans. Owen had been off to the east side of their camp. He'd left the rest sleeping. Owen's shot would have them moving by now, but he should be ahead of them. That made anyone out here a Duncan.

Morgan would never open fire, not with folks, good and bad, spread all over these woods. But he might just whack someone over the head and then be sorry later if he'd given the wrong person a headache.

Inching forward, he realized the person he hunted was heading toward the camp. The varmint would crawl right past him in another few seconds.

He had eyes as sharp as a razor. Despite the dark night, with thick clouds covering the moon and stars, trees overhead, he didn't close his eyes as some folks did when they

206

couldn't see anyway. Rather, he kept them riveted on whoever was coming, hoping for one tiny clue that'd tell him who it was.

Soon the person was even with him, and he smelled the varmint and was sure. Without a sound, Morgan brought his gun butt down with a wicked chop that landed square on his head. He'd judged the man's position just right. The man slumped to the ground, the only sound being the dull thud of his body hitting the dirt. He lay facedown and didn't move.

Morgan turned the man over and searched him. He had a heavy beard, so no one from their group. Morgan found a gun, a knife in the coyote's boot, another in a sheath under his shirt. Stripping him of all the weapons, he used the man's belt to bind his hands behind his back.

Ready for trouble as always, he yanked a length of rope from his waist. He carried six with him, one to tie up each Duncan's hands and feet, and a spare for a surprise outlaw. He tied the man's feet together, used his kerchief to gag him, then moved on.

Three more to go. If he had to capture all three himself, he would.

＊＊＊＊＊＊

Delaney moved fast while fighting to keep silent. She'd been pulled into a game of hide-and-seek, except in this case the stakes were life-and-death.

She'd played the game in the woods with Boone most of her life, and she'd won as often as not. Always pretending they were being chased by rebels or outlaws or sometimes a mountain lion. Whatever struck their fancy.

It would rile Boone when she'd snuck up on him and yank his hair before he knew she was anywhere nearby.

Suddenly, listening for any slight sound that didn't fit, she heard someone. She was as good as blind and so depended on hearing alone. Of course, the sound could be coming from someone in her own group. She eased closer to where she'd heard the rustling. Then the clouds parted overhead, and for just a few seconds, she saw . . .

"Ma?" The word came out as a breath, not audible a foot away.

And her ma was closer than that. She turned her head and smiled. Then she put her finger to her lips and pointed, and the moon went dark again.

Delaney didn't think she'd've squealed and hugged her ma under the circumstances, but she was so thrilled to see her, it'd been tempting.

Delaney couldn't hear a single noise. Even the natural sounds of the woods at night were gone. Not a chirping bug. Not an owl. Not even the near silence of a hopping rabbit. That silence in the woods was even stronger proof that someone was out there. But Delaney had been distracted by seeing Ma, and Ma had been paying attention to something else.

Delaney, silent as a ghost, slipped around to line up beside her ma, who had her gun out. Delaney did the same.

They inched forward slowly, listening. Ma apparently had heard something, and there was no one in the world Delaney trusted more. A few she trusted as much, but none more. Thinking of the few, she knew if Ma was here, that meant Pa was, too. No, he hadn't brought the entire cavalry company from his fort, but still, her heart lifted, for she felt as if the cavalry *had* arrived.

Then finally there was the least little shift in the brush right in front of them, and Delaney knew someone was there.

But who was it? Did Ma know it wasn't Pa? Did she know it wasn't Boone or Owen or anyone else she hadn't oughta be attacking?

There wasn't time to tell her that now.

❖━━━━━━❖

Owen felt himself being frisked, and then when whoever had him found the Marshal's star, the search abruptly stopped. Very quietly he heard, "Ralph Bridger. I'm here to find my kids."

Then the weight was gone, his mouth was free, and Owen was glad to have the help. He was also humbled that he'd been so neatly caught.

He reached for the man's hand, trusting this stranger when he probably hadn't oughta. Owen tugged Pa Bridger forward and pointed in the direction of the man he'd heard, the man he'd been hunting.

Whoever it was, it was a bad guy. He hoped.

He thought of Morgan, who'd talked of how skilled Delaney was. He wondered if he'd have time to learn whatever Pa Bridger might share with him. Delaney had to have learned those skills from somewhere.

Then Owen saw whoever it was had edged right past him, and he struck. Hard, sudden, ruthless, the gun butt came down on the man's head.

The man howled, alerting the whole woods to trouble.

Owen quick slapped his hand over the man's mouth and bashed him in the head again, finally putting him into a deep sleep.

But it was too late.

18

Delaney braced herself to take a reckless dive at whoever was ahead. She was grimly determined to do it before Ma.

Then a few paces away, a man howled like a wolf on the hunt, and then the howler fell silent seconds later.

"We got 'em." Morgan spoke out loud from right in front of them. "Two men, both knocked cold."

"Is everyone all right?" Ma shoved herself off the ground with a groan. Delaney would tease her ma about getting old if she hadn't groaned herself when she stood.

"Everyone except our prisoners." That was Owen speaking only a few feet away. "They ain't so good."

Morgan said, "I'm going to check the camp. Marley, come along. Owen, bring the prisoners."

It was all happening in darkness.

"I've got one of them." That was Pa, and she wanted to jump and scream and maybe cry. She was so happy to see her parents. Not that she could see much.

Ma dragged Delaney into her arms. "Are you all right?"

"Boone was shot and knocked cold. His head was grazed, but he's up and moving. He'll be fine."

"Don't be saying I'm fine, baby sister." Boone moved Delaney firmly aside, then hugged Ma. "How am I supposed to get any tender loving care from Ma if I don't tell her how grievously wounded I am?"

She heard bodies being dragged along. She hadn't seen Pa yet, but she saw Owen go past with someone tied up behind him.

Ma slung an arm around Boone on one side and Delaney on the other. Then Pa was there hugging Boone, then hugging her.

"I'm so glad to see both of you. How'd you find us?"

Pa had her between him and Ma, both of them with an arm around her. She felt so safe, she felt the burn of tears in her eyes. And she didn't let a single one fall.

Ma said, "Lots of stories to tell. Let's make sure these men are tied up tight before we start yarning."

They walked back to the camp together. Roz had the fire going. Jesse was busy stoking it. Boone had a coffeepot filled with water and heating up.

Ma got the skillet heating up as well while Delaney found what she needed for making biscuits.

"Morgan Sawyer, I'm Colonel Bridger. We met in the war."

The two men clasped hands and shook warmly.

Marley came up next. "Name's Marley Tweedt. I served in the war, spent some time at Vicksburg and ended up marching to the sea with General Sherman. I heard tell of you, Colonel. We've been on short rations for a while. Hope there's enough coffee left for me to have myself a cup."

"We've got plenty, especially since we're cutting this trek through the mountains short. We're getting out of here." Pa looked around. "If anyone knows how."

The men all laughed. Delaney didn't think it was that funny. She got biscuits on to bake using Ma's pans and flour while Ma got some bacon frying.

"Roz," Morgan said, "how far would you say it is to town? We could maybe go back the way we came now without those fool Duncans on our backtrail."

"We'll meet up with a good-sized trail tomorrow. That'll take us almost straight to the road that leads north to Fort Collins."

Morgan's brow furrowed. "Why didn't you tell us we were so close?"

Roz shrugged. "Hard to judge how long it'd take with us having to stop and chase prisoners, or tend the wounded, or search for missing Marshals all the time. But I reckon we can put in a good solid day tomorrow and make the trail to Fort Collins. It'll be late, but we should be in Fort Collins tomorrow night."

Owen came over from where he'd been tending the prisoners. "I started this journey with one prisoner and am ending it with four." Owen reached over and shook hands with Pa. "I appreciate the help."

"It came at a high price. You lost a man. And I can see Marley's leg is hurt, and Boone got shot in the head." Pa rubbed his hand over his eyes, then straightened and looked at Owen.

"Yep, a youngster. Stan. A Deputy Marshal who worked with Tex." Owen stopped talking.

"And another Marshal was with us, Tex Mitchel. Tex went after Stella Duncan when the three prisoners we took earlier escaped."

"They had a woman outlaw?"

"We're not outlaws!" Sly Duncan hollered.

Owen had all the Duncans bound and separated by plenty of space.

"Stella's gone?" Another shout, this voice slurred, probably from the whack on the head. "Where is she? Is she alive? What happened to her?"

Owen ignored the questions. "That old coot had his daughter running in the wild with him. All three of them busted loose and went their separate ways. Marley joined Tex in going after Stella, and he saw them disappear over a cliff. Long fall into the river. No way to get down there. We're going to have to go to Fort Russell, drop off these Duncans, and if Tex hasn't turned up, we'll ride back here and search for him."

"Wild land to get lost in." Pa had the right of it. Delaney saw the first black of the night give way to the darkest gray of impending sunrise.

Ma said, "Coffee's ready and bacon. Delaney, check the biscuits."

They were all eating in a few minutes. Begrudgingly, the men even gave the Duncans a biscuit each.

"I'll admit that when I said there was plenty for everyone, I wasn't counting these outlaws," Pa commented, looking around.

"You can't starve us. And I told you—we ain't outlaws." Sly Duncan was talkative for a man tied up and under arrest.

"You can defend yourself in court," Owen said.

Delaney saw him scowling as he gathered food for the Duncans. He walked around and gave each Duncan a drink of water. Then, with Morgan beside him, he untied their hands to let them eat a few bites.

Delaney heard some muttering between Owen and one of the outlaws. She heard the name Stella but nothing else. She was surprised when Owen and Morgan came back to the campfire with an older man, not Sly, who'd been their prisoner for days.

"What are you doing, Gord?" Sly asked suspiciously.

The man, whom she could now see strongly resembled Sly, said, "I'm asking about Stella. Shut up, Brother. I care what happened to her even if you don't."

Sly grumbled but quit his hollering.

19

"I'm Gordon Duncan." The man had a deep red welt on his forehead. "Can I sit, please?"

His knees wobbled, and Owen caught the back of his shirt as Gordon sank to the ground. Owen had left his hands and feet untied, but Morg stood behind him, watching him close.

"What happened to my Stella?"

"Is she your daughter?" Owen asked.

"No, she's Sly's. But she's mine in all the important ways. Sly never wanted nuthin' but boy children, so she found a place in my heart." Gordon's head and shoulders bowed as if the weight of the world had settled on him.

Owen decided to make the story short. "All three of your kin made a break for it. They chose three different directions and ran at the same time."

"You hadn't found the razors in their clothes, and they used them to escape. Is that right?"

"Yep." Owen held up his hand so Gordon could see the wound. "I found one when I cut myself on it."

Owen accepted a cup of steaming-hot coffee from Delaney, gave her a grateful nod. He felt about half asleep even with his eyes open. He sipped the coffee gratefully, then returned to his story.

"I went after Clive, Morgan went after Sly, and Tex and Marley went after Stella. Your Stella is tougher than her brother and pa, I'd say. We corralled those two and brought them back fast, but Tex and Stella didn't come back with Marley. He saw both Tex and Stella go flying off their horses over a cliff after the critters skidded to a stop." Owen shook his head. "It was a long way down to a rushing river. Marley saw no sign of them and no way to make it down to the river. He came back for us, brought the horses and all the gear, including Tex's rifle. We went to see what was what, but after a longer search, we found no way down to the river either. And there was no sign of any bodies."

"My Stella . . ." Gordon sounded anguished. Then his head came up, and hope flashed in his eyes in the firelight. "What if she survived? She's a tough woman. If anyone could ride that river and get herself out, it's Stella."

"Tex too," Owen said. "But we had no way to go after them short of mountain climbing, and we couldn't hang on to our prisoners if we tried that." He might have attempted it on his own if he'd thought he could get down there. The decision not to had nearly torn him in two. "We aim to look for them both after we bring the lot of you to Fort Russell, where we'll turn all of you over to the law."

Gordon reached out an unsteady hand and touched Owen's wrist. Owen tensed up, but the look of fear and grief in the man's eyes made him allow the contact.

"Listen to me, please. I know you don't believe us, but we truly aren't outlaws. We're . . . well, we think of ourselves as a tribe. We've always loved the wilderness life. We roam, do some work from time to time to earn cash money, mostly just hunt. We can live off the land forever. When Sly got married, his wife refused to come with us. She didn't know what she was getting into when she married my big brother.

"Sly built her a cabin and left her to live in it, though we visited. I envied him that life, so I rustled up a wife and married her and built her a cabin too, right next to Sly's. We'd stay there when we weren't roaming. As our young-sters grew up, they'd come with us. We've had a few ride off and find their own life, and I suppose the rest will, too. My youngest two left when Leland, Sly's son, opened fire on you Marshals. Leland was a headlong fool. We didn't set out to shoot anyone."

Gordon's brow furrowed. It was then Owen realized the dawn was pushing back the night. It wasn't just the firelight now that let him see Gordon clearly.

"I've heard the name Duncan," Morgan said. "You're known men. I've seen wanted posters for bank robbery."

Gordon shook his head fiercely, glancing at Morgen. "No. I've heard the talk. The wanted poster you've seen is for my youngest brother."

"There were three of you?" Owen had to admit he couldn't remember a first name, and there was no picture.

"Yep, Leonard. We call him Lenny. I think his wanted poster calls him 'Wildcat Duncan.' Never seen the poster, but I've heard tell."

Owen nodded. "Wildcat Duncan, that's it."

"And Wildcat had sons, so there's a group of them. That's the Duncan Gang. Our cabins were built in a high-up camp alongside the Outlaw Trail west of Denver. The trail is secret and has a lot of twists and side trails. Few men know how to get up there. We left our wives there with the youngsters, and those men, outlaws or not, treated them right."

"You may be able to talk your way out of a bank-robbery charge, Gordon, but it was you and your kin, the ones right here, who busted Clive out of the stockade at the fort. That's a crime, and you're wanted for it."

"That was Leland."

Owen's jaw tightened. Gordon had an answer for everything.

Gordon said, "Leland was the sneakiest of us and a hothead to boot. That's why he opened fire on you."

Owen didn't respond beyond saying, "A Deputy Marshal was killed. It's mighty convenient for you to pin that murder and the jailbreak on the one among you who's already dead."

Gordon shook his head. "I'm real sorry that anyone died. We think of ourselves as masters in the woods. We slip around silent as ghosts, wily as cougars. Leland especially could sneak in and out of a fort and open a locked cell and sneak out again." Gordon swallowed hard. "We take pride in that, how sneaky we are, as if that isn't shameful. We should have stayed to home. Cared for our wives and children."

Gordon looked over his shoulder at his family, tied up, all of them headed for jail. He turned back to Owen. "But what Clive did was self-defense. Finlay MacNeil was a soldier, but he was a bully and a man known to be cruel to women. Our Clive stopped him when he dragged a woman off the streets of Cheyenne. Finlay pulled a gun. Clive was faster. Clive is no killer. It was a fair fight. Except there stood Finlay's cousin Calan MacNeil, who swore with his hand on the Bible that Clive had attacked, intent on stealing the money he'd lost at poker. The woman ran off and didn't come forward to speak up for Clive. They found Clive guilty."

A strange mutter came from Colonel Bridger. "Um, Owen, I have to admit, I've heard this story. It all happened after the shooting, long after Clive escaped. Calan MacNeil, a private at Fort Russell, was in a fury when Clive escaped, ranting about his cousin being murdered. He said in front of witnesses—and I've talked directly to the men who heard it—that he'd set out wanting to avenge his cousin's death. That it was a stain on the family name to be beaten to the draw. Others heard of the woman, and someone even found her and talked to her. I heard this from men I trust. Clive was long gone, but I've talked with the judge who oversaw the trial and sentencing. He said the rumors had gotten back to him, too. When you brought Clive back, I was going to insist on a new trial, and the judge had agreed to it."

Owen couldn't quite take it all in. Clive might've been wrongly convicted. The only true criminal, Leland, a killer and the man who'd assisted in the jailbreak, was dead now. Deputy Marshal Stan Ross, dead for nothing. Tex and Stella, missing and possibly dead for nothing.

Even Clive, who'd probably been watching out the stockade window as they built a gallows for him . . . hard to blame the man for escaping when he got the chance to do it.

Anger bubbled and brewed in Owen's gut as he considered what to do now. He locked eyes with Morgan, then Marley, who was lucky he still had both his legs.

Morgan gave his head a firm nod. "We'll iron it all out when we get to Fort Russell."

Owen sighed and shoved himself to his feet.

"I think it's close enough to daylight we should get moving." Roz started packing up her bedroll.

Owen, in the mood to give orders, snapped, "Let's get on the trail."

That was when Owen noticed Jesse sitting on the ground between Boone and the colonel. He seemed to be fascinated by them. He was sure seeing all the broad swath of humanity on this trip.

They got to work breaking camp and were on their way within the hour.

They'd be in Fort Collins by bedtime. One more long day's ride from here and they'd all be safe and sound.

As they began winding their way out of the treacherous mountains, Owen had to wonder if Tex and Stella had survived their terrible fall off a cliff into rushing water. And if they had survived, likely without horses or guns, without food or the tools to get food . . . if they survived all that, then where in heaven's name were they?

20

"Where in heaven's name are we?" Stella reached the top of a long, steep climb.

They were determined to head east, and they did it whenever they could.

Now here they stood at the top of a mountain, the next in what seemed to be an endless line, and stared out over wild hills that rose and fell and rose again, as if the whole world were one big mountain.

The day had been overcast beginning around noon, and the land treeless for the most part. The sun was completely hidden. They'd walked in and out of fog, some of it quite dense, especially at the mountaintops where they had to nearly crawl.

Now they'd reached the peak of another one, and Tex saw the sun flash a bit of red as it set below the clouds. They were walking straight toward it.

"We've been heading west." A boulder nearby was irresistible, and Stella collapsed on it, dejected, her shoulders slumped. "Will you think less of me if I break down and cry like a baby?"

Tex joined her on the boulder. "Yes. I would."

Stella gave a half smile and said, "That's fine. I'll think less of myself, too."

They were breathing hard. Tex turned to look behind them. "If we just climbed this mountain thinking we were heading east—"

"I know we were heading east around noon."

"I'm sure of it, too. But somehow we got turned around once the sky became overcast and the fog rolled in. To go east, do we have to walk back down the mountain we just walked up? Because I'll be dad-blasted if I'll do it, and yet what else can we do?"

"Right now, if a gang of outlaws came charging out of the distance trying to kill us, I think I'd be happy to see them."

"Even if they started shooting?"

Stella didn't answer.

Tex wasn't completely sure himself. He wasn't inclined to nag her to start moving, especially since he hardly had the strength to start moving himself. "Let's rest here a few minutes."

"We need to get down off this mountain peak before the sun sets." She turned and looked him in the eye. "Which way should we go, Tex? East isn't working out very well for us. Should we go west instead? Maybe we'll cross a trail somewhere?"

"I hate to mention it, but—"

"Then don't," Stella said, cutting him off.

He quit talking, and the silence that followed lasted long enough he thought he noticed the sun dipping lower. Which was pretty slow, so it'd been a while.

"Okay, just say it," Stella said, "whatever it is."

Tex knew she had to be worn clean out. Worse, she was hungry and thirsty. There'd been no sign of water since early that morning and for certain no game.

"We need food. We need water. We need to find a place to sleep, and we need to do all of that before the sun goes down. We've sat here long enough, and because I'm feeling particularly stupid right now"—he pointed down the slope in a direction the sun said was north, though he'd begun to think the sun was playing games with them—"let's go that way."

Stella should have demanded to know why. She should have told him that that was no direction they wanted to go. But that direction was the easiest for them to go at this point. A slope less sheer than what they'd been tangling with. And it wasn't the direction they'd just come. He was pretty sure it was north.

In truth, it led toward woods, which might mean water and trees for shelter and possibly a few rabbits to cook up. But it sure didn't lead them anywhere they wanted to go.

"I've lived in Colorado all my life," Stella said. "Deep in the mountains most of the time. I've hunted and fished when Pa was gone, and now I wander over hill and dale with him, living off the land. I'm tough and know the ways of living wild." She sighed so deep that her shoulders rose and fell, then turned to face Tex. "And I want to go that way, too."

"At least it's downhill." Tex tried to sound perky.

"We're standing on top of the whole stupid world, Tex. Everything is downhill."

Tex nodded, not saying anything. Yet he was pretty sure they were reading each other's minds by now, so why bother to talk? Instead, he stood, offered her a hand to tug her to her feet, which she took, and they started downhill as if there were no other option.

"I wonder where Owen and Morgan are?" Tex said. He didn't expect an answer.

"I wonder if they hanged my brother yet. It's honestly a shame. Clive isn't a killer. He's a half-wit and completely lacking in common sense, but if they hanged folks for that, the world would be mostly dead people."

Tex conceded her last point while disagreeing about the murderer part. "If we get to Fort Russell before they hang your brother, and if we can hide from your family well enough, I'll see that you get a chance to talk to the fort's commander. That man is Colonel Bridger, Delaney and Boone's pa."

Thanks to the slope, they were making good time and had made it to the woods before too long.

Looking around at the trees and bushes, Stella got her sling and stones out and ready.

Tex drew his knife. He was good at throwing it, although he hadn't seen much game close enough to hand to have his knife be of much use.

As they walked on into the encroaching darkness, Tex said, "Will you think less of me if I break down and cry like a baby?"

Stella laughed, which turned into a giggle so high-pitched a woman might use it as a birdcall. Once she had herself under control, she replied, "Yes. I would."

<hr />

The day went well by Delaney's measure.

Ma's food wasn't going to hold up, but they had found

the hidden blades in Gordon and Johnny Duncan's clothing, ripped them out, and then set out, and it wasn't long before Roz found a trail.

"This is a trail for wagons." Pa scratched his head, staring down at it as if he were seeing a ghost. "What's it doing way out here?"

They rode straight east on it like their tails were on fire. Delaney was just so happy to see they were getting out of the wilderness.

After a few hours moving at a faster pace, Morgan, riding beside Roz, pulled his horse to a walk and pointed north. "I know where we are. That's Horsetooth Peak."

He laughed in a way that was a little giddy. Delaney got the impression Morgan Sawyer hadn't had a lot of experience being lost.

Owen, towing three horses behind him, all with hog-tied Duncans on them, said, "I know Horsetooth Peak. We'll be in Fort Collins in an hour, maybe two."

"Two," Morgan said, "because we've got to give the horses a breather."

"We can have the sheriff lock these men up overnight and get some sleep and a good meal." Owen looked over his shoulder and smiled at Ma, the kind of smile that spread all the way across his face. He was feeling mighty relieved.

Delaney smiled back, even knowing the smile was for Ma. "Not a word of that is a criticism of your good cooking, Mrs. Bridger, but maybe you'd like a meal you don't have to cook."

"The best seasoning for any meal is hunger," Ma said. "No offense taken, Owen. I'd be glad for a meal that wasn't laced with trail dust."

Owen let his eyes slide past Ma to study Delaney. She felt the warmth of them all the way to her heart. Even with a row of outlaws strung between them.

He turned forward and walked along, leaving her warmer than was comfortable for a July day in the Rocky Mountains.

21

"Here now, what's all this?" The sheriff, sitting with his bootheels resting on his desk, shot to his feet.

Owen dragged two prisoners with him. Morgan came behind with one, while Colonel Bridger had the other.

"I'm a U.S. Marshal, Sheriff, transporting prisoners to Fort Russell. I need a place for them to stay the night."

The sheriff looked annoyed. Owen thought the man might have gotten used to sitting at the desk and preferred no disruptions to his usual routine.

Colonel Bridger handed his prisoner off to Boone and then reached out a hand to the sheriff. "Lieutenant Isaac, you're sheriffin' in Fort Collins now?"

"Yep. When they closed the fort, I mustered out and stayed here. You're involved with all this, Grizzly?"

Owen had to give that nickname some thought. It didn't make the man sound all that friendly.

"Yep, one of 'em"—he pointed at Clive—"is an escaped murderer. The rest busted him out of the stockade at the fort. That was before I got assigned there. They rounded him up in Denver after he'd been running free for a year or so, and while transporting him back for a hanging—"

"I did *not* murder anyone. It was self-defense," Clive insisted, shouting the same thing as always.

"The rest of his family," Bridger went on, "tried to break him free again and managed to kill a U.S. Marshal, and they wounded my son who was riding to Fort Russell with the Marshals. The man among them who did the shooting, they claim he's dead. But the rest were with him, and that's its own crime."

"Leland wasn't supposed to shoot anyone. We didn't expect that. Yes, we were going to stop the Marshals and help my son escape, but no one was supposed to open fire." Sly had a love for the sound of his own voice.

Colonel Bridger had managed to sum the whole mess up fast and gain the sheriff's cooperation.

Owen decided to give the sheriff a break, too. "I'll see they get a meal and get someone from the nearest diner to bring it over to them."

The sheriff nodded and led the way into the back room. There were four cells. Fort Collins was an up-and-coming town indeed.

"One apiece. You can each have your own room." The sheriff plucked the keys off a nail and led the prisoners down the row to the farthest one. He unlocked the first cell and shoved Clive inside.

It took only moments before they were all locked up.

Gordon said again that he wished Stella were there with them.

For a man who had a rule against worrying, Owen let his thoughts swing toward Tex often enough. How in the world would he find his friend, or find his body, in the vast wilderness of the Rockies? Maybe it was grief he was feeling rather than worry. Because he feared the worst.

Owen said to his group, "Let's have a meal sent over here, eat ourselves, get some sleep, then hightail it to Fort Russell. We need to ride back out there and find Tex."

He didn't mention Stella's name. He was annoyed with himself because of his reticence. He wanted to judge her harshly. He couldn't think of the Duncans and not think of Stan, Tex's Deputy Marshal. A good man was dead, and he shouldn't let a soft heart toward women sway him. Well, if she was still alive to find, Owen planned to see her locked up with her family. Or at least have a judge decide what should happen to her . . . to all of them.

"I appreciate you handling the food, Marshal. There's a diner across the street that'll send over fried chicken that's good enough for the prisoners. But go on down to the Mason Hotel to get yourselves a better meal and rooms for the night unless you're planning on camping out."

Owen looked around at the weary faces, then smiled. A feather bed would be mighty welcome after so long on the trail.

Colonel Bridger nodded, and everyone else agreed.

"Ask them at the diner to run over to my deputy's room and tell him to come here and spend the night. I should have some backup with this many prisoners locked up."

"They do seem to have a talent for escaping, but all those who helped with the escape are locked up with them. I'll send word to the deputy."

Owen led the way out of the jailhouse. Everyone headed for the hotel while he jogged across the street to ask them to deliver meals to the jailhouse. He threw in an extra few meals for the sheriff and his deputy and then wondered if he was being wise, considering the sheriff's opinion about the food there.

He was soon settled in a chair at the restaurant in the Mason Hotel and felt the ache in his bones from so long on a hard trail. No doubt about it, he was getting soft.

Which led him to the notion that had been gnawing at him for quite a while. "I don't think I'm going to ask to be reappointed to the Marshals Service." He looked at Morgan, who grunted. "I might not even get the job," he went on. "The man who appointed me before has since moved on. The new man in the office may have his own ideas."

"Can women be Marshals?" Delaney asked.

She might as well have tossed a cannonball onto the table.

"No. Women cannot be—" Owen began, but then was shouted down by Delaney's pa.

"It's no proper job for a decent woman—" Delaney's pa was drowned out by Delaney's ma.

"You're tough enough to do the job and you know it, but no daughter of mine is going to—" Her ma's words were lost when Boone started laughing.

The laughter, more than anything else, made Delaney narrow her eyes.

Owen kicked the lunkhead under the table. Boone glanced at Delaney and tried to cut off the laughter, but it wasn't easily done.

In a tiny break in the uproar, Roz announced, "I could do the job, too. I'm going to apply."

Morgan, grinning as he took a drink of coffee, spit it

across the table into Owen's face. "Are you out of your mind?"

Owen glared at his friend, who was glaring at Roz. Morg didn't even notice Owen's soggy state.

Dragging his kerchief off his neck, Owen dried his face. At least the face full of coffee made him quit his grumbling. Everyone else was doing well enough without him. Morgan was involved now. He'd thought it was funny when Delaney said it.

But Roz? That he didn't like.

Owen listened to the racket, glad they'd gotten in late and the hotel dining room was empty. And glad they'd already rented a bunch of rooms. Otherwise, the hotel owner would've likely tossed them all out.

As the ruckus finally settled down, Delaney was left with a satisfied look on her face. Owen couldn't figure out if she was happy with her notion of becoming a Marshal or just liked to stir up a fuss with her family. Maybe it was her job as the youngest to be a pest.

Changing the subject, Owen said, "You know, when Boone got shot, we were all scared for him and . . ." His throat grew tight then, which made talking near to impossible.

"You're lucky to be alive, son," Hester said, rescuing Owen.

Boone nodded. "I don't remember much, but I woke up with a mighty sore head."

"I thought he was dead," Delaney whispered.

Owen could see she too was fighting tears and wished now that he'd never brought it up.

She gestured toward Marley, who looked full of food and ready for bed. "We were afraid Marley was going to lose his leg, but thankfully the bullet didn't break the bone. It was bad enough, though. Boone was lying there in a pool of blood, Tex had been shot in the arm, and Deputy Ross was dead. They shot Clive too, a gutshot. The bullet missed anything serious, but we figured he might die, too. But he was just too ornery."

"That pack of polecats is claiming *one* of them shot four people?"

Owen shrugged. "Doesn't ring true, does it? Leland Duncan. That's Clive's brother, and a hothead according to the Duncan family. Morg and Tex kept watch over them at night, and we'd left very little to track, so they were coming slow. It gave us time to bury Stan and patch the rest of them up enough to ride. Once we were ready, Morg and Tex went back to them, captured two of 'em standing watch, and stole all the horses, setting them afoot."

They talked together for another few minutes, and then Marley said, "Well, I'm turning in."

Morgan pushed back his chair. "I'm all in as well. If you Bridgers have a hankering to catch up, you don't need me. Roz, if you're ready to call it a night, I can walk you and Jesse up to the room we got you. Owen, you coming?"

Owen looked around at a family he had nothing but respect for. "I might stay here a little longer and listen to the Bridgers spin a few yarns, if you folks don't mind."

"Marley and I are in the room right at the top of the stairs," Morgan said. "You're in the room next to ours, Owen. It seems right we stand guard, but we've got a tough crowd here. They can handle any robbers we may get."

The Bridger family nodded.

Colonel Bridger said, "We appreciate your care of our family, Marshal Sawyer, Marshal Tweedt. Thank you."

Morgan gave a firm nod of his head and headed out with Marley. Roz and Jesse trailed behind them.

Owen spent an interesting hour listening to tales of the travel west with Delaney and Boone, and life at the fort with the colonel and his missus. And he did his best not to let his eyes settle on Delaney for too long.

Good chance she wasn't going to get to be a Marshal. He wondered what she would end up doing with her life. Living at the fort with her ma and pa sounded a little tame for the woman he'd come to know and admire. No doubt the men would come flocking to her. That made him grind his teeth together. He realized he'd been looking at her for too long and shifted to stare at his rough, callused hands.

What was he going to do with his life?

What was he fit for? Ranching maybe? Tex was a top cowhand. Owen wasn't as good, but he could hold his own. But being a cowhand was a long way from being a rancher. It took money to set up ranching and probably more smarts than he had.

He could drive a stagecoach or ride shotgun on one.

He could be a lawman, but a local sheriff instead of a Marshal. He found himself wanting to stop wandering, to put down some roots.

But he'd wait to take root until after he found Tex.

A slap on the shoulder that was a little too hard to be exactly friendly drew him out of his thoughts. That was when he realized he'd quit looking at his hands and was looking at Delaney again.

Boone, sitting next to him, had disrupted his daydreaming.

"Sorry," Owen said, "I was thinking." No one else at the table seemed to have noticed. They were busy sharing tales of their eldest brother, Bowie. Then he had a second to wonder if they had in fact noticed him staring at Delaney. The Bridgers were a noticing kind of family, but they either hadn't noticed or were pretending they hadn't. Owen preferred it if they hadn't.

"Yep, I saw that you were." Boone patted his shoulder again, this time with less force. "Maybe it's time we all went up to bed. I'm about asleep in my chair."

Chair legs scraped as they all got to their feet. Owen thought it was his duty to bring up the rear.

Mrs. Bridger had plans to sleep in a room with Delaney, Roz, and Jesse. Colonel Bridger was next door in his own room. Everyone claimed he snored like a hibernating bear. Boone had the room on past his pa.

That left Owen alone. He could have slept on the floor in Morgan and Marley's room, but they'd rented every room on the second floor, and Owen wanted it like that. No one to move in next to them. Not that there should be any danger, but a man got used to being cautious.

And the thought of a bed was too tempting to deny himself. It struck him again that he was getting soft.

He was the last one upstairs and the last one to reach for a doorknob. A heavy hand settled on his shoulder. He looked sideways to see Colonel Grizzly Bridger, gripping his shoulder. Beyond him he saw Boone right before he stepped into his room. He gave Owen a quick glance and looked to have something like sympathy in his eyes.

The colonel nodded toward the stairway. Owen's stomach twisted in a way it hadn't since he was about eight years old. He followed Grizzly back down the stairs.

22

"Delaney, we need to talk for a few minutes." Ma was sitting on the edge of the bed, wearing her nightgown. She should have looked sweet and loving and kind.

Ma was all those things . . . well, a little light on the sweet. But right now, what she looked like was grim, dead serious, and intent on speaking her mind.

Roz was asleep, so Ma kept her voice low. Yet it didn't matter if their voices disturbed Roz's sleep. They were having this talk either way.

And Delaney had a notion of what it might be about.

Ma stood from the bed with her arms folded across her chest. "You seem to be taken with Owen," she began.

Delaney had accepted long ago that her ma could read her mind. She sometimes read things in her mind that Delaney hadn't read yet.

"Taken?" Delaney was buying time to think. So far she hadn't thought of much.

"How much time have you spent alone with this boy?"

Boy? Delaney almost smiled. But her self-preservation instincts prevented it.

Then, because she hadn't thought of a thing, and Ma was the smartest woman she knew, in truth the smartest *person* she knew, she said, "We haven't hardly spent any time alone, but he's a man I respect, Ma. Tough and smart. Hardworking and savvy in the woods. He and his Marshal friends did the very best they could in a terrible situation. They kept their heads, all of them, but Owen . . ." Her voice faded as she looked up at Ma. "I'd like to spend more time talking with him, to get to know him. He is a fine man, Ma. You know the men I've grown up around. They're all hard men to measure up to. I haven't met many men in my life, and until Owen came along, none have measured up to Pa and my brothers. I think Owen does."

Their gazes held. Delaney thought she'd maybe surprised her mother. Maybe she hadn't expected such straight talk from her.

Ma tilted her head slowly, as if she were trying to get whatever she was thinking to balance itself. "Are you in love with Owen?"

Delaney hadn't actually considered that—well, not much because she didn't exactly know what being in love felt like. "I feel . . . drawn to him. Interested in him. And tomorrow we're going to ride to Cheyenne, and as soon as he turns over the men he's arrested, he's going to ride off. And as skilled as he is, it's going to take a long time to find Tex. If they do find him . . ."

She felt the burn of tears behind her eyes, and Delaney never cried. Not even when she thought Boone was dead, although later she'd gotten around to it once she was alone. And it was Owen who'd helped her get through it. She'd started wondering about him then.

Ma nodded and sat beside her on the bed.

"I need more time with him, Ma," Delaney went on, "but he's going to ride off real soon." The tears spilled over. "I may never see him again."

Ma pressed a handkerchief in Delaney's hand, and she wiped her eyes with it.

In a quiet but firm voice, Roz said, "I'm gonna stick like a bur to Morgan."

Delaney lifted her head and saw that Roz wasn't asleep but just lying there still. She'd heard everything.

"In the end," she continued, "he'll marry me just to stop me from chasing him. If Morgan rides off tomorrow to search through the Rockies for the rest of his life, I'm going with him. You oughta do the same."

Ma added, very sternly, "You're not riding off into the wilderness with two men."

"We'll see about that," Roz snorted.

Ma frowned, while Delaney almost smiled. It was more than clear that Roz didn't consider Ma to be in any position to issue orders.

"I was only fourteen when Morgan rode off, heading to a war of all the stupid things. But I loved him with all my heart. I think I married that worthless Herman Beck because my heart wasn't working right then—I was too young to know better. I also figured Morgan would never come back. His pa was as mad as the fires of Hades over him fighting for the North. He told Morgan when he left to never come back. And when Morgan's brother died, it would've been dangerous for him to go back, and he never did. The only good thing that no-account Herman ever gave me was my son. I never thought I'd see Morgan again. Now that I have, I'm not letting him out of my sight."

"Do you think you could get Morgan to marry you tomorrow?" Delaney asked Roz. "That's the only way it's proper for you to leave with him."

"Doubt it. He's so all-fired worried about Tex, he ain't thinking of much else. Either way, when he comes back from his searching for Tex, I'll be there. And then he'll marry me."

Delaney envied the woman for her confidence . . . or was it stubbornness? She wasn't sure which. "W-what should I do, Ma?"

"Nothing right now," Ma said with a yawn. "Let's sleep on it, see what tomorrow brings. Good night, Roz." She then lay down on the bed and scooted herself toward the wall.

Delaney gave a long sigh, then slipped in beside her ma.

◇━━•━━◇

The dining room was empty and dark.

Owen followed Grizzly. What a name that was. When he first heard it, he'd thought it amusing. Now he had to wonder just what attributes the colonel had to earn such a nickname. He was about to find out.

Up until now, Owen had been addressing the man as the colonel and not Grizzly. Should he keep doing that?

Owen braced for trouble . . . and for questions he didn't know the answers to.

"So you're thinking of not requesting reappointment to your Marshal job?" Grizzly the colonel asked.

Owen was braced so hard, he almost fell forward. He quick sat down at the table farthest from the door into the lobby. Then he looked up at Grizzly. Was he wrong in what he'd expected?

He studied the colonel for about five seconds before he knew he was *not* wrong. At least the man had started with a question he could answer. "Yep, I've always had a wandering star hanging over my head. Until the last year or two anyway. I haven't made this decision lightly because I like the job of Marshal. I think I'm good at it."

The colonel didn't respond, so Owen went on. "I don't have the usual Marshal's job. I don't act as guard at trials, nor do I deliver subpoenas and summonses, or reward money to folks who helped catch wanted outlaws. Somehow I've ended up chasing outlaws and, like with Clive, delivering prisoners. It's part of that wandering star, I reckon. Not many men want those kinds of jobs, and I've stepped forward when they ask for volunteers and get picked for the job. Morgan, Tex, and I have teamed up steadily for the last few years and gone after men who broke out of jail and outlaws wanted on federal warrants."

"And you don't want to do that anymore?"

Owen surprised himself, and maybe the colonel too, by smiling. "I guess that wandering star has set along with the sun. I don't feel it hanging overhead like I used to. Nope, I don't want to do that anymore. I haven't quite figured out what I'll do next, but I'm capable of plenty. I've got another couple of months left still in my four-year term, so I've got time yet to consider the future while I go searching for Tex. I wired the man I receive assignments from and told him what happened. He knows I'll be gone awhile and approved it. He wants to find Tex, too."

The colonel nodded, then locked eyes with Owen. "What

about my daughter? Whatever this new job is you're gonna do, are you planning to do it with Delaney at your side?"

Silence hung between them.

Owen felt like a young buck being chastised. He hadn't thought of himself as young for so long, he almost liked it. Yet he wasn't a young buck, and he figured he'd best make that clear to Grizzly right now. He wasn't sure what was the right or wrong thing to say, nor how to say it. He just said what was on his mind.

"Your daughter, Colonel, is as fine a young woman as I've ever met. Fact is I've never known a woman as wise and brave and kind as she is. Yes, I feel like there's something very special between us. I have an inclination, once I find Tex, to ride to Fort Russell and see if your daughter would . . . would have an interest in going for a walk with me. We've spent some time together and have already gotten to know each other a bit."

Grizzly stared at him. "Are you not going to ask for my permission to spend time with my daughter? That's what I was expecting."

Feeling a little confused, Owen said, "I was hoping you'd be willing to have me underfoot, but no, what I'm thinking of is between Delaney and me. We'll be making our own choices about the future. If we decide we suit each other, I won't be asking anyone but her for permission. I wouldn't mind your blessing, though, Colonel. If she needs your permission, well, she can ask for it herself." Owen paused, then added more firmly, "But you withholding your permission won't stop me from chasing after her."

Grizzly's eyes narrowed. Clearly his last statement didn't please the colonel. Owen didn't want that. He liked this man.

240

He liked Delaney's whole family. He had to admit he'd never done much thinking on how to impress a sweetheart's pa, especially not one called Grizzly.

"You know, I have the power to appoint U.S. Marshals to serve at the fort. I could use another judge advocate, too. But you'd have to join the U.S. Army for that to be possible. And once you're in the Army, well, you can be ordered to move to other places. It's an interesting life, but it can separate you from your family. Of course, the Frontier is so settled these days, you'd likely be allowed to take your wife and children along with you."

Wife and children? Owen swallowed hard. He felt the need to tell old Grizzly here to stop planning his life.

And yet it wasn't a bad plan.

"The Marshal who's stationed at the fort doesn't roam around much. We keep him plenty busy doing federal work. And I've just received word we can appoint a second Marshal. I could put your name in for consideration. You'd still be a Marshal, but you wouldn't be wandering."

It was a *really* good plan.

"I appreciate the offer," said Owen, "but I'll need to think about it. It'd sure make all my decisions easy . . . including courting your daughter."

"What I've seen of you so far has impressed me, Son."

Son? It reminded Owen he hadn't seen his own family in a long time.

"For now, I've got to go find Tex." And he *would* find him. He might be gone awhile, though, searching for him. If that stream he'd fallen into connected to the Colorado River, Owen might have to ride all the way to Mexico to find him. Would Delaney wait for him? Every man in that fort and the whole town of Cheyenne was sure to be interested in her. He wondered what she'd think of going along with him, helping him hunt for Tex.

"What I've seen of you has impressed me, Colonel. You've raised some fine children. Boone, I could see myself being good friends with him. Bowie, he's almost legendary. You've spoken of your sons, Crockett and Jedediah, and they sound like fine men, too. You've brought up Delaney to be the best kind of woman there is. And Mrs. Bridger could tame the West single-handedly."

"Whatever my young ones have grown up to be is more owing to Hester than to me. I was gone too much, and those times I got back home, I'd be so blessed by my children I was humbled." Grizzly stood from his chair. "Let's get some sleep now. Oh, one last thing before we turn in. If you treat my little girl wrong, Son, I'll kill you. And no one, not even your tracking friend Morgan, will ever find your body. In fact, I'll arrange it so he'll be afraid to even look for it."

Nodding, Owen said, "Somehow that doesn't even surprise me. In fact, I'd be disappointed in you, Colonel, if you hadn't said it."

He followed Grizzly up the stairs. After saying good night, Owen went to his room. He locked the door behind him, though it was probably a waste of time. If Grizzly or anyone in his fierce family decided they wanted to get to him, they'd for certain find a way. On the other hand, he hadn't treated Delaney wrong yet.

He hoped.

Stripping down to wash up, he put clean longhandles on for the first time in way too long. Then he finally got to lie down on a bed.

23

At breakfast the next morning, Owen asked Morgan, "What do you all think of Gordon Duncan's story?"

Morgan took a sip of steaming coffee, then said, "It has the ring of truth, especially taken with what Colonel Bridger told us. We need to look through the posters to see if any of these men are wanted or if it's all just their kin Wildcat Duncan. I know there were other Duncans involved, but maybe he runs with his sons like Gordon and Sly do." With that, he went back to his coffee.

Owen chewed on a biscuit. "What should we do then?"

"Even if you believe their story, you can't just let them go," Delaney said as she cut a chunk from her flapjacks. "They broke Clive out of jail. They were right there when Stan was killed and Boone shot. Even if none of these Duncans did that, they rode after us with the intention of getting Clive back from us."

Morgan nodded. "Lots of things happened around those coyotes. Chasing after us into the wilderness could be named a crime. And if they got turned loose, they'd probably go back to trying to break Clive free, and then we'd have to go riding into the mountains chasing after them for another week or two."

"Why not just turn them over to the law at Fort Russell?" Grizzly said. "Let the court there decide what to do with them. No doubt the judge has heard the rumors about the MacNeils, and I know the man who heard Calan and his family talk about making Clive suffer. We can get the men who heard that talk to testify in court. And you can testify to what Gordon's told you."

"I will if it's absolutely necessary," said Owen, "but I've got to get on the trail after Tex. It's eating at me that I rode away from him. Will Delaney and Boone being there to testify be enough? They witnessed the shooting, and we only know what Gordon has told us. Not sure he can be trusted to tell the truth."

"Give us one day, Owen." Grizzly looked so serious that Owen took it for a threat.

"One day." Owen finished his biscuit and rose from the table. "The sun's up. Let's get to Cheyenne."

While they rode, Owen had a talk with Sly. Gordon, Clive, and Johnny listened in.

"You know," Sly said, "if we'd just let justice run its course, we'd've gotten to the fort a long time ago. Colonel Bridger would've been there and told his story, Clive might well be free by now, and my son Leland would be alive."

Owen wanted to bash every one of the Duncans on the head. Stan would still be alive too, and that burned something terrible. Tex wouldn't be lost somewhere in the wilderness, or Stella either.

"If we'd let justice run its course, Clive would've been hanged long before word got around about him being innocent."

244

Owen had to admit that would've lit a fire under anyone.

"I talked to the judge advocate, and he said he was going to call for an appeal. He didn't like the MacNeil witness and had some suspicions. And the truth came out real quick because Calan MacNeil has a big mouth. He'd've been fine."

"I don't believe—"

"Keep quiet, Sly, or you're riding to Wyoming wearing a gag." Morgan always had a way with words.

They pushed harder, and the Duncans caused no real trouble. They'd be riding into Fort D. A. Russell in time for the evening meal.

<hr />

Delaney was glad to see the backs of those blamed fool Duncans. Even if they all walked away free men, Clive included, they'd no longer be her problem. They had a big enough group with Boone and her that Ma and Pa couldn't handle the crowd in the very comfortable fort commander's house. Roz and Jesse would stay with them, while the Marshals got assigned to the guest quarters.

Owen, Morgan, and Marley headed there after Pa invited them to supper.

As they split up, Delaney felt a tug on her arm, and she turned to see Owen studying her. "After we've eaten, Delaney, would you like to take a walk with me?"

Owen had asked her right in front of her family.

She was impressed by that. Owen was an even braver man than she'd suspected. Of course, they'd been together all day, but nothing even close to being alone. They hadn't spoken one word to each other, that is, short of "pass the biscuits" and such.

Delaney didn't even look at her parents to see how Owen's question affected them. She wasn't going to let them decide her answer. And besides that, she was sure she'd hear what they thought. She just hoped they waited until the Marshals were gone to start in.

"I'd like that, Owen," she replied. "I'd like that very much."

He got a somewhat dazed look in his eyes, as if she'd answered all his prayers in that brief moment. He smiled at her, but then Morgan grabbed his arm and pulled him away.

She was pretty sure she heard Morgan mutter, "You need a bath and a set of clean clothes."

Good advice. She'd take it herself.

Ma then grabbed her arm and pulled her away.

◇—•—◇—•—◇

Owen enjoyed supper. They even let him sit beside Delaney. When it was over, Delaney started to clear the table.

Her pa said, "You go on for your walk, girl. We'll take care of the dishes."

Owen almost reached for her hand but stopped himself. Seconds later, he had to check himself again when he moved to rest his hand on her back.

He felt all those cold Bridger eyes drawing a bead on his spine, and so he kept his hands to himself as they walked outside and down the few steps to the fort grounds. Neither of them had visited the fort before, so Owen had no idea where a man and woman oughta walk to. But Delaney turned to the right, and they walked together to the edge of the house. Then she stopped suddenly and turned to look up at him.

It was a clear night, and the stars shone as though God himself were beaming down on them from heaven.

Her face was beautiful in the starlight.

Taking his hand, she led him to the back of the house, where she turned to him once more, this time holding one finger to her lips. "Shh," she said.

They hadn't stood there a full minute when the back door opened, and Boone stepped out.

"You can go right on back inside." Delaney had the kind of cold, cutting voice that made a man back up.

Instead, her brother grinned like a knothead.

"Aw, Delaney, I just wanted to take a little walk myself." Boone didn't even try to act innocent.

Delaney stood there, arms crossed, toe tapping. "I'm waiting. You know I can make you sorry you ever started this. In fact, I can make you sorry you were ever born."

That one made Boone laugh, almost as if he wasn't one speck frightened by her serious threat. But he went back inside the house nonetheless.

Delaney grabbed Owen's hand and walked quickly toward a wooded area behind the house. Once they were among the trees, they stopped and waited for a bit. The back door hadn't reopened. Delaney moved deeper into the woods. She slowed down some but still held his hand.

"They're still coming, don't you think?" Owen had liked it better in the bright starlight. Here, shrouded in the trees, he couldn't see how pretty she was. He remembered just fine, though.

"Oh, most definitely. But maybe they'll be a little stealthier about it."

"Well, we'd better do this right away then," Owen said. He turned her in his arms and kissed her.

He'd meant to steal just one kiss, but he didn't count on how nice it felt.

The next thing he knew, her arms were around his neck and he forgot he'd ever had a plan. Kissing her became an end in itself.

He wasn't sure how much time had passed when he pulled back enough to say, "Delaney, your pa had a talk with me last night."

Delaney laughed and buried her face in his chest. "How bad was it?"

That got a smile out of him. He kissed her on the forehead. "I like your pa. I like and respect your whole family. And I'm a little afraid of them, too."

"You oughta be."

Owen and Delaney jerked apart. Delaney turned to the nearest tree. "Boone, you get out here right now, you low-down snoop!"

He stepped out into the open.

"Are you all hiding out here?"

"Nope, only me." But Boone's tone didn't ring true.

"And me." Her ma walked over to stand beside Boone.

Owen slapped himself on the forehead. "Hester?"

Delaney leaned against him, clearly struck dumb.

Owen could think of only one thing to ask. "Delaney, I thought of asking you to wait for me while I go search for Tex. But I can't help imagining a dozen men, maybe a hundred, won't be chasing after a woman as pretty and brilliant and sweet as you. I trust you, but I think I'd better just wrap you up tight before I go."

"W-what are you saying?"

"Will you marry me, Delaney?"

She grinned. "Yes, but only if I can go with you."

Ignoring their audience, Owen slid his arms around her waist. "You can absolutely go with me. And I want to leave tomorrow. Maybe the next day if the trial stretches out. Is tomorrow too soon for a wedding?"

She smiled at him in a way that made his heart burn with love for her. She remembered Roz declaring last night that she was planning to stick with Morgan no matter what. She wanted to do the same. "Tomorrow is perfect."

"Now, Delaney, tomorrow is a little fast. I think—"

"Ma, stop. You don't get to vote on this. Owen and I decide, and I vote *yes*. Tomorrow it is." She sounded just as tough as the rest of her family.

Owen glanced over to see how serious Hester was about voting, but she and Boone had left and were walking back to the house.

Delaney wrapped her arms around his neck again. They stood there together in the dark, truly alone finally. "I want to spend the rest of my life getting to know you, Delaney. I haven't had a chance to tell you this yet, but your pa offered to appoint me to be Marshal at the fort. He said I wouldn't be traveling around, that there was enough work to keep me busy here. We could live in Cheyenne where you would be close to your family. I don't want a job that takes me away from my wife all the time."

Delaney giggled. "Sounds like you've got our whole life planned."

Owen froze. "Is that wrong? I've never proposed to a woman before. I was hoping you'd like it that I wouldn't be wandering. But if you want me to be gone more, then maybe—"

She touched his lips with her finger, and he shut up, not sure what to say anyway. "I love your plan, Owen."

"Actually, it's mostly your pa's plan."

Delaney laughed out loud. "Well, I approve of it, and I like the idea of you not being gone. I would enjoy living near my parents—that is, if they don't pull up stakes again. But maybe next time, when there's a big decision to be made, you'll come and talk to me about it first, and we can decide together. Don't forget that I'm a sensible, capable woman. You can trust me to cooperate with you to make those decisions. Most likely I'll agree with you since you're also very sensible and capable. But if I don't agree with you about something, then you should still listen to me because I might have a good reason for disagreeing."

"You make a good point," he said with a broad smile. "How about we decide where to live once we're married?"

"Agreed. I think if you're not in the cavalry, but you're employed by them, you can live off the fort grounds. I'm just not sure."

"I'm not sure either. We definitely need to look into what's possible and decide together." Then Owen leaned close. "I like your family a lot, but can we not live with your parents? I think we might be more . . . comfortable with a little space between us."

He waited for her to give her opinion.

"Space sounds wise. Again, I agree."

He drew her even closer and kissed her soundly. He wanted to show her just how much he appreciated her being so agreeable. As the shadows of the trees and the night breeze and birdsong wove romance into his soul, he got another idea.

"I'm thinking maybe we shouldn't wait until tomorrow, Delaney. We might be able to find a preacher yet tonight."

She eased back enough that their eyes could meet. She caught herself staring at his lips and decided her soon-to-be husband was a genius. "Yes, tonight sounds even better than tomorrow. Good idea, Owen."

"Let's go tell your family and my fellow Marshals we're going to hunt up a preacher for an evening wedding. I think there's a chaplain here at the fort."

A grin spread across her face. She nodded, and they walked hand in hand back to the fort commander's house.

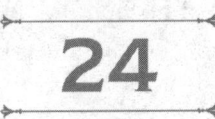

24

Delaney had to give her parents credit. When she walked into the house holding Owen's hand, then asked someone to run and get the chaplain, announcing they were getting married immediately, the explosion was a mild one.

Ma recovered first. She hurried off to fetch the chaplain, and it surprised Delaney that she latched on to Pa's arm and dragged him along with her.

"I don't think Ma wants to give Pa a chance to say anything. We probably don't want to hear what he thinks about a wedding tonight." Delaney watched as her parents appeared briefly in the window. She could make them out in the starlight.

It looked like Pa might be sharing what he had to say to Ma outside in private.

Owen was watching them, too. "I doubt your ma wants to hear what he has to say either."

Delaney saw that Morgan and Marley were both there, which meant their wedding party was complete.

"I suppose we oughta invite Clive." Owen scratched his

chin. "It was him who brought us together . . . sort of like a matchmaker."

"So you're really getting married?"

Delaney narrowed her eyes at Boone. "You should've gone with Ma and Pa."

Boone grinned. "I knew it from the first. You two were made for each other."

Owen rolled his eyes. "You were unconscious for those first two days and dazed for a couple more. You didn't know anything."

Roz came up to Delaney with a huge smile and hugged her. "I'm so happy for you two. I didn't know it from the first like Boone, but I think it's a wonderful idea either way. Where are you going to live once married? Maybe you could come live with me."

Delaney was glad they'd found Roz and brought her to civilization. That's when she really noticed Roz. "Look, you're wearing a dress."

"Yep, Mrs. Bridger made me put it on. She'd gone shopping the minute we got back. She bought me a riding skirt and a shirtwaist as well." Roz's pretty blue dress was sprinkled with white flowers among green vines.

Delaney shook her head in wonder. "And your hair, Roz. It's all tidy and perfect, and you smell like a rosebud."

Roz laughed. "All Mrs. Bridger's doing." She leaned close and whispered, "I'm gonna have to start calling her ma. She insisted, and she was fierce about it."

Delaney hugged her again. "Well, if she's your ma, that makes us sisters."

"And she cut off a bunch of my hair," Roz went on, "although I've still got plenty as you can see. Then she made me take a bath with her sweet-smelling soap and helped scrub my hair."

"That's Ma for you. She's a woman to take charge."

With her back to Morgan, Roz slid her eyes toward him, then arched her brows at Delaney. "Jesse's all dressed up nice, too. We're ready to head back into the mountains with you and Owen to search for Tex."

"You're not going, Roz." Morgan came up beside her, took her arm, and turned her firmly to face him. "This is Marshal work. We don't take women and children along." He looked at Owen. "I'd welcome your company, but now that you're getting leg-shackled, you should stay here, too. I'll go find Tex and bring him home."

"I don't think you can—"

"Owen, let's not argue with Morgan. He can go search for Tex and Stella. We'll go too, and if he doesn't want us along, we can split up."

Morgan sputtered and missed the look Roz shot him. She didn't seem to appreciate him ordering her to stay home. Delaney figured that unless he locked her up somewhere, Roz was determined to tag along on the search for Tex regardless of his opinion.

Then the door swung open, and Ma, Pa, and a man wearing a white collar came into the room.

"Are you the happy couple?" The chaplain looked at Roz and Morgan, who was still holding her arm.

Morgan let go like he was gripping the business end of a red-hot branding iron.

"It's us," said Owen, taking Delaney's hand. "Delaney is Colonel Bridger's daughter, and I'm the U.S. Marshal who escorted her from Denver to the fort."

"That's only a two-day ride. Sounds like you're rushing into this. Maybe you should wait a bit before getting married."

"The ride took more like three weeks." Delaney suddenly felt exhausted and dreaded a lengthy explanation.

"Let's just get on with the vows, Parson." Owen dropped her hand and pulled her arm through his elbow.

"It's Chaplain Moore."

"And it's Owen Riley and Delaney Bridger," Owen said.

Nodding at his commanding officer, the chaplain faced the couple before him and began, "Dearly beloved . . ."

Chaplain Moore must've decided that if they were going to rush things, then he'd do the same. Delaney noticed, with some tiny bit of relief, he didn't ask if anyone objected to the marriage. Why ask for trouble?

The vows were spoken in just a few minutes. It made Delaney wonder what normally went into wedding vows. She hadn't been to a wedding in a long time, but it seemed like the vows usually took longer than a couple of minutes.

"I now pronounce you man and wife. You may kiss the bride."

Owen looked at her with the biggest smile she'd ever seen. She knew her own expression matched it. The kiss was polite and brief, probably because her father stood nearby glowering at them.

Delaney was sure that her pa was in favor of the marriage; he just wasn't happy about the haste in having the wedding tonight.

Then Ma pulled Delaney into her arms and gave her the biggest hug of her life. Next came Pa and Boone and Roz.

All of them but Roz shook Owen's hand. Morgan, Marley, and Jesse stayed well back.

After the chaplain left, Morgan and Marley headed for the guest quarters without Owen. Boone went to bed, followed by Roz and Jesse. Which left Owen, Delaney, and her parents.

Delaney considered it the most awkward moment of her life.

"This way." Delaney held on tight to Owen and led him toward her room. It was down the hall from her parents, who followed along.

She got the two of them inside with the door closed and leaned against it with a huge sigh. The awkwardness should be over, except there was Owen—standing in the room with her, smiling at her.

He drew her into his arms and kissed her, and suddenly everything made sense and seemed so perfect.

Owen pulled back just an inch. "Delaney, considering we're in a room with your folks on one side of us, and Boone on the other side, if you're all right with it, I think we should put off . . . married things until we have more privacy."

Delaney nearly sagged to the floor as the tension rushed away. "I'd prefer that, Owen, thank you. But I am, well, looking forward to *married things*."

"As am I, Mrs. Riley. Now, would you like me to step out while you get ready for bed? Then you can do the same for me."

"Yes, please. I won't be long."

"Before I go, can I help you take the pins out of your hair? I'd like to see it around your shoulders."

Delaney kissed him; she couldn't help it. This time it was all her idea.

He smiled. "I'll take that for a yes."

She went to the dressing table in her room. She'd barely seen this room before today, but her folks had it set up nicely for her. She sat down in front of a mirror with her brush and comb laid out neatly in front of her . . . and then felt her husband touch her hair.

She had some vague idea of what was ahead of her. The intimacies of marriage. Ma had found a few minutes to talk with her about it.

It sounded rather dreadful honestly, but then Ma had talked about the "two becoming one" and the delight of such closeness. When Owen touched her hair and drew out the first hairpin, she could only imagine how much more wonderful it could be.

He took his time with letting her hair down. She studied him in the mirror as he did so. Handsome, clean clothes, freshly shaven, hair trimmed. He must've taken a bath. He looked in all ways civilized. And he was all hers.

After he'd brushed out her hair, he stepped out of the room and left her to undress and pull her nightgown on. It couldn't be more modest. Dark blue, flannel, it covered her from neck to wrists to toes. And yet she'd never felt more exposed in all her life as she moved to the bedroom door and cracked it open for him.

Owen stood there looking almost as nervous as she felt.

"Your turn." She stepped out, and he went in.

He was back quickly and opening the door for her. Reaching out his hand, she took it and let him draw her inside. They lay down together, his arm around her shoulders. The strangeness of holding a man so close was a marvel. He lowered his head and kissed her, and the strangeness faded away. Then he nestled her head against his shoulder and said, "Thank you very much for marrying me. Sleep now, Mrs. Riley."

With so much ahead of them, and so much between them, Delaney prayed and then drifted off to sleep.

25

The judge didn't rush through the trial.

He heard from everyone, including the woman who'd been absent from Clive's first trial and the men who'd heard Calan Finlay brag about getting revenge against the man who'd killed his cousin.

Calan Finlay was no longer posted there and so couldn't tell his version of events.

The woman's testimony settled things for the judge and jury.

The Duncan family talked about Leland breaking Clive out of jail, and Leland killing Marshal Stan Ross. No one took that lightly. The family blamed everything on Leland and took no responsibility for themselves. Like innocent little lambs, they were.

Owen didn't like it.

In the end, the jury accepted the testimony of men who benefited greatly from their version of what happened. But the woman accusing the Finlay cousins of assaulting her did ring true. And since all the madness had descended from that, Owen didn't protest—not out loud anyway.

The Duncans were set free.

While Owen didn't like it, he figured it was probably the right thing to do.

The instant the trial was over, the Duncans all hurried toward the courthouse door, likely hoping to leave town before the judge changed his mind.

All of them but Gordon ran off, who approached Morgan and said, "I want to help you hunt for Stella."

Morgan shook his head. "Nope. We're ready to be shut of you Duncans. We'll find her and then reunite her with you, if that is her wish. She said a few things that made me wonder if your rugged life agreed with her. We'll make sure she's safe whatever she chooses. We'll leave word for you here at the fort, so you can stop in and see if she wants to join up with you again."

Gordon stared at Morgan for a long moment. He must've decided that talking to Morgan was hopeless because he then turned and grabbed Owen by the upper arm. "I love that girl. She's more my daughter than Sly's. You'll note he's left without even asking about her. Clive and Johnny, too."

Owen met Gordon's eyes. He read sincerity there. "I believe you want to help, that you care about Stella like we care about Tex. But you can't come with us."

"I can help. I promise I—"

"Your promises are worthless," Owen said, cutting Gordon off. "Simple truth is we don't trust you. I'm not going to spend this whole journey looking over my shoulder. Wondering if I dare to sleep at night. Wondering if you lied your way through the trial when really you were all for Leland unloading that gun on us. If you always stay together, your 'tribe' as you call it, then what was Leland doing alone in

Fort Russell? He may have gone in alone, but where were you at the time? Just out of town, holding his horse?"

"Hold on. That's not—"

"And if you try to come with us, Gordon, I'll get my father-in-law, the fort commander, to lock you up for a week or so. That way we can ride far ahead of you. You'll be on your own then. Go hunt for Stella if you want to, but it won't be with us."

Gordon's shoulders sagged more and more with each word. Owen saw genuine concern in his eyes, yet that didn't change his decision. Finally, Gordon turned away and left the courthouse.

Owen glanced through a window and saw him talking with his brother and nephews. They all mounted up. They took their horses, as no one could prove they'd been stolen by anyone but Morgan and Tex, and then rode off.

Owen and Morgan might accept that the Duncans weren't all criminals, but they still had a bur under their saddle about Leland shooting Stan, and they weren't ready to trust the men in a clan like that. Gordon had chosen his wild life and had left the niece he loved like a daughter behind. He'd also neglected to tell Owen to make sure and leave word for him about Stella.

Owen looked at Morgan and saw disgust, which had to match his own. "Nothing wrong with having a wild life. Nothing wrong with choosing to live with no ties to the world outside those mountains. But Gordon and the rest of the Duncans, when they had to choose . . . they chose wrong."

Morgan nodded. "You chose ties too, Owen, when you took on a wife. I'm going after Tex on my own."

Owen snorted. "Don't think of it as us coming with you, Morg. Think of it as you coming with us. Try and keep up."

It was midafternoon. Plenty of time still to gather up his wife and some supplies, then hit the trail to go find Tex.

EPILOGUE

It was a successful wedding and a joyful, if chaste, honeymoon. Now they were galloping away from the fort. Delaney had a new name and felt like a new woman, and she was glad for it.

"Oh, just come on up here," Morgan called out. "You're being a stubborn, ridiculous little pill."

Roz was tagging along, behind them about fifty feet away, with Jesse riding beside her. Delaney had to admit that she *was* acting like a stubborn little pill. She didn't think "ridiculous" was fair, though. Delaney admired Roz's grit.

But Morgan had absolutely forbidden her to come along with them. Roz had smirked at that, waited for Delaney, Owen, and Morgan to ride off, and then she and Jesse mounted up and followed them at a distance.

Marley had stayed behind to let his leg finish healing up. He wasn't up to the search for Tex, and he wouldn't be heading back to Denver for a few weeks either. Maybe he'd wait until the train was running again. He wired the man who'd appointed him to his post and was ordered to stay put until he was well again.

Boone and her parents had opted out of the search, too.

Boone's head still hurt too much to ride a horse for any length of time. As for Delaney's parents, they'd've probably gone along just to keep an eye on Delaney. In the end, they decided to trust Owen to take good care of her.

Owen told Delaney later that he was honored by their decision.

Grizzly said he was going to put the word out about Tex and Stella being missing, so if anyone saw them, they'd report it to the fort commander.

Shaking his head, Owen had said to Delaney, "If anyone sees Tex, they wouldn't need the word put out, would they? Tex would just talk to them and use what information he gleaned from that to catch up to his comrades. It's not like Tex is hiding from us."

"Do you suppose he's come across other people out there in the wilderness?" Delaney was going on the assumption that he and Stella had survived the fall and their river ride. And she recalled how utterly amazed Roz had been to see them. Not many folks up there among the peaks.

As they rode southward, they soon came into view of the Front Range of the Rockies. How were they ever going to find Tex and Stella in such vast and rugged mountains?

"I need to get back home and fetch my cows," Roz said.

"We ain't bothering with your livestock until we find Tex," Morgan said. He could sure be a cranky man, although at the same time he'd let Jesse ride along on his right, Roz riding on his left.

"I meant *after* we find Tex." She gave Morgan a wide smile, who seemed to forget he was being cranky as he locked eyes with her for a long moment.

Owen and Delaney brought up the rear. Owen had told

her that Morgan was the man they wanted in charge once in the wilderness. Delaney, figuring this way she could get more attention for herself from Owen, didn't protest.

She reached her hand out to Owen, and he took it. "Are we going to call this our honeymoon?" she asked.

Owen looked at her and chuckled. "Nope, we're not. But when we're done here, and before your pa puts me to work at the fort, I thought we might head to Iowa and look up my folks. We could take the train, which would be a faster way to travel there."

Delaney said, "I'd like that. And if they've moved on, we'll see if we can find them maybe."

Owen leaned over and kissed her. "Any honeymoon we go on isn't going to have three extra people along. I'd prefer your undivided attention, Mrs. Riley."

The look in his eyes and the warmth of that kiss made Delaney's heart race. "Besides getting ambushed by the Duncans and driven deep into the mountains, I'd say more than anything, you ambushed my heart, Owen. And I'm thankful for it. Going to Iowa to visit with your family for a bit sounds just right."

Holding hands, stealing a kiss now and then, talking quietly, planning their future together, they rode along while enjoying the summer sun—until Morgan turned the group toward the west and into the wild.

For more from Mary Connealy,
read on for an excerpt from

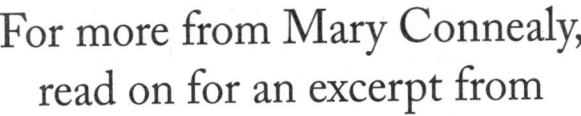

Book One in the
BROTHERS IN ARMS
series

Available now wherever books are sold.

ONE

AUGUST 1870
BEAR CLAW PASS, WYOMING

Kevin Hunt came awake with a snap. A metallic clink. He didn't need to figure out more. He slid a hand over his little brother's mouth and felt Andy wake up instantly.

An inch from his ear, Kevin hissed, "Hide."

Not a word from Andy, not a question. Nothing but instant obedience. It made a big brother both mighty proud and sad. A shame the kid had learned such ugly lessons. Silence, fear, danger, death. Stay hidden. Move, move, move.

Ugly lessons they'd all learned well.

In the darkest night Kevin had ever known, he crawled on his belly around the campfire, its ashes burned down until they didn't even glow. The sky was a starless, moonless black mass. Not even a sliver of light.

Wind whistled with a mournful howl through the rolling hills and waving grass. The reminder that soon cold weather would return to push back the warmth that now ruled August in Wyoming.

Fighting for silence and speed, hoping the wind covered when he failed, Kevin reached Molly on the far side of the campfire. Even though she was his sister, she said it was improper to sleep by the men. It was a cool night, and Kevin regretted Molly held herself apart from her brothers. She'd learned her own bitter lessons, and holding herself apart wasn't all about being proper.

He felt more than heard her wake up and stir just a bit. She judged the silence correctly and maintained it without his covering her mouth.

Bleeding Kansas had taught them a lot. Even all these years later, they remembered. All that teaching might save their lives tonight.

Kevin whispered just louder than a breath, "Hide fast."

Molly was moving before he said the second word, Kevin right behind her. His brother and sister were no kids. Molly an adult woman of nineteen. Andy fifteen. The three of them were on their way west, abandoning the town that'd turned on them.

Kevin crawled after Molly, scraping on his belly like a low-down cowardly worm, and it burned him to retreat. He'd like to stand and fight, but he couldn't fight what he couldn't see.

Summer grass closed overhead, but it wasn't tall like the prairie grass back in Kansas. Still, it was tall enough to cover a person lying on their belly. The grass rustled as they crawled into it, but with the wind covering their movements, Kevin hoped whoever was sneaking up on their camp wouldn't notice.

If they could just be silent and stay hidden in the grass, they had a good chance of surviving this night.

He listened. His vision was keen in the dark, but it was useless tonight, so he relied on sound and smell.

He heard a clink of metal again and a faint creak of leather. The very fact it was so quiet alerted him. A faint jingle of a horse's bridle, but not close. A brush of footsteps. More than one person. Whoever they were, they'd left their horses behind, sneaking up.

Not native folks. There wasn't usually metal on their hackamore bridles. And if it'd been an Indian, Kevin doubted he'd've heard them coming.

He turned back, crawled to the edge of the grass, not sure just where he'd be visible should the clouds part and the moon shine down. When he'd gotten as close as he dared, he waited, breath held, wondering where Andy was now.

An explosion of movement came from the far side of the camp. Two dark forms silhouetted against a black night leapt into the clearing and fired an instant after they appeared. Their deafening guns poured lead right into the blankets where Kevin and his family had slept.

Kevin saw the flare of light that accompanied each shot. Smelled the gunpowder, sharp and acrid. One of the men roared as if he were more beast than human. Their horses, tied somewhere nearby, whinnied as the noise of pistols blared.

Kevin forced himself to stay still. Any movement could bring those guns around to shoot at him.

The guns clicked on empty chambers. Then silence. Kevin's hand went to his holstered pistol. He could get them both before they reloaded.

Weight hit his back like a load of sod.

"No!" Molly's hiss was hidden in the breeze, only a hair from his ear.

She was a skinny little thing and couldn't have stopped him. But remembering all he stood to lose if his bullets missed and they reloaded in time to shoot back made him release the gun and relax when he wanted to fight.

"They're gone!" One of the men kicked the blankets aside before kicking at the campfire. "It's gone stone cold. Are you sure this is where Hunt was camping?" A doubting Thomas who'd just told Kevin this wasn't a simple robbery.

Not two men sneaking up on strangers to rob them. No, these men were hunting Kevin. And he knew just who one of them might be.

"Yep, three of 'em," the other man replied. "I spotted them in Casper. Coming like we figured. Made sure they took the main trail west, straight for Bear Claw Pass, then I came for you."

Like I figured. Very few people knew Kevin was coming out here. Very few people would profit from his death. Only one in fact.

A brother he'd never heard of until three weeks ago.

Kevin owned a share of Wyatt Hunt's ranch. Or rather their pa's ranch. Pa had been dead for less than a month. Again.

Before he'd left Kansas, Kevin had torn down the memorial headstone they'd put up for Pa twenty years ago. Tore it down and smashed it to pieces.

"If Hunt set up this camp and left, then they're on to us. Let's git." Doubting Thomas whirled and strode back into the grass. His saddle partner hesitated for an instant, then went after his friend.

Kevin's fingers itched to go for his gun. Letting Wyatt Hunt ride away unscathed didn't suit him.

But shooting from cover in the dark didn't suit him, either. Kevin wasn't a killer. But folks killed who weren't . . . if they had reason enough.

It wasn't long before Kevin heard two horses gallop away. On toward Bear Claw Pass.

Murderers were waiting on down the trail west.

"Another half hour, I'd say, and the sun'll rise." Molly climbed off him and patted him on the back. "Could you see their faces so we can recognize them?"

"Nope, but I think I'd recognize their voices." Kevin rose to his feet. In a low tone, he asked, "Andy, you all right?"

"Yep, Kev." Andy emerged out of the grass.

The clouds scudded along, and for a second, the moon peeked out. Kevin made out his little brother. Andy was still a gangly boy, but he was getting his growing on and stood taller than Molly, near Kevin's six feet. He was all coltish awkwardness, as if he hadn't learned what to do with his long legs and arms. It struck Kevin that his little brother was close to the age Kevin had been when Ma had died, and Kevin had become the father of two.

Running one hand through his brown curls, Kevin looked at his brother and sister. Good-looking blonds. They took after their pa, while Kevin looked like Ma. No sign of Kevin's father anywhere.

And wasn't that just the truth.

"I wonder what that was about?" Andy dropped his gun into his holster.

Molly tucked her gun away, too. They'd all learned to sleep armed. Hard lessons for a fact.

"Probably my brother trying to kill me."

That brought silence to both of them.

Finally, Molly, a quiet woman, said into the black night, "Wyoming's about as friendly a place as Kansas."

<hr/>

Andy fetched their horses. Those men had been bent on murder, or they'd've taken the time to hunt up the horses. Kevin had them well-hidden away from the camp, but a thief would have searched for them.

Kevin, Molly, and Andy made short work of loading the three packhorses and saddling the other three before setting out. Those two would-be killers would stick to the trail and ride straight toward Bear Claw Pass, the town nearest the ranch. They'd figure Kevin and his family were ahead of them.

That didn't mean Kevin was going to be reckless. They moved along slowly, sticking to the trail, but he could smell the dust of the riders ahead. They must be galloping to kick up the faint trail.

In a hurry.

Must be trying to catch up to Kevin before he could claim his land.

Kevin didn't see any way not to go where he was going, so he moved forward, grimly hoping he wasn't riding his whole family straight toward death.

Well, not his whole family. Wyatt was family, too, he supposed.

Another brother.

Huh.

Hard to get used to that.

It wasn't a long ride west from Casper to Bear Claw Pass. But Kevin was sickened by what this ranch meant.

Worse than the almost certainty of a fight with a brother he hadn't known existed, it was the shocking, undeniable proof his pa was a cheat and a liar.

A son in Wyoming. An abandoned family in Kansas. Kevin had gotten a telegram from some lawyer in Kansas, telling him his pa—rather than being dead all those years—had owned a ranch in Wyoming. Kevin got a share. The only mention of a brother was telling him Wyatt Hunt, Clovis's son, lived there now. It added up to Pa leaving his family, taking up with another woman, and being a man with no honor.

Not something Kevin wanted to believe about his pa. Better to believe he died exploring the West. That didn't help Kevin's ma get food on the table, but being an explorer had a heroic, thrilling kind of lure. Kevin had understood why Pa had wandered off. Well, some days he'd understood. Other days he'd wanted to punch Pa right in the face.

Pa was no hero. He was a cheat. Old Clovis Hunt had a son with another woman while Kevin's ma was still alive.

That made Pa a no-account varmint. No lure in that to Kevin. Only shame.

Now the siblings rode along, all three of them paying sharp attention. Kansas had been a dangerous place the last years before the Civil War had broken out. Some said that Bleeding Kansas was the Civil War on a small scale before the big scale came along. And the danger hadn't stopped just because the war did.

They'd learned to sleep light, stay sharp, and hide away on short notice to escape renegade night riders thieving and killing in the name of their cause. And their cause was slavery, a free state, and abolition. In truth, outlaws used anything to justify their crimes.

The trail they'd been following widened just as the sun pushed back enough of the darkness to make out fresh tracks from two horses. Stretched out as if the horses were running. It didn't look like the riders had plans to dry-gulch Kevin and his family. They probably figured they'd do that later.

In the early light of dawn, Kevin saw a town ahead. It had to be Bear Claw Pass. Kevin had brought his sister and brother along to their new future. And now it looked like he was leading the two most important people in his life toward death.

Two

You've got to go." Winona Hawkins slapped both hands flat on the kitchen table she sat beside.

At the head of the table, Cheyenne jumped.

Winona knew her lifelong friend Cheyenne Brewster wasn't a jumpy woman in the normal course of things. But this was no normal day. And anyway, Win wasn't talking to Cheyenne.

"There's no getting out of this." Winona shoved her chair back, irritated beyond belief that they were so stubborn.

She understood why, but— "You're like an ox kicking against the goad, Wyatt. You're wasting time and energy better used for roping cattle." She added more gently, "And that's not like you. You're a man who accepts things as they are."

The betrayal of Wyatt's father had rocked Wyatt and Cheyenne.

Win had been there the day Clovis died, and she'd been there for the reading of the will.

Carl Preston, the lone lawyer in Bear Claw Pass, had come with news that still echoed in Win's ears.

He'd ridden up to the ranch house just as Wyatt, Cheyenne, and Win came back from unceremoniously burying Clovis Hunt—away from the family cemetery so as to keep Wyatt and Cheyenne's grandpa from spinning in his grave.

Carl had taken a step toward the front door. "Let's go inside. I have to go over some details with you."

"You can just leave it, Carl." Wyatt had been so calm about the burial, good riddance about summed it up. Then he calmly handled this detail. "I'm sure Ma's wishes are all in order. She told us both how she'd split things up."

That earned a grim look from Carl that shifted between Wyatt and Cheyenne. "These aren't your ma's orders, Wyatt. They're your pa's."

Win's heart had stuttered a bit. She knew too much about poor men marrying rich wives and outliving them.

Wyatt frowned and looked sideways at Cheyenne. "Pa didn't own nothing I've heard tell of."

Shaking his head, Carl said, "That's not true. A man and his wife are co-owners of any property in the marriage. In fact, the man is the sole owner by law. Clovis Hunt came to me and wrote his own will after your ma died."

Win's stomach twisted. What low-down thing had Clovis Hunt done now?

Wyatt had gotten the door and held it while Cheyenne, Win, and Carl went in.

◇—••—◇

"Brothers? What brothers?" Wyatt shoved himself to his feet.

"Your father, Clovis, left this land, the Rolling Hills

278

Ranch, all the cattle, horses, bank accounts, everything, divided in three equal parts, or rather, technically, kept in one large part with three equal owners. It goes to you, Wyatt; a brother named Falcon, who lives in Tennessee; and another brother, Kevin, from Kansas. Your father explained things very clearly to me, and there's no other way to say this. It appears he was married to three women, a-all—" Carl cleared his throat—"all at the same time."

Cheyenne stood and turned from Carl to pace toward the window.

Win knew just what she saw. The beautiful rolling hills that had given the ranch its name. It was a landscape that looked out on a huge log barn, well-built corrals, the bunkhouse, the foreman's house, and the ramrod's house. This ranch had forty thousand head of cattle spread over fifty thousand acres, bought up by Wyatt's grandpa over many years, spending every penny and every bit of strength in his back to build his ranch and build a life for his only daughter and her two children.

Nothing like how Win's pa had gotten his ranch. The grand and lavish ranch house was built by others, and the land bought in one huge parcel, paid for with Win's ma's money.

Over here at the RHR it had been work. Years and years of work done by Wyatt's grandpa, Jacques LaRemy, followed by Wyatt's ma, Katherine, and her first husband, Nate Brewster, who were Cheyenne's parents. Then Nate Brewster died, and Katherine remarried and had Wyatt—who grew up fast and went to work, too. They'd poured blood, sweat, and tears into this ranch. Absolutely none of the work had ever been done by Clovis Hunt, who'd outlived Jacques and Katherine and, without telling anyone, altered the will his wife had left behind.

"And as instructed in this will, I immediately telegraphed another lawyer in Casper to inform him of your father's death. He'll contact your brothers and—"

"Don't call them that." Wyatt hammered the side of his fist on the desk. Carl jumped and quit talking.

Win's heart clutched as she waited for Wyatt to launch himself at Carl. Wyatt visibly struggled to get ahold of himself . . . and then his eyes went wide.

"What about Cheyenne? She was supposed to inherit the land from her father. Surely Clovis has no ownership of Nate Brewster's land."

Carl swallowed hard. "He does. I'm sorry. The law says any property brought into a marriage by a wife immediately becomes the property of her husband. Clovis never exerted any property rights over your mother's land, but according to the letter of the law, since the day they married, your father has been the owner of all Katherine Hunt's holdings, including those left to her by her first husband."

"That land was meant for Cheyenne."

Carl shook his head helplessly. "Intent doesn't override the law. When your grandfather died, his will left everything to your mother, but by law he really left it to your mother's husband. He, that is, Clovis, wasn't even here when your grandpa died."

"I remember that. He hadn't been around for years. Most of my growing-up years."

"He came around once in a while," Cheyenne said bitterly.

"Yep, and we were all mighty glad to see him go, which he always did." Wyatt began to pace the huge office.

"But it'll take time for letters to reach them, won't it?" Wyatt stopped pacing to look at Carl.

"The lawyer in Casper wired back before I rode out here and informed me he had clear instructions of his own. He sent telegrams to the towns closest to your broth—uh, that is, uh, your father's other sons. He was fully paid to hire riders to take the telegrams directly to their homes to make sure they knew of their inheritance."

"Fully paid with my mother's money."

"That's correct." Carl ran a finger around the collar of his white shirt as if it were choking him. "The brother in Kansas may know already and be heading here. The other one, the oldest, Falcon Hunt, lives in a remote part of the Blue Ridge Mountains of Tennessee. But included in the telegraph were precise directions to Falcon Hunt's home. Your father kept track of his sons and thought of everything."

Carl paused. "I'm not aware of the . . . condition of the other wives."

"Other wives, good grief." Wyatt paced faster, his fists clenched.

Cheyenne remained utterly silent, looking out. Win waited for her to start shooting. Cheyenne wasn't known for taking bad news cheerfully.

"It's possible your br—" Carl coughed suddenly, then continued. "That is, your—that is, Cl-Clovis's other sons may be bringing his wives—their mothers—here as well. In addition, they could be married men. They could have children."

Wyatt slapped himself in the face. There was an extended silence.

Carl didn't break it. Cheyenne kept staring out.

Win sure enough wasn't going to speak up.

281

Finally, Wyatt's head came up, his hazel eyes flashing fire. "I want you to find a way to break this will."

Carl's mouth pinched tight as he shook his head. "The will is finely and carefully drawn, including caveats that make it almost impossible for your father's other sons to sell—if they could be convinced to sell their parcels back to you. I wrote it up, but Clovis took it to Casper and had it gone over to make sure there were no weak spots."

"Cavee-what?"

"Caveats. What it comes down to is, if any of the three brothers sells his parcel within the first ten years of Clovis's death, the entire ranch must be sold, and Clovis arranged to donate the full amount, bank accounts and everything, to the state of Tennessee to build a monument to the Confederacy."

Win rubbed her mouth for a few seconds before she said, "Did he write the will before or after the South lost the war?"

Carl winced. "After, I'm afraid. About a week after Katherine's death."

Wyatt swept a hand wide. "That don't matter. My pa's other sons won't sell out anyway, leastways not for less than a fortune. They'll be like him. They'll come out here and move in like a pair of locusts, chomping it all down for themselves."

"I did have one notion."

Win started. Cheyenne turned around.

"What's that?" Wyatt asked.

"If your father had another living wife when he married Katherine, then he couldn't legally marry again. That would make his marriage to your mother bigamous. If that's the case, then he'd have no legal standing to inherit her land."

282

Wyatt—just told he might be the offspring of an unmarried mother—looked wildly hopeful. "What can you do to track this down?"

"Well, we can see if Falcon Hunt arrives with his Tennessee mountain ma. If she's living, then the will is void."

"And if she's not living, we'd need to know when she died," Wyatt said. "Not likely Falcon would aid in his own loss of the ranch."

"If he won't cooperate, I suppose we'd need to hire investigators of some sort."

Wyatt's mouth got tight, and he frowned at the lawyer. "I guess we can pay for that out of my third of this ranch's bank accounts."

"Let's wait until Falcon arrives. His mother is the first marriage and possibly the only legal one. Once he's here, we'll know more. While we wait, I'll try and figure out how to handle things if need be. Finding investigators and such. We'll talk about it as soon as I have some advice for you." Carl left a copy of the will on the table and gathered up his satchel.

Win watched him go, left in the house with two very unhappy people.

But they didn't start raging.

Yes, the telegrams had gone out to Wyatt's brothers.

Yes, the ranch was in the hands of two strangers who might be as worthless as Clovis.

But those two things could be endured because, at least for now, they had hope.

And now the time had come to meet the brother from Tennessee.

Falcon was coming in on today's train. He'd gone to the lawyer in Casper. Apparently, he was instructed to do that. The lawyer sent him to Bear Claw Pass and wired ahead to Wyatt with the news.

"You. Have. No. Choice." Win could only say what was true even if it was the worst kind of dirty shame.

Wyatt Hunt was the same as a little brother to Win. A full-grown man, of course, but she had a hard time not thinking of him as a kid. A stubborn kid. She was tempted to give his ear a good twist.

Cheyenne was Winona's lifelong friend. They'd spent their younger years picking on Wyatt, and he'd done the same right back. It was hard to get out of the habit of growling at him. Bossing him around. Insulting him. Tormenting Wyatt was her favorite thing to do.

There was just no use for him acting like this.

"You have to go to town." Win tried to use small words so the poor idiot would listen. "It's the right and decent thing to do."

"There's nothing right nor decent about this ranch being stolen from Cheyenne. I'm mad clean through, and I don't have one speck of interest in making this easy for anyone else. Pa was a coyote, and we all knew it long before he died, but I never thought he would sink this low."

Win closed her eyes. She had to say it, and it caused her pain, dread really. But Wyatt was digging in his heels, and Cheyenne wasn't about to go to town. That was just too much to ask.

Mary Connealy writes romantic comedies about cowboys. She's the author of the BROTHERS IN ARMS, BRIDES OF HOPE MOUNTAIN, HIGH SIERRA SWEETHEARTS, KINCAID BRIDES, TROUBLE IN TEXAS, WILD AT HEART, and CIMARRON LEGACY series, as well as several other acclaimed series. Mary has been nominated for a Christy Award, was a finalist for a RITA Award, and is a two-time winner of the Carol Award. She lives in eastern Nebraska with her very own romantic cowboy hero. They have four grown daughters—Joslyn, married to Matt; Wendy; Shelly, married to Aaron; and Katy, married to Max—and seven precious grandchildren. Learn more about Mary and her books at

MaryConnealy.com
facebook.com/maryconnealy
petticoatsandpistols.com

Sign Up for Mary's Newsletter

Keep up to date with Mary's latest news on book releases and events by signing up for her email list at the link below.

MaryConnealy.com

FOLLOW MARY ON SOCIAL MEDIA

Mary Connealy   @MaryConnealy   @MaryConnealy